Nightflight

WILLIAM JEFFREY PATUS

Copyright © 2013 by William Jeffrey Patus
First Edition – August 2013

ISBN
978-1-4602-0763-5 (Hardcover)
978-1-4602-0761-1 (Paperback)
978-1-4602-0762-8 (eBook)

All rights reserved.

No part of this publication may be reproduced in any form, or by any means, electronic or mechanical, including photocopying, recording, or any information browsing, storage, or retrieval system, without permission in writing from the publisher.

Amanda Robillard, front cover artist, Mixed Medium Artist
amanda.robillard33@hotmail.com

Jerry Zolner, front cover photography and graphic arts,
www.jerryzolner.com

Produced by:

FriesenPress
Suite 300 – 852 Fort Street
Victoria, BC, Canada V8W 1H8

www.friesenpress.com

Distributed to the trade by The Ingram Book Company

CHAPTER 1

JAMESTOWN, OHIO. SEPTEMBER 11, 1987.

Tom Forbes wheeled his Jeep Cherokee four by four into the freshly paved driveway of the Busy Bee Day Care Center. He stopped up against the curb, put the shift lever in park and killed the engine. Once again, it was time for the big drop off. In his mind, Tom crossed his fingers and hoped things would go smoothly. You could never tell with kids and new situations. He took a deep breath and got out of the Jeep.

Tom walked around to the passenger side. Safely strapped in the rear booster seat was his little angel, Tiffany Amber. Tiffy was a month shy of her second birthday. With long wavy blonde hair and blue eyes, she possessed the energy level of a small tornado. Or, she was sleeping and inert. It was usually one or the other; the kid seemed to have no middle gear. Tiffany had been wriggling in her car seat since they left the house. She was beyond ready to get going.

Accompanying the little girl was her ever-present, red stuffed elephant. The elephant was as old as the owner. Fraying had occurred around the long nose and stitching repairs had been required in a few places. Otherwise, the stuffed toy was holding on to its distinctive color, and maintaining its full belly. Tom had never seen a red elephant in his life. Nor did he ever expect to. The red elephant reminded him of those silly, colorful creatures on Sesame Street.

Tom opened the door, tipped the seat forward, reached in and unbuckled his precious girl. He hoisted her out of the Jeep and up against his shoulder. Tom bumped the door shut with his hip and walked towards the main entrance.

Greeting all visitors was a beaming, yellow happy face painted across the glass double entry doors. Above the doors, the bright yellow motif continued with a huge bumble bee, smiling of course and trimmed with black. Tom couldn't help but grin at the colorful balloons and streamers plastered over the front of the handsome building. Today was Parent's Day. The kids would be displaying their many talents.

"Down?" came the little request, along with the associated squirming and kicking from the energy kid.

Tom gently set Tiffy on the ground. She ran ahead to the front doors, clutching her red elephant. Tiffy stopped, and with a large loud smack, she planted a kiss on the yellow happy face. Tom grinned again. What a kid.

Tiffy tugged at a door handle, not quite strong enough to pull it open.

"Daddy, daddy," she called.

Dad hustled up to the door and drew it open.

Tiffy scooted inside.

The Busy Bee was a brand new, comfortable, solid brick building. Its design put the facility at the leading edge of the growing day care craze. The building contained an office, a large eat-in kitchen, a quiet room, washrooms, and a spacious common area. Portable partitions divided the common area into different activity centers. Each center was decorated with bright colors and popular cartoon characters.

Attached to the side of the building was a beautiful green outdoor space. On the perfectly manicured lawn sat a jungle gym, a swing set, a teeter totter, a sandbox and an assortment of large plastic toys. A gleaming, silver, chain link fence, about three and a half feet high, fronted the outdoor area on the street side. The rest of the yard was enclosed by a wood plank barrier, topping out at six feet in height. Smack dab in the middle of the yard, a massive oak tree stood guard. The oak tree offered welcoming shade during the humid, energy sapping days of summer.

The Busy Bee was operated by Joe and Marie Danton. The Dantons were the key component in the successful transition from home to day care for the anxious little ones. The kids melted within minutes of contacting either Joe or Marie. They were indeed, the magic couple with the magic touch.

Joe was tall, slim and bearded, a thick pony tail trailing down his back. His smile was infectious, and his eyes were clear and piercing. He seemed to be someone everybody knew. Joe possessed a quality of comfortable familiarity about him.

Marie was a petite girl with dark hair and beautiful olive skin. There was an extremely gentle aura about her. The couple seemed to be 'good people'. Honest, hardworking and trustworthy. The last attribute was the most important. Because this couple was taking charge of, taking care of, and taking responsibility for, all of these children. The Busy Bee was only three months old, yet word of mouth had already produced a long waiting list.

Joe Danton was lingering inside the front doors, anticipating, watching for his charges to appear. The door swung open, the blonde tornado shot in. Joe knelt down and held out his arms to Tiffany Forbes. She went right to him, waving the red elephant in the air. Joe was rewarded with an enthusiastic hug.

Tiffy was so excited.

Then immediately, she saddened.

Tiffy realized her daddy would be leaving. She turned away from Joe, dropped her elephant, and ran back towards daddy, who was now entering the building. Tears were flowing down her chubby cheeks.

"Up, up," she pleaded.

Tom lifted his little girl, wrapping his arms around her. This was only day five of the Busy Bee experiment. Today, it might not work. He certainly wasn't going to force her to stay. Tom could take Tiffy to grandma's house if he needed to.

Joe Danton walked over, wielding the magic power of the red elephant.

"Good morning, Tom."

"Hey Joe, how's it going?"

Tiffy quickly produced a smile and climbed from dad back onto Joe. She reached for her red elephant, grabbing on to the toy pachyderm as if it was a talisman.

"What an amazing day out there. Not too many of these left," Joe offered.

"Incredible," Tom agreed.

So it was. Seven forty five in the morning. Sixty-eight degrees and pure sunshine. A week and a half into September.

Tiffy broke in.

"Bye bye daddy," she called, waving her free hand.

Everything was okay now. Everything was safe. It was play time. The energy kid was ready to roll. The tears were already drying, the drama had passed.

"Bye-bye darling. See you real soon," Tom replied.

To Joe, "Thanks a million. Again."

"No problem, she's a great kid."

Tom slowly backed out through the happy face door, waving and smiling at his little girl.

He stopped.

A strange sensation washed over him. Tiffy looked happy enough to be with Joe. Yes she did. Parked there in Joe's arms. With her favorite toy. For the last four days, make it five now, she had clung to Joe or Marie, or romped with the other kids. She seemed to be fine with it.

Though she was awfully young to be away from her parents, wasn't she?

No, there were younger kids in this day care, and it was a great facility. It was such a clean, vibrant, happy atmosphere. She's good here. Yes she is. Safe, at ease, content.

Was he seeing *something* in her eyes?

Let it go Tommy. She's fine. She's more than fine. The Busy Bee is a great place with great owners and a fantastic, engaging program. Leave it alone. Let her grow.

However. Her eyes seemed to be speaking to him. Her eyes seemed to be saying, 'I understand this is the way it has to be, even though you and mommy are my two most favorite people in the whole, wide world'.

Jesus. That *really* is enough. Easy now big guy. Let's not make a big deal out of this. You are not abandoning the kid. Abandonment. What an ugly word. Tom shuddered.

Tom Forbes had one stark recollection of abandonment. He couldn't have been more than six years old. He had to stay overnight at the local hospital following the removal of his tonsils. The fourth floor. The children's ward. It was a different time. Parents were not allowed to remain with the kids. Eight o'clock in the evening and all visitors were required to leave. Eight o'clock sharp. Out you go. No exceptions. The nurses and orderlies had work to do. The little patients had sleep to do.

Tommy and the kids were all in lockdown beds, really glorified cages, set up in one giant room. As the parents began to leave, the fear in the room became palpable. The sniffling came first, then the tears, and finally the all out bawling and wailing. Mommy and daddy were going home, and you were being left with the strangers. You were terrified of staying with these busy, official people, and you were sore from what these people had done to you. You were in a very strange place, a place that made you hurt. A place full of scared kids. Trapped in cages. Everybody was feeding off each other's fear. You had been forsaken by the only people in the world you had ever trusted. Your mommy and daddy.

Not a good memory. Tom shook it out of his mind.

Certainly, abandonment was *not* happening here. Tiffy was with great people in a great place. The kids were always playing and laughing, or drawing or finger painting or doing something fun. There was no hint of sadness or anxiety or fear in the Busy Bee. None at all.

Except, her eyes.

CHAPTER 2

Joe set Tiffy down. She ran on and joined the rest of the kids in the common room. The air was filled with the busy sounds of children playing and laughing. Busy, buzzing sounds, hence the name, Busy Bee. Joe chuckled at the irony. The kids were such fountains of joy, energy and curiosity.

He looked around the common room. Four of his instructors were engaging the little ones in different activities. Everybody was involved. Everybody was occupied. It all looked good and right.

Tiffany Forbes was indeed a great kid. Kids were his job. Job number one for Joe Danton. Joe would take care of this little girl as if she was his own. This is how he felt about all of these children. Joe was captivated by the kids, almost obsessed with the kids. He found them to be amazing, unadulterated creatures, full of wonder and potential and awe and belief. Undamaged and unfettered by life experiences. Pure, innocent and vulnerable.

Joe didn't appreciate the 'vulnerable' part. No he didn't. This is why he was here. To watch over the kids. To keep them safe.

Joe found Jamestown to be an attractive, successful, progressive city. Hard working and chock full of optimism, a true community. Jamestown boasted many well attended churches, service clubs and volunteer organizations. Everything local was supported to the hilt, including the farmer's market, school sports teams, artisans, crafters and fund raising drives. This was not the big metropolis up the interstate, or Detroit, or Las Vegas or Baltimore. The rot was already deep in the fabric of those places, emerging, multiplying and insidiously eating away.

When Joe first arrived here, it had taken him only days to sense the seeds of rot *had* been scattered all over the town. The seeds, they were desperately trying to grow. It was their job to grow. However, the seeds required nourishment and acceptance in order to cultivate. At this moment in time, the ideal growing conditions did not exist. So the seeds were sitting dormant, waiting, biding their time. Patient.

If the seeds began to grow, well, Joe had seen this before. Many times. As a moth is pulled to the light, Joe would be drawn into the struggle. So far, Jamestown showed none of it. From the outside at least, Jamestown appeared to be Pleasantville, USA.

Joe stroked his beard and contemplated. He had hoped things would begin to stabilize, but the world was changing again. Quickly. Joe had seen it in the other boomtowns he had passed through. The hard work, the rapid growth, the speedy accumulation of wealth. The blinders being put on. The success would never end. There could be no rainy days coming. So keep the pedal to the floor.

Cleveland, Pittsburgh, Detroit, St. Louis, Buffalo. These cities had all raced to the top. They were all tumbling, or would be tumbling in the very near future. Because with the success, came the over-indulgence, and of course, the celebration. We earned it. Yes we did. Self congratulations all around, and continued good fortune to us. The alcohol was never enough. It wouldn't get us to the plateau we were seeking. We needed more. Weed, pills, powder, crystals, heroin, crank, E. Gangs would bring these rewards in. Street punks would sell it and collect the cash. Everybody would celebrate.

With the celebration, came even more spending. Why don't we buy a whole pile of crap we don't need, and can't afford? Why not? The next union contract will pay for it all. The union contracts always go up, and we always get more money. The ever expanding economy means our wallets are full and our credit card limits keep rising. One and the same, right? Double the cars, double the garage, bigger houses we will only use half of, cottages and boats, and skidoos and vacations.

Why don't we bring a casino to town? Let's have some real, big city entertainment. Why not again? We earned it, didn't we? The casino will bring casino-type amenities, such as loan sharking, strippers and prostitution.

Now the mayhem begins. Because the money is going out faster than it is coming in. 'Negative balance' the bankers call it. Which leads to insolvency. Bankruptcy. Despair. Depression. Destruction. Society changing, becoming uncaring, cold and violent.

Why did we need to 'have it all'?

Why did we need to go so fast?

Even the day care business. Joe couldn't understand why parents would let complete strangers raise their kids. Were the parents too busy? Too busy for their own kids? So they could make more money to pay for their stuff? To pay for their entertainment? To pay for their escapes? To pay for their mistakes?

Can't we slow this thing down?

Was there anything more important than raising your own kids? Building a family? Building a community? Wasn't this the reason for being? For the entire human race? Sure it was. Or it should be. Everything else is noise and wallpaper. Everything else is distraction. Everything else, is emptiness. So why was everyone chasing the new religion, the almighty dollar? Greed was good. Greed was God. People dancing with debt, so strung out. So dangerous. So unpredictable.

While all of this is going on, *who is watching the kids?*

Who indeed?

Somebody is watching the kids.

Somebody is *always* watching the kids.

All of the signs were pointing to this time, and to this place. Yet, Jamestown was proving to be a conundrum. Booming and growing, but incredibly and unexplainably, peaceful and crime free. Joe had met the town sheriff and had been blown away by the power and strength of the man.

Could one man make all the difference? Could he? Could one man hold back against the tsunami of temptation and greed? The wanton desire for drugs, prostitution and gambling? The desire for more and the awful price to be paid? The violence of the gangs and the corruption of humankind?

Joe wondered.

Some people had a resolve, a belief, an inner strength which superseded the norm. He had seen it before. He was seeing it right now. Anything in this world was possible.

The sheriff was doing an extraordinary job. However, something was definitely afoot in Jamestown. Joe could not yet pin it down. He sensed a probing, a watchfulness, as if something or someone was ready to leap at the first sign of weakness. He could only hope he would be in the right place at the right time to help. Even so, Joe didn't know if it would be enough. The odds were not stacked in his favor.

They never were.

Joe made his way to the rear exit. The kids would be moving outside soon. He gazed through the glass door at the morning sun. Marie joined him and together they stepped out into the unfolding, glorious day. They fixed their eyes skyward. Marie wrapped her arm around Joe's waist, pulling him tight against her. She knew something was bothering her husband. He had been preoccupied over the past few weeks. Usually, he was so carefree and upbeat. Marie watched as Joe stared at the sky, his eyes slowly scanning, and then closing tight.

"Hon? What's wrong?" she asked.

Joe opened his eyes, and put his arm around Marie's shoulder.

"I don't know. I'm not sure."

For a brief second, Joe looked very different to Marie. As if something passed through him. And between *them*.

A wall.

Cutting her off from him.

The feeling chilled her to the very bone.

Then poof, it was gone.

What on earth?

"Honestly, I don't know. I feel a little off. Maybe it's the change in the weather."

"Do you feel sick? Are you okay?"

Joe sensed the alarm in Marie.

"No, no, no. Not that way. Physically, I feel fine. I can't really explain it. I just feel different. Not a big deal."

They were silent. The touch they shared helped. It always did.

Except.

Except for the wall going up between them a second ago. Such separation had *never* happened before.

"Look at the sun," Joe continued.

"It's so bright. So pure. So high in the sky. As if this is the first day of summer. And the sky. It's so blue."

Marie had been simply enjoying the unexpected warmth of the early morning. This was such a luxury before the long, cold, damp winter locked onto Ohio. The sun did look, unnatural. It was not where it should be. In September, the sun was always slanted way off in the sky, following a less direct, autumn trajectory. Right now, the sun was nearly straight up above them.

Was this some sort of solar phenomenon? Had the earth tilted on its axis?

The drone from the giant Morgan Iron and Steel Works disrupted the moment. Joe and Marie looked at one another. The factory smoke. Where was the smoke? The blast furnaces were pounding away, albeit muffled by distance. The ever-present reverberation was rumbling in the ground beneath their feet.

So where was the factory smoke?

It should be smothering the city, what with the lack of wind and breeze.

Wait a second.

Something didn't quite fit.

Joe again looked to the sky. In the distance, three seagulls wheeled, buffeted by what looked to be a strong wind. The seagulls were struggling to maintain their flight. Joe scanned over to the property next to his. The leaves on those tall trees were definitely moving. He looked past the plank fence into the railroad lands. The evergreen bushes were rustling their branches as well. Joe stared at his own giant oak. His eyes ran right up to the very top. The leaves weren't moving at all. Not a bit.

Not a single, solitary leaf showed any motion.

Strange.

Joe felt a tingling sensation slip down his spine. The breeze, the wind, it was not blowing in *his* backyard. The breeze was stopped dead in this little square of property.

It was eerily tranquil.

Joe looked around again. The seagulls. The tall trees. The evergreen bushes. All outside his yard. All in motion. All being impacted by the currents of the wind.

What on earth?

Joe walked with Marie past the great oak, to get a better view to the north. What they knew they would see behind the brown leafed behemoth were lazy, thick emulsions curling out of the factory stacks.

They saw nothing.

Nothing.

The furnaces were blasting away. The sound from the factory seemed to be increasing in strength with each reverberation. As if a slow footed, but massive beast, was stalking their way. They looked at each other once again.

Where was the smoke?

The stillness in the backyard was beyond comprehension. Even the sounds of the kids, laughing and squealing as they tumbled out the rear door of the Busy Bee, seemed far away.

Joe had seen or read somewhere about the dead quiet arriving immediately before a massive weather or seismic event. The giant tsunami devastating Thailand. The colossal eruption in Columbia. The 'Quake of the Century' in Queensland. The locals who survived those events had all remarked on the supernatural sensation of peace and quiet. Before all hell broke loose. Was it National Geographic? Or the History channel? Joe couldn't remember.

So what was going on here? What was coming their way?

Suddenly, the coldest breeze Joe had ever felt shattered his thoughts. The breeze ran right through his being, shaking him to the core. Why was the breeze so cold on this unseasonably warm morning?

The breeze moved on to the oak, rattling around the heavy branches, dropping fall leaves to the ground. For only a fraction of a second, the leaves seemed to suspend themselves in time. A true freeze frame.

Joe blinked and the leaves began to fall again.

His brain box began to fire.
Yes, he could hear them.
The whispers in the wind.
Muted, but he heard.
They were coming.
And.
The numbers were back.
Three. Seven. Eleven.
Whispering through his mind.
For sure they were coming.
In fact, they were almost here.

CHAPTER 3

Tom Forbes was heading towards the city center. Not so bad, right? A short moment of trepidation and a few crocodile tears. Tom never thought he would see the day dawn when Tiffy was comfortable with the drop off. His little girl so loved to be glued to her parents. At home she was always underfoot, always trying to keep up with mom or dad. Whether it was vacuuming, or doing dishes, or raking the lawn, or polishing the new Jeep. There she was, underfoot. The little bundle of blonde business.

The drop off separation was definitely happening. So quickly. The Dantons were proving to be miracle workers. Tiffy especially loved Joe. Without a doubt, Joe Danton had the 'Pied Piper' effect on the kids. It was all good.

Except.

Except for the look in her eyes. Eyes flashing years of sentiment and trial. Eyes flashing sorrow, and perhaps fear. Fear? Fear of what? Stop being an idiot. You are making too much out of it again, Tommy. She's two years old. She's a kid. She's okay. Otherwise, you would be going right back to the Busy Bee and taking her out. Yes you would.

End of story.

Okay then.

Tom swallowed a deep breath and exhaled. Right. Let it go. Stop being such a punk. What's with all the emoting anyway, Mr. Forbes? She's a kid in a day care, with many other kids in a day care. Everybody was doing the day care shuffle. So calm yourself down, you are marching right on point with the rest of America.

Fine then.

Relax.

Tom sat back in the comfortable bucket seat of his 'fresh off the assembly line' Jeep Cherokee. This was not some piece of crap made in Japland. No sir, this was American made. Union made. The big Jeep projected a manly, virile, sporting veneer on its driver. In fact, this was the exact tagline spouted by the dealership salesman. Probably used at dealerships all the way across the country, Tom surmised. Well, in this case, the salesman was bang on. Tom Forbes was the poster boy for Jeep. You bet he was.

Tom was married to the trophy wife, they had produced the super cute kid, and he wore a shirt and tie to work. Come the weekends, the warrior now had the four wheel drive which allowed him to assert his freedom. Along with an amazing new-car smell, the Jeep came with many bells and whistles. The stereo cassette deck/compact disc combo, the quad speaker sound, the high up ride, the bush bars, the flex top and the giant knobby tires all shouted to the world, 'Here comes Tommy Forbes'. It was a little vanity, but why not?

These were the boom times, so it was time to boom.

Tom lowered his windows as he slowly motored into the downtown. The Miracle Mile they called it. Actually, the road was much longer than a mile, but the heavy commerce of multiple story brick buildings ran an exact mile.

Tom was working the quad stereo system to the max. Ohio's best rock, 92.1 CITI FM ruled the airwaves. U2 was blasting away, having a hard time finding what they were looking for. Five months after the song debuted, it was still in the top ten. Tom figured the Irish rockers were going to finish the year at number one with this tune. Good for them. It was a great song.

Along with U2's unsuccessful search, Jon Bon Jovi was trying to live on a prayer and rockin Bob Seger was running a shakedown. 1987 is becoming a big year for Bob Seger. Shakedown has moved into Billboard's top slot on the strength of Beverly Hills Cop 2. Indeed, Eddie Murphy is still the comedic bomb of the decade.

Tom noticed all the shiny new vehicles on the road. So many different colors and models. Red, yellow, white, blue, purple, green and brown. Ford, Mercury, Chrysler, Pontiac, Dodge, Plymouth, Chevy, Buick and Cadillac. Made in America. Made with pride.

Tom spotted the odd foreign car. Which of these is not like the others? The foreign cars stood out, sore thumbs on the roads of the American heartland. Ugly designs, ugly colors, thin looking stamped metal bodies. Cheap, poorly made, pieces of shit. Send the garbage back in the containers they came in. Or better yet, take them to the crushers and turn them into toys. Not a chance they would catch on in this country. Americans would spend more money on Slinky Toys than Jap made cars. No doubt.

The new cars were a good indicator of the money Jamestown was hemorrhaging. Thanks mainly to the giant steel factory gushing union wages to thousands of workers. A grade ten education could get you a nice fat paycheck from Morgan Iron and Steel. With overtime and bonuses, there was almost no limit on the take-home pay. Everybody was spending the generous take-home pay. Yes they were.

Tom rolled on through the core area of Jamestown. Already, most of the stores were open. As usual, business was looking good. The sidewalks were thick with early morning shoppers. Every parking space was full. The vehicles were angle parked on both sides of the Miracle Mile. From high up, it must have resembled a giant metallic arrow pointing straight towards Lake Erie.

The great, All American city of Jamestown, Ohio was beginning another day. Hectic, bustling, noisy and productive, Jamestown oozed vigor and victory. The population has passed the 68,000 citizen plateau, earning Jamestown the title of 'Fastest Growing City' in the United States. The populace is spreading out into sprawling subdivisions, while the downtown is bursting with commerce and civic pride. City planners have so far held the line against ugly, wanton commercial expansion. They have not allowed those soulless, power malls to be built, thus keeping character, business and hometown pride right where it belongs. There is zero occupancy in the downtown core, there is zero urban blight and there are no transients taking up quarter.

Thanks to the huge Morgan Iron and Steel Works factory at the north end of Jamestown, there is another zero number. The unemployment rate.

The mill employs fourteen thousand workers. Spin off jobs and supply networks employ another sixteen thousand. The government bureaucracy, the education system, the health care sector, service industries and white collar firms employ everybody else. There are strong rush hours into and out of Jamestown slowing the interstate traffic to a crawl. Workers are commuting from up to a hundred miles away to grab a piece of the boomtown.

Jamestown is proof positive, Americans *can* build the best stuff in the world, right here at home, and still pay honest wages to honest workers. Made in America pride is contagious. The red, white and blue of old glory flutters from nearly every business front and house porch in the city. Morgan Steel and the city fathers are determined to find a way around the outsourcing disease reaching into the soul of the country.

Jamestown has the highest unionized workforce in America. The big union means big wages, which means big local spending, which means big business taxes, which means great local amenities.

The roads are constantly being paved, swept and line painted. The roads are black and smooth and clean, and are a pleasure to drive on. The city provides gleaming chromed parking meters, ornate wrought iron benches, hanging flower pots in the summer, glowing decorations at Christmas, a state of the art arena/pool complex and a beautiful urban park. In the urban park is a pond which freezes up in winter to become a skating rink. When the seasons change, the locals get to trade their fishing poles and sun tanning blankets for steel blades and hockey sticks.

A brand new high school has opened, the largest in the state, because the city is growing so quickly. Negotiations for an Ohio State University campus have wrapped successfully. This is without a doubt, Buckeye Country. The shovels will be going into the ground in January for a Medical Center of Excellence, the new term for hospital. The old hospital is a crumbling mess and can no longer serve the population growth. The good times are right here, right now, and a bountiful future beckons the city of Jamestown. Millions of tax dollars from the steel mill are boosting city coffers, paying the way and lining the streets with gold.

Despite being only an hour and a half down the freeway from the metropolis of Cleveland, Jamestown has remained relatively crime free, drug free and gang free. Where Cleveland was once a busy, honest, broad-backed working town, decay has begun to hollow out the big C. The manufacturing outsourcing sickness has latched on, throwing thousands and thousands of men out of work. Idle men are not good men. Drinking and drug abuse is on the rise. The demand for drugs is being filled by the gangs. This is not the way Jamestown wants to go.

To prevent this ugly scenario, the city hired their latest town sheriff away from one of the southwest Sunbelt states. The man has proven to be an intimidating deterrent to crime. He is a very large man, and he much resembles a cowboy. The sheriff suffers no fools, and runs a zero tolerance program. The big man makes Jamestown a safe place to raise a family, to live in, and to grow old in. The sheriff is determined to hold the line against the Cleveland rot.

As Tom drove on, he had a perfect view to the north. He was following the giant metallic arrow pointing towards the lakeshore. This would be a fantastic day at the beach, what with the sunshine and the blue sky. After the Parent's Day visit, he would take the family to the sandy shores.

Because this particular September morning is proving to be an extreme rarity for Jamestown. The sky is crystal clear. A steady breeze, blowing from the southwest, started late last evening. Meaning, the legendary smoke columns continuously belching from the big factory are being pushed right across the lake into Canada. Cross border polluting. It's a good thing our northern neighbors are so tolerant.

The breeze is a blessing.

The city right now, is completely smog free.

A small miracle.

Most every day, the giant factory blackens the sky with thick, acrid smoke. A myriad of tall, brick pipes spew the crap heavenwards twenty-four hours a day, seven days a week, fifty-two weeks of the year. The smoke usually combines with the natural humidity from Lake Erie to cast a soupy pall over the city. The sky is rarely clear, or rarely blue. Nobody has seen a star in the night sky for decades. A minor inconvenience on the path to riches and success.

Throughout the year, individual furnaces are suspended on a rotating basis for maintenance. However, the factory continues to churn, never missing a beat. One furnace down while eighteen others fire make no difference to the Jamestown skyline.

There is one special day in the year. Christmas day. A day steeped in tradition, going way back to the whims and desires of the city founder, James Peter Morgan. James Peter Morgan was the king of Christmas, and nobody in his employ would be working on the revered day. The tradition continues, and the giant factory completely shuts down once a year. Christmas is the day the locals call 'the Clear Day'. No operating plant, no smoke. No smoke, clear skies.

Today, is a bonus day. The sky is blue. The sky is clear. The sun is beaming, bright, round and yellow.

The sun is shining with all its might.

Today, is the last gasp of Indian summer.

Today is September the 11th, 1987.

CHAPTER 4

Work for Tom Forbes is a mundane, eight to four job in the office of Burns, Henderson Chartered Accountants. Tom is number six on the totem pole of power. At the top of the pole are the two senior partners, and right below them, three of the sons. Then there is Tom Forbes. Number six. The top five are pure numbers nerds. Thick glasses, thick waistlines, big brains. They live for the ledgers and columns, the profits and losses, the tax codes and IRS regulations.

Not Tom. Tom was the jock, the sports dude who settled on this career. It certainly wasn't his number one choice. After his pro sports flame-out, Tom's options had shrunk. His old man wanted him to work at the factory, to carry on the family tradition. The factory owned his dad, his grandpa, his uncles and cousins. Not him though. No way.

A couple of years in community college and here he was. Tom's new white collar career was unfolding before him. Slowly. Very slowly. He was five men and honestly, a couple of veteran secretaries away from the top. Or in hockey terms, he was number eight on the depth chart. Ouch. A third line player.

Tom pushed paper and played with numbers. Nothing creative, nothing fun, he made sure the numbers got in the correct columns. The job was so simple he could do it in his sleep. The job did not pay very well. At least, not yet. Not at his current position in the company hierarchy. The pay wasn't even close to the money he should be earning playing in the big leagues. Or the money he could be earning in the steel factory.

Tom had toiled in the big smelly factory as a teenager. He endured the driving heat of dead summer, the ear splitting noise of the foundry, the physical grunt labor and the incredible repetition of line work. The work sucked but the money was excellent. Most of the grunts were making thirty to forty grand a year. The mindless, dirty, tiring work was another story. This was not the life he was going to choose. Instead, he chose white collar, non-physical, repetitive paper pushing.

Thank goodness for Karen's job. Karen's better job. Ouch again. Her sales position at the Jamestown Evening Tribune enabled them to bring home enough cash to keep the bills at bay. The three bedroom split level with attached double garage, the finished basement, the two cars, dog and cat, ate up every penny they earned. The Busy Bee had been a tough decision to make, but right now, the eleven per cent mortgage rate was huge, the utility bills were huge and the car leases were huge. The money didn't stretch as far as it should have.

While the household income had not risen this year, the outflow of cash had. Never mind why. For now, this was it. Both parents working. If their little girl began to suffer in any way, they would pull her out of the day care and go to plan B. The day care option was working so far, except for the guilt which the parents carried on their backs. The Forbes' were not totally comfortable with the fact their little girl spent most of her waking hours with strangers, and not with them. Even though the strangers were fantastic people. They seemed to be fantastic people, anyway. Tom truly knew nothing about the Danton's. Nothing at all. The excellent word of mouth spreading through the city was his only awareness of the Danton duo. There had been one conversation when they signed Tiffany up. Plus, a few short chats over the past four days.

In reality, the Danton's were still, strangers.

What about Tiffany's little eyes? The windows into the soul? Even for a child? What were those eyes really saying as he backed out of the doorway? Yes, she was smiling and she looked happy, perched there in another man's arms. Clutching her red elephant.

Shit, wasn't it his job?

To hold his little girl?

Was it more important to be pushing stupid numbers around?

Not going there.

Besides, work *is* a necessary evil of life.

No work, no cash. No cash, no bills paid, no food to eat. No Jeeps to buy. No day care to afford.

There. Done. Let's pack it up, for the fifth morning in a row.

She is fine.

Tom parked in the back alley behind his office building right at eight a.m. He took his usual slot against the newly bricked complex. Yes, slot number eight. Tom got out of his Jeep, shut the door, stepped back and admired his new ride. The rich, emerald green paint glistened. How did they get those sparkly things so deep into the finish?

She was a beautiful, beautiful machine.

Tom looked past his baby. He saw only one other car. A red Ford Escort. The Escort was small, kind of boxy ugly, insignificant and puny. Especially when it was parked next to the power Jeep. The owner of the Escort was anything *but* ugly or puny. When the owner of the Escort was behind the wheel, she transformed the red box into a Corvette. She sure did. Funny, how a good looking girl could improve everything around her. Make everything look so much better, richer, happier, perkier, brighter, more colorful. More fun. More playful. More hopeful.

Tom turned away from the Escort and walked towards the rear office door. Happy to sad, in half a second. He sighed. Seeing the office door underscored the somber fact that he was number eight on the depth chart.

Crap. Another lackluster work day was about to begin. Yes, another great day of the numbers game. He would need a jolt of some kind to stay focused. At least until two this afternoon. The big show at the day care was starting at two. Good stuff. The show would be a nice break from the tedium. Tom had already arranged with the bosses to skip the last half of the afternoon.

The office lights of Burns, Henderson Chartered Accountants were already on. As the lowest man in the office, Tom got to start at eight. The secretaries would be in at eight thirty. The rest of the boys would wander in around nine, after their big power breakfast at the country club.

Oh well, it was time for the first jolt, and through the open back office window Tom could smell the coffee.

Or could he?

★★★★★

How the mighty had fallen. Tom's dream had been to parlay his teenage hockey skills into a free ride at university, then take a run at the National Hockey League. The university free ride part worked out perfectly. After an outstanding four year, award winning college career, Tom stood on the verge of realizing his professional dream. He was taken in the second round of the big league draft by the Pittsburgh Penguins. A nice signing bonus put him on cloud ten as his life was about to change forever. Good grief, he was actually going to play with the French Canadian wunderkind, Mario Lemieux!

The step up to the premier league proved to be an enormous one. Tom had to transition from pampered college boy to full grown man. This chasm proved too vast a distance for him to bridge. Professional players were not college boys. The pros were hardened men. They were much bigger, stronger, tougher, meaner and so much faster. They lifted weights, boxed and took steroids. They played with tough injuries, bleeding stitches and missing teeth. Tom was not prepared for the physical pounding, the air travel, hotel food, hotel beds, homesickness, after game parties, groupies, celebrity, and the constant, unyielding pressure to produce for money.

In college, his teammates had all been mates. All for one and one for all, the happy, camaraderie stuff. In the pros, his teammates saw one another as job competition, everyone trying to take food off of someone else's table. Cripes, the opponents were worse. Nobody wanted to give up a goal, or take a loss, or lose a puck battle for fear of being benched, sent to the minors, or released outright. The two way contracts most everybody signed were brutal. A nice six figure salary, five star hotels and comfy jets were the rewards of playing in the big league. Twenty grand a season, eight hour bus rides and Motel Six were waiting for you in the bush leagues.

When Tom failed to make the grade at the pro level, he skulked back to Jamestown to live out his life. He had some street credibility left, and was popular in the bars and around the slow pitch diamonds. Tom met Karen after his not so triumphant return. She was able to re-light his fire.

Was she ever. Karen was drop dead gorgeous. Tom thought she was far too good looking for him, way out of his league.

Especially after five of his front teeth had been knocked out of his mouth, courtesy of a Tiger Williams punch. Thanks a lot, you asshole thug. The toothless bastard must not have wanted anyone else to have teeth. Right after the infamous punch, Tom was shipped down to the minors. As a result, the NHL dental plan was not available to him. The minor league plan was. The inferior dental work didn't help a lot. The demotion to the minors was the last straw. The dream was over.

He did end up with the girl.

Tom always harbored an uneasy suspicion he did not deserve Karen. Besides her incredible looks and body, she was so bloody nice. Sensitive. Gentle. Caring. Generous. What did Tommy Boy bring to the table? Unable to follow his dream? Unable to cut it in the big show? Coming home, a loser. With busted up teeth. Wow. Did he ever catch a break with Karen. They married and had Tiffany. For a while, he was a very happy camper.

For a while.

*****

Tom keyed the back office door and went in. Yes, it was coffee he had smelled. For the third time this morning, a smile came to his face. Because this dead end job did have one rather amazing perk. Lisa, the office filing clerk, was the amazing perk. Only nineteen years old and fresh out of high school.

Tom re-locked the door. Walked down the narrow hallway leading towards the main reception area.

There she was. Young Lisa. Bent over the refreshment table, stirring sugar into a coffee mug. Humming to the radio.

Wow. What a view.

Lisa was wearing black high heels, black panty hose, a black mini skirt and a white fluffy sweater. As she bent, the white sweater ran up her back, exposing perfect young skin. Tom started.

What the hell?

On her skin, some sort of tattoo was peeking up above the top of her skirt. Tom had never seen a tattoo on a girl before. He stared hard. Crept closer. Some sort of stalker, his eyes on the prize. His eyes on the ink.

Yes, it was the matching spread wings of a butterfly. At least the top of the wings. Tom figured the completed butterfly must reach right down to the crack of her ass. And what an ass.

A butterfly. Really? What did the butterfly suppose to mean? What did it represent? Something about Lisa?

Who drew it on her?

Man, lucky bastard whoever did it.

How do you get into this line of work?

It would be a lot more fun than pushing numbers around.

Lisa was a striking brunette. Thick, rich, cascading hair. White, white silky skin. She was tall, at least five foot ten. Long, forever legs. Young, fresh and perky. No baggage. She drove a red, boxy Ford Escort, and she loved Tommy's hot new Jeep.

Tom saw the time on the round face clock. The office didn't open for another fifty-nine minutes. The secretary gang wouldn't be in for another twenty-nine minutes. He glanced around, searching for co-workers. No one else was here. There wouldn't be. There were only two vehicles parked outside. Therefore, only two people could be inside. They were alone.

Tom continued his stealth approach, the plush new carpet absorbing any sound from his shoes. He stopped right up behind Lisa, slipping his arms around her tiny waist. An inch separated the front of his crotch from the curvy back of her miniskirt. The one inch space wouldn't be there much longer.

Their 'thing' had been going on for months. They had never gone further than playful touching and ridiculous flirting. It had been fun.

Lisa laughed and turned, handing Tom his morning coffee. Her dark eyes, full red lips and brilliant smile filled Tom with the juices of life. He could devour her right here and right now. Alas, it would take some planning to actually pull it off. Discretion would be required. He was still a family man.

"Good morning, *Mister* Forbes," Lisa laughed.

"Enough of the Mister crap," Tom responded.

Sadly, he relinquished his grip and took the coffee. The hell with it. Tonight would be the night. It was time to step past this silly flirting stage. He had to have this girl. *Had* to. She sure wanted him. They had sent enough signals back and forth. He couldn't picture her with those fumbling young boys from her own peer group. Lucky not to get it off before they even got it out. No, this girl was years beyond them. She needed a real man. She needed Tommy.

Tom would figure something out. How about the old Flamingo Inn? He hadn't been there in ten years. No, the Flamingo was a dump. Christ, it had been a dump ten years ago. It was the one of the best pieces of real estate in the city, but Benny the Innkeeper ran it so cheaply. He never painted, never upgraded and barely cleaned. No, the Flamingo was not good enough for Lisa and her perfect body and her perfect, unblemished white skin. Or her fancy ass tattoo. The Flamingo was no longer good enough for Tommy. He wasn't some sixteen year old stud, rutting in the dark, a Romeo even back then. Tommy would find something much better. Something with clean sheets. It would have to be out of town. He was still pretty well known in Jamestown.

Cleveland would work. It was only ninety minutes away. The big Holiday Inn. One of the honeymoon suites with the heart shaped hot tubs. The king sized beds. Yes, a little planning was in order. Lisa couldn't leave her car here. They sure couldn't be seen leaving work together. He could pick her up at her place. No, her place wouldn't work, she didn't have a place, she lived with her parents. Remember, nineteen years old. He would have to meet her somewhere, possibly at the theatre. Whatever, he would figure it out. He was a clever guy.

So clever in fact, he would still fit the little beach excursion into his schedule after the day care show. And then, he would sneak off to the big city, with Lisa. After dinner, of course. This boring day suddenly got, a whole lot better.

"Why don't you drop by my office around four? Maybe we can...."

"Sounds great, *Mister* Forbes."

Lisa smoothed down the collar of Tom's white shirt and adjusted his new red tie. She undid a button on his jacket.

"There, perfect," Lisa said, still smiling.

The red tie was a birthday present. From Karen. First time wearing it. Tom thought the red tie looked kind of sharp against the white shirt. Red, a toreador fending against a charging bull. All macho.

Lisa patted the tie down against his chest. He tingled at her touch, and her smell, and her closeness. It was all so damn intoxicating. So illicit. So dangerous. So rewarding? Lisa slowly ran her tongue across her upper lip, and Tom nearly exploded. He didn't care about the obvious bulge in his pants. He was rather proud of it.

The phone began to ring on the switchboard.

Lisa turned on her heels and wiggled towards her desk. Tom sucked in his breath and stared. Indeed, what an ass. When she was out of his radar zone, he walked back down the narrow hallway, stepped into his office and closed the door. The things he could do with her butterfly tattoo. Damn, the crotch of his pants was near bursting. Right now, this second, Tom was Hercules.

He growled to himself and flipped his light switch, the ceiling fluorescents crackling with energy. He sat down in his fancy roller chair. Reaching way to the back of the bottom desk drawer, Tom pulled out a whiskey flask. Poured a nip into his coffee, a habit recently picked up. Carefully, he swirled the liquids together in the cup, took a sip and closed his eyes.

Fantasized about the night ahead.

Tom opened his eyes, excited about the other trick he had up his sleeve. He rummaged inside his jacket pocket and fingered the glass vial of white dust. This was another new habit. A very expensive new habit. Tom had picked up the vial at the Indian Sports Bar in Cleveland. Amazing what you could buy in the big city. For an amazing price, of course. Tom had taken half a dozen little rides in the past two months. It was powerful, wicked stuff. Totally non-addictive, his contact had assured him. This was the recreational version, designed for the occasional high. Not a lifetime dependency. There was no need to become a worthless, loser junky while pursuing a well deserved buzz.

Tom would show little Lisa what the big stud was made of. Tonight was going to be awesome. The nineteen year old filly was going to get a full ride, courtesy of the magic dust. Yes she was.

Tom had not felt this good in……..well, he wasn't hurting in the girl department, was he? Not with Karen at home.

Anyhow, with Lisa, he was suddenly carefree, unburdened, virile, and alive.

A champion.

A winner.

Tom placed his fantasy on hold and picked up the phone. He called his bookie to get the latest sports lines. Yes, another new habit. Yes, still more cash going out. Being such a sports hero, Tom figured he would be a natural at the betting game. For the life of him, he couldn't figure out why he kept picking losers. His luck had to turn. It certainly seemed as if it was going to turn.

Tonight.

CHAPTER 5

Tom listened to the recorded sports lines.

As he did, he admired the beautiful Hobey Baker Trophy commanding center stage of his desk. The trophy recognized him as the best college hockey player in the land. The best.

On one side of the trophy, a gold framed picture of Karen kept an eye on proceedings in his office. What a beautiful lady. She was stunning. Movie star stunning. What a great picture of her. Lucky man, Tommy, you are one lucky man.

So, you want to screw around with Lisa because?

Let's come back to this later. In fact, let's not revisit this at all. Why bother?

Instead, let's admire the trophy a bit more.

Yes, the trophy. What a fine piece of hardware. Heavy polished wood, gleaming gold accenting and plating. Impressive. Powerful. Handed out to only one person, once every year. By winning this trophy, Tom had put himself in rarified company.

On the other side of the trophy, sat a matching, gold framed picture of....

Wait a second.

Where was the picture of his little girl?

This wasn't right.

To: Al, Poppy, Dad... and Xuen

We thought you could enjoy some time reading and learning together!

Love,
Seth + Angela

Bridge mixture from kids!!

handwritten notes:
faith
goodness
knowledge
self control
patience
service to God
kindness
love

SCENES OF ABBOTSFORD
Mill Lake

HOUSE OF JAMES

2743 Emerson Street
Abbotsford, BC V2T 4H8
Ph: 604-852-3701 • Fax: 604-852-3734
Toll Free: 1-800-665-8828
www.houseofjames.com

Tom had not felt this good in…….well, he wasn't hurting in the girl department, was he? Not with Karen at home.

Anyhow, with Lisa, he was suddenly carefree, unburdened, virile, and alive.

A champion.

A winner.

Tom placed his fantasy on hold and picked up the phone. He called his bookie to get the latest sports lines. Yes, another new habit. Yes, still more cash going out. Being such a sports hero, Tom figured he would be a natural at the betting game. For the life of him, he couldn't figure out why he kept picking losers. His luck had to turn. It certainly seemed as if it was going to turn.

Tonight.

CHAPTER 5

Tom listened to the recorded sports lines.

As he did, he admired the beautiful Hobey Baker Trophy commanding center stage of his desk. The trophy recognized him as the best college hockey player in the land. The best.

On one side of the trophy, a gold framed picture of Karen kept an eye on proceedings in his office. What a beautiful lady. She was stunning. Movie star stunning. What a great picture of her. Lucky man, Tommy, you are one lucky man.

So, you want to screw around with Lisa because?

Let's come back to this later. In fact, let's not revisit this at all. Why bother?

Instead, let's admire the trophy a bit more.

Yes, the trophy. What a fine piece of hardware. Heavy polished wood, gleaming gold accenting and plating. Impressive. Powerful. Handed out to only one person, once every year. By winning this trophy, Tom had put himself in rarified company.

On the other side of the trophy, sat a matching, gold framed picture of....

Wait a second.

Where was the picture of his little girl?

This wasn't right.

Tom thought the big trophy in the center, with the matching gold framed pictures on either side, brought a nice Feng Shui to his desk.

With his free hand, Tom moved papers and ledgers, searching. He punched the speaker phone button so he could continue hearing the sports lines. He cradled the receiver.

Working with both hands, Tom lifted the large blue Spectrum computer monitor out of the way. The damn thing still wasn't hooked up. Burns Henderson's big step into the future. Tom didn't know why they needed computers anyway. His Texas Instruments T2 calculator worked fine. What about the keyboard attachment for the computer? Geez. He would be learning to play a damn piano. There was also something called a mouse. Really? A mouse? Tom could see no gains in efficiency or speed by entering the computer age with a mouse.

The picture of his little girl was not behind the Spectrum. Tom replaced the monitor and pushed his chair back. Deep, under his desk he saw something gold and shiny lying on the carpet. Aha. Tiffy's gold picture frame. It must have slipped off the back of the desk, along with some papers. Oops. Whose paperwork was missing from whose file, and for how long? Might somebody owe more taxes or have earned less profit than he thought? Oh well. It was only numbers. Stupid, penciled numbers.

The sports line was now at its end; Tom hit the speaker button to kill the connection. He bent down, slid to the front edge of his chair, and reached under the desk, stretching his arm and fingers.

Stretching.

Almost there.

Stretching some more.

He bent down even further and leaned forward a bit more, barely sneaking his head under the desk top. Tom was precarious on the front edge of the chair, his position and weight compressing the large spring under his seat.

Almost.....

Almost.....

Nearly.....

Only a tiny bit further.

Got it!

Tom snagged the picture frame with his fingertips.

On his way back out, the chair spring boomeranged, sending him up fast.

WHAM!

Tom cracked his skull on the underside of the desk!

Stars filled his field of vision.

Woozy, Tom much more carefully pulled himself the rest of the way out from under the desk. He reached behind his head and felt warmth. Blood? There was nothing on his fingers when he brought his hand back. Tom's stomach began to burn, a bad reaction to the coffee, the whiskey and the smash to his skull. He felt dampness under his arms, down his spine, even in his formerly bulging underwear.

Tom was about to straighten up in the chair, when he caught movement out of the corner of his eye.

He had hit the desk hard enough to cause the large trophy to teeter back and forth on its undersized base. The trophy was quite heavy, the fine cherry wood and polished brass plating. It was a big trophy for a big man. The base of the trophy, Tom had always believed, was far too small for the body above.

Tom was too slow.

He could not react in time.

Down came the trophy off its base.

The trophy landed.

SMASH!

On his skull!

On the *exact same* spot he had cracked, one and a half seconds ago!

Dark spots swam across Tom's eyes. He thought he was going to pass out.

He fumbled back in his chair, one arm flailing for the arm rest, the other clinging to the picture frame. Tom got his butt safely seated, and carefully began to rub his head. Again, he was checking for blood. He was in a world of pain, but at least there was no blood.

There *was* another round of flop sweat. He could really smell himself now. Disgusting. Settle it down, big guy, settle it down. A bunch of cleansing breaths were needed. Inhale through the nose, exhale through the mouth, inhale, exhale, inhale, exhale. The cleansing breaths seemed to work. How ridiculous. What the hell, was he planning on giving birth?

Never mind. He was not going to pass out, he hadn't yet puked, and he didn't shit himself. But wow, did his skull ever sting. Okay then.

Tom picked the trophy up off the carpet.

No wonder it hurt so much. He had forgotten how heavy the bloody thing was. The metal hockey player at the top of the trophy had impacted his skull. Tom saw the golden hockey stick was badly bent. Shit sakes. He slammed the heavy trophy back onto the desk top.

In his other hand, he still held tight the picture of his little girl.

He glanced at the picture.

Something wasn't quite right.

Tom tilted the picture slightly. Then he picked up the picture of his wife. The frames and the glass were identical. However, Tiffy's picture looked sharper and more focused. More intense. Almost radiant. Almost, alive. Tom had looked at these pictures hundreds of times. He had never noticed a difference. As he pondered this slightly disturbing phenomenon, he did not see his office door begin to open.

The door continued moving, ever so slowly, creeping, oozing. The door was of new construction, perhaps not set properly in its jamb. Tom did not notice because he was wondering why he was feeling so disturbed. About the difference in the two pictures. He fully understood why he was feeling disturbed about his head. His head hurt like hell.

The gold picture frames and the glass had come from Ace Hardware, two blocks away on the Miracle Mile. The frames were identical. $4.97 each. Six inch by four inch. Why were they different now? Tom set both pictures face down on the desk, and shuffled them around as if they were playing cards. He closed his eyes and rubbed his tender skull. He cracked one eye open and peeked at his fingers. Still no blood. A good thing. He closed the eye again. Kept shuffling the pictures around.

Stopped.

Lifted both pictures to his face.

Opened his eyes.

This was amazing!

Tiffany's picture was definitely brighter. Much brighter. It had almost a liquid feel to it. As if it had a third dimension. He could only stare at the picture, not comprehending. It reminded him of Jaws 3D, how freaky that movie had seemed. Things jumping off the big screen, right into your face.

A bone chilling wind shot through Tom's office, whipping papers around, badly startling him. He dropped his little girl's picture facedown onto the hard surface of the desk. He heard the loud 'crack' of the glass being violated.

"Damn!" he exclaimed, looking to his now open office door.

Where did the wind come from?

Why was his door open?

Had he not closed the door when he came in? After Lisa? With his coffee? Yes, of course he had.

Tom looked back at his desk top. He turned his little girl's picture over. The picture glass had cracked, sending spider webs across Tiffy's little face. Spider webs?

Tom returned his attention to the open door.

Who was there?

Lisa?

Playing with him?

No, he could hear her all the way across the office, talking on the phone.

This was something else entirely.

What was going on?

Confusion reigned.

A horrible feeling of black moved in on Tom. From all directions. From the top, from the bottom, from the sides. Surrounding him. A suffocating, overpowering sensation. Black waves. His bowels dropped. His guts began to roil. Tom reached down for his trash pail as his mouth flew open, spewing Karen's breakfast and some of Lisa's coffee and a nip of his whiskey. Miracle of miracles, the liquid mess hit the can perfectly. Good grief. Maybe he should have played basketball instead of hockey.

Or basketbarf.

Tom wiped the sleeve of his crisp, white shirt across his mouth. He stared again at the damaged picture. The spider webs continued to spread, rippling, covering his little girl.

Taking his little girl.

How was this even possible?

Tom heard faint whispers.

He whipped his head around to look behind. Bad idea. The sharp movement sent new pain through his skull. He kicked off with his feet and rolled his chair to the doorway, looking around the main office. He saw only sweet Lisa at her desk, still talking on the phone. Nobody else was present. Nobody. So who was whispering? Why was his bloody door open?

Tom rolled back to his desk. The effort afforded even more sweat to break out across his forehead. His whole body was soaked. He was standing in a warm ocean. A mild panic began to set in. For a split second, he was completely lost. Tom did not know who he was, where he was, or what he was. He was transported somewhere he had no comprehension of. A slipstream of some kind.

In the slipstream, nothing was everything. A foggy mass of nothing.

Suddenly.

Everything focused.

Clear and sharp.

Tom was moving through a corridor. It was dark. It must have been nighttime. His feet were gliding, almost as if he was back on skates. This was such a surreal feeling, but it was definitely satisfying. Tom was happy to be skating again, enjoying his first memories on the outdoor ponds and rinks of his youth. As he got older, he graduated up to the competitive ice surfaces in the crisp arenas. He performed before ten thousand fans in the collegiate ranks, and twenty thousand fans in the big league. What a rush. Twenty thousand fans packed in a rectangular box, cheering and screaming for him.

Tom skated on through the slipstream. Open doorways lined both sides of the corridor. Tom was able to peer inside as he glided past. Behind the doorways were long, narrow rooms. Weak fingers of candle light flickered in the rooms. Tom tried to put on the brakes but he had no control. He simply skated on past.

In the flickering light, Tom could see glimpses of people. People huddled in the deep recesses of these rooms. The people looked dirty and cold and malnourished. Tom couldn't tell for sure, because he was unable to slow down. In fact, he was speeding up. The doorways were passing him by, faster and faster. The weak flickering lights were growing brighter and sharper, taking on a strobing illusion. Between the bright lights and the darkness, Tom could see faces turned towards him.

Pleading, begging, needy faces. The faces of damaged poverty and capacious despair. The faces of something gone horribly wrong. Not true faces though. Not faces we know or understand. It was more, outlines of faces. Where faces should have been.

Skeletal faces.

On living people.

Still surreal, but no longer satisfying.

There was only one more doorway ahead. Tom was barely able to peek in. At the back of this room their appeared to be a little girl. The girl's hair was long and dirty. Possibly blonde at one time? At the exact moment Tom whizzed past, she looked up. The little girl possessed the same skeletal features and the same filthy clothes as the others. The same despair and haunting emanated from within her. She was suffering the same awful condition as the others. The girl was clutching a dirty rag or something. It might have been an old toy. A hint of red stuck in Tom's mind. He was past the doorway in a flash.

Tom was hurtling down the corridor now. He could see he was fast approaching the end. At the end of the corridor, a giant mirror waited. The mirror reflected Tom's rapid approach. This was not a good development. A ferocious impact was imminent. Into glass. Pointed, wicked shards of mirror glass. Tom had broken a mirror once. In his panic to clean it up, he had cut himself to ribbons on the tooth-sharp ruins. The mirrors came with a sinful glass, yes they did.

Tom felt a sudden super charge of strength and energy. His veins had been lit up with octane. He braced himself to throw a mighty body check. Yeah baby, bring it. He was going to plaster this son-of-a-bitch right through the boards. Tom actually left his skates as he charged at the mirror.

Abruptly, he was right back in his chair, free of the slipstream.

The disconcerting second passed.

Tom shook himself out. He felt chilly despite the mad sweats he was experiencing. His undershirt was now stuck to his back. His underwear was strangling his balls. His noggin began to throb, well past the headache stage. The throbbing was more of a reverberation, a sensation he knew, but could not immediately place. What on earth had just happened to him? Was still happening to him?

The clamor of employees entering the main office jarred Tom out of his stupor. With a near silent whoosh, the slipstream, the whispers, everything, was gone. He pulled a handkerchief out of his pocket and dried his face. He concentrated, trying hard to retrieve what had happened.

There was nothing.

Empty space. Zero. Zilch.

Except the giant headache, and the stench from the garbage pail, and the broken glass on the picture frame. The glass was not rippling now. Had it ever been? Was it his imagination? Was it the effects of a mild concussion from the suicide trophy?

How about the effects of the magic, non-addictive white powder?

Six trips already, right Tommy?

In only two months?

With no side effects?

The dealer *promised* there would be no side effects. The dealer wouldn't lie, would he? Not to Tom Forbes, a good customer.

Were we even going to consider this as part of the problem?

No.

Not going there.

Tom set up both pictures on the desk. He made a mental note to replace the cracked glass, and to get his precious trophy repaired. The trophy was still important to him. The trophy validated everything he had once been. The part of his life when he had been wildly successful.

Tom fished in his top desk drawer for aspirin and picked up the trash can. He carefully stood up from the chair. He was a little dizzy, but he was fine. Tough guy, ex hockey player and all. Tom headed to the washroom for water, a gargle, and a garbage can cleanup. He had six hours of paper to push before he picked Karen up. After all, it was Parent's Day at the Busy Bee.

What could be better?

CHAPTER 6

Joe Danton watched his wife chase Tiffany Forbes around the lush green backyard. They were both kicking at a soccer ball. Tiffany was squealing in delight as the large black and white dots rolled in front of her. The little girl clutched the red elephant in one arm as she ran. Joe helped a youngster down from the swing and surveyed the scene. There was so much energy. Kids running, climbing, laughing and shrieking. So busy. Expending so much raw joy. Such happy sounds on such a gorgeous day.

Joe found himself staring at the sky again. A mesmerizing sight. Joe was drifting. Drifting away, into the blue yonder. The sky approximated a painting, the artist having purposely altered the colors to create an abstract dimension.

Joe was thinking again about the factory smoke, or the lack of. Had the big steel plant taken a second Clear Day? Why would they? No, they didn't. They couldn't have. Because the thumping was still reverberating through the ground. So the furnaces were still running hard.

What about this surreal calmness in his backyard?

The cold breeze rattling through the oak tree had evaporated and disappeared. All was quiet again. All was calm. Too calm.

The birds were gone from the sky, but the tall trees and evergreen bushes were still showing movement. Did the birds know something? On a primal level? Had they gone to ground?

"Joe?"

The sound of his name brought Joe back to earth.

"Joe? Come over here," Marie called.

Marie and Tiffany were near the back plank fence, stooped over, looking at the ground. Tiffany was pointing at something. A marble? A worm? What little bit of fascination had caught the child's eye?

Joe walked towards them.

"Smell that," Marie said to Joe.

Joe stopped beside her, bent over and inhaled.

"I can't smell............"

He sure smelled it now.

A fountain of death, spewing up from the ground.

Joe's eyes began to water.

"Good grief! What on earth is it?"

"Smells as if something has died," Marie offered. "Isn't it awful?"

Joe could not even answer. He was focused on not vomiting.

Tiffany was hunching right over, seemingly oblivious to the smell, pointing intently at the ground. Joe covered his nose and managed to move closer. Together, he and Marie swept the immediate area with their eyes; they could see nothing in the grass. There was no little insect, or crawly creature, or lost ring capturing the child's attention.

There were no remains of an unfortunate accident spewing such an odor. The grass blades were standing straight up, thick and green and dewy. Joe scoured the ground and the plank fence for traces of blood, fur or feathers, looking for something indicating an animal in distress. Still nothing. He stepped to the high fence and stretched up on his toes. Looked over the fence and on into the adjacent Burlington Northern Railway property.

Whew! The smell was overpowering, it stayed with him right to the fence. He scrambled up and over the wooden planks.

Joe searched in the messy overgrown vegetation on the Burlington side. As he moved away from the fence, the smell disappeared, completely. Odd. When he rummaged back towards the fence, the smell returned. An invisible wall of stench.

Joe found nothing in his search. As he hoisted himself back over the fence, his eyes were very much watering, the odor was so bad. Joe stepped away from the fence. No smell. He inhaled deeply, almost furiously, and still no smell. Then he moved slowly toward the fence. About three feet from the fence, the smell hit his nostrils and brain box, akin to a strong steel hammer. The smell was hanging. A thick, suffocating death curtain. The smell carried on to the fence and over into the Burlington property for another couple of feet. Joe looked at Marie. They were dumbfounded. The only thing Joe could think of was the rotting of a corpse.

Tiffy was now squatting, pointing from the ground to the fence, back and forth, forth and back. Marie was holding her sleeve over her nose. She got right down beside the little girl.

"Tiffy? What is it? What do you see?"

Joe also knelt down. It was hard to keep from blowing his breakfast, the odor was so ghastly. Tiffany was speaking, but without sound. The death reek seemed to have no effect on the child. Joe was fascinated with the little girl's efforts. Her tiny lips moved, mouthing words. Joe stared. He could almost make out the words. It was as if she was speaking in a different language. Joe was so close to being able to translate, but it wouldn't quite come. Marie was watching the little girl as well. Marie finally shrugged her shoulders.

What was the child saying?

Still kneeling, Joe looked around the yard. Something was calling him. Not verbally, and not anything he could perceive with his ears. This was a different calling.

This, was a warning.

Okay, so where are you, you bastards?

I know you are here.

Joe's eyes stopped at the big oak. The branches and leaves were not moving. They were hushed. Static, or tension crawled across the air. It felt as if a spider was running across his bare back. Joe was sure he could hear whispering in the wind. However, there was *no* wind.

A faint tremor of panic ran through him. This was definitely a warning, but for what? Joe looked from the tree straight back to Tiffany. The whispering continued. It had to be the little girl.

The whispering stopped, as if in confirmation.

Tiffany stood, waved her arms and ran off. She found the soccer ball and attacked it with a new burst of energy. Marie stood, shivering. Joe stood, and together they backed away from the fence, and the smell. They held each other for warmth, on this warm, sunny day.

"What do you make of it?" Marie asked.

Joe shrugged. He didn't have a clue about the awful smell, but he did have his first clue about the warning. His mind was still processing things. For sure, he would have to watch the kids closely. Especially Tiffany Forbes. Something was happening, and it was happening right now. His whole body felt flush.

Marie could feel the heat coming off Joe. She felt the same sensation of separation she had felt earlier. Almost as if, it wasn't *her* Joe. Someone else was occupying Joe's body. Had replaced her Joe. Someone she did not know. Her Joe had left his body and was now somewhere else. She didn't like this one bit. No sir.

Joe was looking towards the sky again. The blazing yellow sun was offering no warmth to his face, his body, or his soul.

"Joe?"

Joe's mind was muddled. Thinking, thinking, going back. Going sideways and going forwards. Searching for clues or points or memories, something to help him now. Joe's thoughts often took him to different places and different times. Sometimes in the past, sometimes a sidestep, sometimes into the future. As if he had lived in those times, or was living concurrently in another space. Joe often felt a connection with yesterday. With many yesterdays and with many tomorrows. He had been through a lot in his thirty-three years on the planet, and his time living as Joseph Richard Danton seemed to be only a fraction of his existence.

The sidestep happened in his quiet moments, when he was trying for sleep. Joe was lucky to get three hours of real shut eye every night. The other hours were spent travelling, wherever his mind would take him. Often, he thought his inability to sleep soundly meant he was living in another dimension during those hours. A whole different life. Or lives. Sounds weird. Who really knows? Anything is possible. We are all a little crazy, aren't we?

At least, that's what he overheard his grade six teacher tell his parents.

Grade six was a tough year for young Joe. Something had gotten into his being, and began to play. Began to play strange games with his mind.

Joe would be walking home from school and he would hear something right close behind him.

Really close.

Right on his neck.

Joe would spin around, almost catching a glimpse of what it was. A shadow. He would spin around three or seven or eleven times, so close to catching up to what was on him. Joe had no idea why something would be following him so closely. Or why he would have to spin three, or seven, or eleven, or seventeen times to get rid of it. On a few occasions, young Joe would hit the ground because he became so dizzy. And look out if the other kids saw him. The other kids and parents did see him, and well, Crazy Joe came to be.

Next came the light switches at bedtime. Joe would turn out his bedroom light and at the *exact* same second, he would almost see what had been following him. He would quickly flick the switch back on. Nothing there. Turn the switch off. There it was again, almost. Joe would have to exhaust himself through the same sequence of numbers he used in his spin-around game as he attempted to capture his tormentor. He never did capture or even see his mysterious nemesis.

The capper was the grass pulling. Whenever Joe was walking across the ball field or a neighbor's lawn, he would get a life or death urge to bend down and pull up tufts of grass. He could sense through the bottom of his sneakers the evil spots on these surfaces, and knew exactly which grass had to be removed. There was a lot of bad grass on his street and the neighbors were not impressed to see their torn up lawns. This bit of madness had something to do with whatever was following him. It had something to do with whatever was waiting for him in the first second of darkness when he turned out the lights. These eclectic actions were all connected to some phobia, somehow.

The grade six teacher noticed Joe's number thing. If Joe was at the blackboard he would tap it three times with the chalk, or seven times, or eleven times. The poor kid was threatening to seizure once he got up past the thirty-three tap mark. The teacher figured there *might* be something wrong with this kid. A problem at home, or epilepsy, who knows? Dr. Phil wasn't around back then.

The numbers meant something to the kid. Something comforting. Or a way out of a bad situation, real or imagined. Some of Joey's homework listed the numbers. Three, seven, eleven, seventeen, nineteen, twenty-three, twenty-seven, thirty-one, thirty-three, thirty-seven. Always the same numbers. Something psychological for sure was going on with this kid.

The teacher called in the parents and the guidance counselor and some kind of behavior specialist. It was time for the big intervention. What was with the numbers and the spinning, Joey? Joe had to look at cards and pictures and answer all kinds of grown up questions. Joe thought he was simply a kid doing crazy kid things, so stop worrying folks, he was fine.

Then Joey's parents were obliterated in a car accident. There were no other relatives to step in but the grandparents. Joe and his sister got two years with the grandparents before the old folks were deemed incapable. Then foster care took over. Splitting the kids as they were entering high school.

Hold on.

Wait a second.

Zip back two years.

A funny thing happened immediately after the car accident. The spinning stopped. The lights on, lights off stopped. The grass pulling stopped. The tapping stopped. The numbers became numbers, once again. Whatever had been coming for Joe moved on when his parents died.

Now, flashes of numbers, the urge to do things three times, or seven times, or eleven times, was back. Joe was much older now. He could suppress the need to whirl around or crank the light switch, or rip up his own grass, but it was taking a toll.

"Joe?" Marie was tugging his arm.

"Can't figure this one out," Joe said.

"The smell is so intense, and so concentrated. The ground shows no sign of disturbance. There is nothing to indicate a dead animal."

"Do you think it could be something buried, possibly chemicals from the rail yard?" Marie asked.

Fresh in their minds were the headlines. Last year, the Garrison Pit in New Mexico owned the newspaper front pages. The Garrison Pit had been a burial ground for the nascent nuclear industry in the forties. Dig a really, really deep hole in a deep abandoned mining shaft and throw bad stuff in. Bury it and forget it.

The central New Mexican water table ran through the pit. Who knew? Birth defects were showing up in disturbing numbers from the counties located around the pit. It had taken forty, long years for the poison to leach into the water table. Affected children numbered nearly five hundred.

The year before, it had been Burns Lake, outside St. Paul, Minnesota. Burns Lake was re-christened Burnt Lake by the media. The lake had been a dumping ground for the munitions business. In the summer of 1985, a violent storm struck, churning up the lake bottom. The following morning, huge slicks covered the surface. An errant cigarette ignited a massive fire, killing boaters, cottagers and lake front home owners. The dead numbered almost three hundred. The Governor of Minnesota tried to call it a forest fire. A forest fire spreading across the water? Hardly. The Army Corps of Engineers filled in the lake and planted a forest.

If you lived in the upper northeast of the US of A, you would never forget the biggie of them all, the Love Canal. The absolute definition of manmade stupidity equaling disaster.

"It's possible," Joe mused. "There's always been plenty of heavy industry here. But the smell. It's a smell of rot, or decay. A smell of death. It doesn't smell of chemical."

"I'll call the city to come out and check. In fact, I will do it right now," Marie offered.

"Good idea," Joe responded.

"Now, let's get back to the gang. It's going to be a big day."

How big was the day going to be? Joe had no idea. His mind was still working the details. The little girl, the oak tree, the whispering in the wind, the awful smell in the ground by the fence. The dead calm in his own backyard.

What was the connection?

What was he missing?

One, two, three.

Four, five, six, seven.

Eight, nine, ten, eleven.

Why was he ticking off numbers in his head?

Three.
Seven.
Eleven.
Was there supposed to be some comfort in these numbers?
A clue in these numbers?
What?
Joe thought back to the death of his parents. Twenty, long years ago. The numbers and the crazy behavior had shown up right before the fatal crash.
A harbinger of sorts.
The numbers were back.
The numbers had not arrived alone.
Joe Danton was not in grade six. He was older now.
He was a soldier.
The numbers didn't faze him.
The numbers did serve as a warning.
Watch the girl, Joe.
Watch the girl.

CHAPTER 7

Tom pushed papers from one pile to the next, scribbled, erased, filed, calculated, tapped buttons and typed. He even glanced at his new computer monitor, and wondered again what the hype was all about. The computer appeared to be a slick version of a television set. Big deal. It was supposed to be the magic box into the future. Oh well he figured, one day the thing would be up and running. He would have to take on a new skill set and learn to operate it. The technical installation team was scheduled in next month. They had been scheduled in last month and couldn't make it. Apparently, demand for the installers was off the charts, and a re-committal had to be arranged. The computer business was taking off. This was going to be one expensive hula hoop.

The day dragged on as Tom processed a blur of financial sheets. To break the monotony, he spent fifteen minutes on the phone with Mike the bookie, going over his weekend sports picks. It was all about the baseball, because his hockey season had not yet started. Those shitty Minnesota Twins were really messing him up. Every time he bet for them or against them, he lost. Every single time. What was up with the Twins? Tom had never been to Minnesota, and knew nothing about the place other than cold snow and Burnt Lake. He did admire the NFL Vikings and their black and blue style of play. But the Twins?

The Twins were leading their division, but barely playing above five hundred. They were actually going to win the division with eighty-two or eighty-four victories. Not right at all. Tommy couldn't wait for the playoffs. He would bet everything he had on the shit Twins getting blown out in round one by a real team. October was going to be fun. Baseball playoffs, NFL start up, NBA and NHL hockey. Opportunity would be knocking in the betting world. Games to wager on, pools to join. Good times for all.

Tom's usual, dull afternoon boredom headache was being overtaken by the double rap he took to his noggin. First from the underside of the desk, and then from the heavy falling trophy. He rifled back three more aspirin, making the day's ingestion a grand total of six. He washed them down with coffee and whiskey. His stomach had settled somewhat, and the whiskey helped cut the awful puke tongue. A roll of breath mints sat on his desk, ready for the trip to the Busy Bee. He could really use a pick-me-up.

Should he slip into the back washroom and grab a snort? No, this wasn't the time. He truly felt like crap, but to run right up to ninety miles an hour was not the way to go. A good, ten minute nap would be a better solution. Besides, tonight with little Lisa? Yes. He would save his snort for tonight.

Tom carefully massaged the pronounced lump on the top of his head. Two blasts to the exact same spot. How fucking ridiculous? No kidding it might be a concussion. If it was, it would be the second one of his life. The first being the cheap shot by the cheap prick on the Vancouver Canucks. Tom remembered the scrum. A typical NHL scrum, two guys fighting, everybody else paired up watching. Tom, the fresh rookie was paired with Canucks superstar Thomas Gradin. Neither one of them was a fighter, neither one of them even dropped their gloves. Gradin had the misfortune of stepping on a discarded hockey stick. As he buckled to the ice, Tom actually tried to pull Gradin back upright.

Tiger Williams saw his captain going down, released his dance partner and skated over to Tommy. Williams wound up and suckered Tom in the mouth. What an asshole. Two months later in Pittsburgh, Penguins tough guy Kevin McClelland ambushed the Tiger, beating him like a rag doll. Tom was in the minors by then. With his bad dental work.

Whatever.

All in the past.

Tom began to yawn, stretching his arms, leaning back in his chair. He had been hunched over his desk for a solid four hours. He needed to relax. He needed to sleep. The doctor was ordering him to sleep, begging him to sleep. The office was unusually warm, a result of the gorgeous day outside. Nobody had bothered adjusting the furnace down. This was not the era of conservation. The monotonous work, the warm office and the aspirin overload finally began to catch up with him. He was tired. No, he was exhausted. A nice catnap was required.

Tom closed his eyes for a second. What relief. It felt *so* good to simply drop those eyelids. His poor eye muscles felt as if they had been holding up a steel garage door. Peace was now flooding over him. It was amazing how a simple, effortless movement could allow you to fall into such a luxurious, deep sleep.

Mere minutes had passed by when Tom opened his eyes. He wasn't tired anymore. Wow. The nice bit of shuteye did the trick. It proved to be the tonic he needed. Thank goodness he didn't take the snort.

He checked his watch.

Good grief!

It was one minute past two o'clock!

So much for mere minutes of napping!

He must have dozed off. No, he did doze off. Actually, he had slept solidly for nearly two hours. Two hours? Two hours of sleeping and nobody came into his office? To ask him a question? To get an opinion? To wake him? To bust his chops? To light his ass on fire?

Was he really so unimportant to the operation of this business?

Never mind, it was time to go.

Tom had to swing by the Tribune and pick up Karen before heading over to the Busy Bee. Parents Day. Should be entertaining. The little tykes showing off their artwork and singing skills and what else. Better not be late. Shit. He was already late.

Tom packed away his sports picks, his booze, his magic dust and his plans for romance. He ripped open the breath mints and put two in his mouth. Then two more. Better make it two more. The rest of the pack went in his pants pocket. It was time for family stuff.

He was heading to the rear exit when Lisa rounded the corner. They nearly collided in the hallway. She seemed troubled by his unkempt, fatigued, messy look. More than troubled.

"Mr. Forbes? Are you okay?"

Alarmed would better describe Lisa's rapidly evolving state of mind. She backed away, almost in revulsion.

"Tom?"

Tom realized he had not seen Lisa since the 'good morning' coffee, six hours ago. The cock of the walk, the super stud, the big green Jeep. He was all that and more.

Not so much now. Seeing the distress on Lisa's face, he realized he must look like crap. The early morning barf, the super soaker sweats, the sewer breath and the nearly caved-in skull. This was not the virile, healthy, sportsman image he wanted to project. Mr. Four By Four in the open top Jeep, rocking and rolling down the highway.

Tom threw up his arms to ward her off.

"Back in about an hour, okay?" he mumbled.

Tom blew past Lisa and hit the door, nearly running. He made for his refuge, sitting right there in the middle of the parking lineup. His pride and joy. Emerald green. The brand new Jeep Cherokee. Big truck for a big man. Tom punched the Jeep out of the parking lot.

It was eight city blocks to the Tribune. Starts and stops. Starts and stops. Traffic was pouring in and out of the downtown. Vehicular gridlock on the road. Pedestrian gridlock on the sidewalks. Lots of commerce.

Tom saw the food joints were all crammed. Two o'clock in the afternoon and people were still eating lunch. Still packing it in. Red Barn, McDonalds, Tasty Freeze, Burger King, the whole lot of them. Chairs all full, lineups at the counters, cars and trucks queuing to get in the parking lots. Everybody happy. Everybody hungry. Hungry for more, more and more.

Flags were fluttering everywhere. The tri-colored American flags were always so festive, especially when there were so many bunched together. The Miracle Mile indeed. So busy. So much money changing hands. Everybody was working hard for their money, but seemly throwing it away as if the supply was perpetual. Tom Forbes included.

Tom saw Karen waiting out front of the Tribune. She was positively glowing, standing in the sunshine. Her long, light hair tousled in the breeze. Her thin dress flapped over beautiful brown legs. Strappy summer sandals completed the look. She was gorgeous. Karen said goodbye to a co-worker and climbed into the Jeep.

"Sorry I'm late," Tom said sheepishly.

Karen reached across the seat and patted his thigh. In an instant she knew her man was off kilter.

She smelled sweat, and……..yuck.

What was mixed in with the sweat?

"Are you okay, babe?" she asked.

"Yeah, I am now. I smashed my head on the stupid desk. Don't ask me how. Did it ever hurt. Pretty much crapped my drawers when I did it."

"Poor baby, what can I do to make it better?"

Tom looked across the seat at her. She was so beautiful.

"Nothing. I'll be okay. Just. Sorry I'm late."

"Tom, she'll be so excited to see us. It should be fun."

By fifteen past two they were nearing the day care.

Late.

Damn.

Tom hated being late.

Especially for an event such as this.

It was bad enough dumping his girl every morning.

Being late as well?

Shit.

Traffic and commotion plugged the road ahead.

"Wow. Good turnout," Karen said.

"Sure is," Tom agreed, surprised as hell at the turn out.

After all, these were the same parents who couldn't ditch the kids fast enough to start their busy days. Again he was included, this time in the group of parental ditchers. Guilty as charged, Tom realized.

This wasn't supposed to be the way. The giant pro hockey contracts were going to put him and his family on easy street. And keep them there. Not so much. Tom got a nice Corvette out of the deal, some bad dental work, and little else. The Vette was long ago sold, a mere blip in his memory.

A hundred and fifty feet from the day care was as close as they were going to get. Tom pulled to the curb and parked. He spotted flashing lights ahead, red and blue, in front of the Busy Bee. They got out of the Jeep and walked down the sidewalk towards the action. The beautiful warm sunshine was gone. The sky was darkening, and a bone chilling wind blew into Tom's heart. Something was wrong. He reached for Karen's hand. For the second time this day, he felt the bottom drop out of his guts.

The red and blue lights were not part of the show. No they weren't. Emergency personnel at a day care in the day time could only be bad news. The large crowd covered the front yard, spilling onto the roadway. As Tom and Karen approached, they saw police, fire fighters, ambulance attendants and anxious parents. Tom and Karen looked at one another. They clasped their hands tighter. Something here had gone off the tracks.

Badly.

Their next door neighbor, Annie Zimmerman, broke from the crowd.

She ran towards them.

She was hysterical.

"It's Tiffany!" Annie screamed. "Tiffany's gone!"

Annie Zimmerman embraced Karen, who quickly moved past agitation and alarm, to panic. What was Annie saying? Tiffany was gone? What? What did this mean?

Two police officers suddenly appeared, looking perturbed at the interference of the neighbor.

"Tom Forbes? Karen Forbes?" the lead cop asked.

Tom nodded a yes. He was beginning to feel numb.

"Your daughter is missing. Joe Danton is missing."

One officer pulled the weeping neighbor away from Karen.

"Tom?" Karen gasped, grabbing for her husband. "Where is she?"

Tom turned to the lead officer.

"Officer?"

"Please come with us."

The cops led the confused parents through the crowd. The crowd parted easily, as if their collective minds were saying, 'It's them. They have the trouble. Stay away from them'. The faces in the crowd stared. Tom wanted to tell them all to F off. He still didn't know what was going on.

An officer from inside the brick building opened the yellow happy face door. Into the Busy Bee they went, and then straight out to the backyard. They walked past colored plastic toys, the sandbox and the swing set. Police personnel were searching the yard and adjacent Burlington railway property. Colored police tape cordoned off an area near the back fence. Inside the tape, a gray tarp covered a large lump. Wisps of smoke curled off the charred fence and singed grass.

What had happened here?

A lightening strike?

The lead officer pointed to the tarp.

"Marie Danton. She was badly burnt. She's gone. There is no sign of your daughter, or Joe Danton. At this point, we have no witnesses who saw what happened here. We have put out an APB for Joe Danton. I need to confirm. Did you drop your daughter off this morning?"

Tom nodded, stumbling the words out.

"Eight o'clock. Yes I did. Joe took her in. Joe was holding…………."

Karen's knees weakened and she leaned against Tom.

Tiffany?

Missing?

Taken from the day care? Joe missing? Marie dead?

Tom spotted something on the fence.

Something not there before.

Something *wicked*.

He could see it as plain as day. He pointed towards the fence.

"What is that?" he shouted.

Tom handed Karen off to one of the cops. He ducked under the police tape and walked towards the fence, pointing. The smell stopped him in his tracks. His eyes began to water. Tom looked down at the curling smoke rising off the grass.

"What on earth is this *smell*?"

The officers followed, stepping under the tape, dragging Karen along. They moved in close, sniffing at the air. They smelled nothing. The cops stared at the fence. The fence was a blackened, charred mess. Nothing else.

Karen was near hysterics.

"What is it Tom?" she managed.

"This!" Tom bellowed, still pointing towards the fence.

"And the smell!"

Tom was losing it. Tears were flowing from his eyes, the odor was so rancid. This must be what riot gas was like. He had never smelled anything so debilitating, so vile, in all of his life. So rank. So utterly evil.

What the hell had happened? Marie Danton was dead? How could anybody die at a *fucking* day care? His little girl was missing? Joe was missing? None of this made *any* sense.

Tom's fingers were now on the fence, tracing an imaginary figure.

"Right here! This!"

Karen could see nothing but burnt wood. She figured she was in shock. Or Tommy was. Or they both were. She wheeled on the police officers.

"Where's my baby! Where is she?"

Tom continued to stare at the fence.

An officer was relaying a report to central station via his radio.

"Possible lightening strike. Fire. One dead. Child missing. Confirm APB for Joseph Danton."

Tom heard the thump, thump, thump of a helicopter looming.

This was all wrong.

It was Parent's Day, for God's sake!

Karen was now plastered to him, shrieking and crying. The officers began to guide them away from the fence. Tom saw a hand protruding from underneath the tarp. A small, woman's hand. Blackened and blistered. He shuddered.

Marie Danton.

Dead?

Marie?

Joe Danton? Vanished?

Tiffy, missing?

Where was his little girl?

What had she known this morning?

What had she seen?

What had he *not* seen?

Right above, the thump, thump, thump of the search and rescue helicopter beckoned to Tom. He looked up. The afternoon sky had darkened so quickly. In fact, the sky had blackened as if night had fallen. The night light above the rear door to the Busy Bee had powered on. The unexpected darkness accentuated the strobing lights of the emergency response vehicles parked out front. The reds and blues were flashing against the brick building, the big oak tree, even shooting across the falling sky.

The great oak, which this very morning had begun to hint at fall colors, was now completely bare. Not a single, solitary leaf remained on its mighty branches. The ground beneath was carpeted with dead, curled leaves. Blackened leaves. How on earth could every last leaf fall from the tree in mere hours?

Way beyond the oak, at the shores of the great lake, lightening streaked from the sky. It had to be landing in the Morgan Iron and Steel Works. The sky above the factory was angry, black and roiling. Heavy clouds were mixing with the thick smoke. Tom couldn't tell one from the other. Or if it *was* one or the other. He had never seen the sky look so alien.

The magnificent clear morning of six hours ago, was now a memory blip.

The temperature dropped further. Tom felt the icy wind. He shuddered. He heard sounds in the wind. Whispering. The same whispering he had heard in his office?

With his eyes, Tom swept from the base of the tree, to his Karen with the police officers, to the ambulance attendants pushing a wheeled stretcher, to the bright toys in the green, green grass, to the empty swing set.

Something began to change.

The darkening sky was draining color out of the world. As the color ran away, Tom frantically looked for the red elephant. He *had* to find the elephant before it too lost color and faded away. His little girl and the toy elephant were inseparable. If he found the red elephant, he would find her. That's how it was.

Tom raced through the backyard in full panic mode. Adrenaline coursed through his veins.

Holy shit!

This was real!.

Not a bad dream.

Not a TV show or a movie.

Real!

Dead real!

Where was the damn elephant?

Where?

Tom looked, searched, hoped.

Alas.

There was no sign of the elephant.

The elephant was gone.

Tom stopped.

Breathing hard.

Heart pounding.

Head pounding.

Skull aching.

Scared shitless.

Quaking where he stood.

He looked back at the charred fence. Wisps of white smoke drifted and swirled.

A message?

Calling him?

Or mocking him?

Where was his little girl?

CHAPTER 8

TIME CAN BE BROKEN DOWN INTO SECONDS.

Insignificant little seconds, ticking away.

Once they tick away, they are gone. Forever.

Whether we eat, or sleep, or work, or play, or do good things, or do bad things, or do nothing at all, the seconds tick away, running off to eternity. Those seconds add together to become minutes. Minutes become hours, hours become days, days become weeks, weeks become months and then years.

Before we realize it, those insignificant seconds have grown into something pretty important.

They have grown into time.

Now, after so much precious time has passed, Tom Forbes is skating again. It felt good to be doing something fun, after enduring seconds and hours and years of gut wrenching grief. If you considered mourning your missing child and your destroyed marriage as fun. Because these two facts would never leave him. Could never leave him. Ever. Regardless of what he was doing. Or not doing.

Sleeping.

Thinking.

Breathing.

Living.

Existing.

Tiffy, gone forever.

Karen, gone forever.

Both still with him, but gone.

At least he knew where his wife was. Sort of. Nobody could tell him where his little girl was. The lack of closure was a dagger through his heart and soul.

How could you not know something so important? How?

Of the half billion fathers on this planet, what percentage *did not know* where their two year old daughters were?

The answer was so minuscule, it did not even have a value.

The answer might be, a bunch of prisoners, some deadbeat dads and Tom Forbes.

Pathetic. Truly, pathetic.

So, before he once again slipped into the depths of despair, it was time for Tom to skate.

Time to have some fun.

Indeed, 'fun' was now a relative term for Tom Forbes.

Skating was undoubtedly something pleasing and exciting for Tom. As far back as he could remember, his best childhood recollections involved skating. Skating right here on the big pond at Ironworker's Park in central Jamestown. By mid November, the pond would be frozen solid. The city workers would keep it clear of snow in the daytime. They even left shovels out for after hours and weekends so the skaters could pitch in with the maintenance. Three or four times a week, Tommy and his dad would lace up the blades, grab their old hockey sticks and shinny around.

Friday nights were special in Jamestown. City workers started the timer for the flood lights at dusk, allowing skaters and hockey players to have their fun right into the late hours. Tommy was allowed to stay out on those Friday nights. Supper done, homework done, hockey time. Then hot chocolate and bed.

The winter weekends were sure magical. Because after Friday night, came Saturday night. Jamestown was close enough to Canada to pick up the Hockey Night feed. Dad had installed the latest new fangled rotating antenna up the side of their two storey house. The action from Maple Leaf Gardens came in crystal clear. Steve Thomas. Wendel Clark. Borje Salming. Sometimes little Tommy Forbes wished he lived in Canada. He loved the Toronto Maple Leafs and couldn't believe those Canadian folks did nothing but play hockey all winter long.

Tommy and his dad on the couch, drinking hot chocolate and watching the game. Tommy in his pajama pants and Maple Leaf jersey. Dad in his trousers and Maple Leaf jersey. Mom tolerating the mundane sportscast, knitting quietly in her rocker, a smile playing on her face.

Great memories.

Great memories of a great childhood.

The kind of childhood everyone should have. Fun, exciting, stable and secure. Mom and dad always there for you. Always there when you needed them. If you fell and scraped your knee, if you got the measles, if you were having a sad day or a bad day, they were always there. You could grow up strong and secure, and then eventually pass this down to your own children. Or your own child.

If you had one.

Yes, a child.

Tom sighed.

Suddenly!

A bullet train blasted past the pond!

Tom actually ducked.

Jesus!

He had forgotten how close to the tracks the pond was. Why were those trains allowed to go so fast through the city? The speeding trains were a catastrophe waiting to happen.

Already, Tom could barely see the tail end of the train. Snow and dirt swirled in the train's path and began to settle onto the tracks.

Back to his previous string of thought.

Children.

It might be fun to have them. Raise them up from infancy. Care for them and nurture them. As they got older, say two or three, the good stuff would begin. Tom could bring his little son down to the rink and they would have a blast. Or, if it was a girl, Tom could bring her down to the rink, and they would have a blast. Boy, girl, either way it would be fun. The boy? He would definitely be a hockey player. The girl would be a figure skater, or more likely, a hockey player as well. Children. Yes. He would want to have them.

Tom gracefully circled the pond. He thought about trying a double axel but had no clue how to pull it off. He would probably land on his ass or break an ankle. As a former hockey professional, Tom could appreciate the skill set required to be a figure skater.

He closed his eyes and for the moment, felt as if he was flying. The breeze buffeted his face as he propelled himself around the rink. The effortless thrust from his thighs and calves produced magical results. Indeed, he was born to skate.

Tom opened his eyes. He saw bits of green poking through the snow. It looked as if winter was going to be done this very day. For sure it was getting too warm for the ice to hold out much longer. In fact, Tom could feel his blades slashing deeply in the slushy surface. He skated two more circuits of the frozen pond and was finished.

Tom sat down on one of the many park benches and unlaced his blades. He pulled off his extra socks and slipped on a pair of black rubber boots. The rapid warming of the day was turning everything to mush. The rubber boots had been a good call.

Tom tied his skates around the end of his hockey stick and placed the stick over his shoulder. He was a hobo hauling his worldly possessions on the end of a branch. He had done this very thing many times, back when he was a kid.

A kid.

Tom sighed again.

From the opposite direction, another bullet trained blasted past!

Again, Tom was caught unawares!

What the hell was with the trains?

Tom realized his stomach was crawling.

Weren't the trains required to give warning blasts as they approached population centers? Jamestown was definitely a population center. Fastest growing city in the country, they said.

Stupid bloody trains.

Tom had to cut across the rink to get home. No problem. He kicked thick slush as he walked across the surface. Thank goodness for the boots. Six dollars for the pair from the local hardware store.

He stopped in the middle of the slowly melting rink. He looked around the entire circumference. Tom knew he was getting old because this pond used to seem so big. Vast and borderless. Really, how many strides would it take for him to get across?

As a kid, with his short little legs pumping hard, he remembered it taking forever. Not any longer. Tom balanced his hockey stick and skates on his shoulder, then stretched his hands out to the sides. In his mind he could nearly touch the outside edges of the rink. He had grown to superman proportions. Kind of how he felt right now, what with the ugly combination of beer and whiskey coursing through his system. A full dozen beers already, and now, he was into the hard stuff. He had to admit, he was sure building a tolerance to the alcohol.

Superman.

Felt good to be superman, didn't it Tommy?

Suddenly, the ice was completely melted.

Wow.

Soft ice to water, in an instant.

Tom found he was terribly overdressed. He pulled his arms back down, unbuttoned his jacket and stuffed his winter gloves in his pockets. What did you call those waves of heat spilling down out of the Rockies? Chinooks? Yes. A Chinook seemed to be what was going on. There was no other explanation for the sudden rise in temperature.

Ohio was nowhere near the Rockies, was it? Arizona was, however. Arizona was on the far side of the Rockies. Why was he thinking of Arizona? Where did his skates and stick disappear to?

What the hell was going on?

Why was everything so jumbled?

So disconnected?

Tom looked around the formerly frozen rink. Only cloudy water remained. The water had spread infinitely in all directions, becoming quite shallow. The water was only up to his ankles, and barely rippled towards him. Despite the alcohol induced sluggishness he was beginning to feel, Tom put himself on alert. The rippling water was ever so slightly betraying its oncoming direction.

Shit, Tom thought.

Here we go again.

He raised a whiskey flask to his mouth, and drank.

Sometimes ingesting this crap helped.

Usually, it didn't.
If it didn't, he had the next level primed and ready to fire.

CHAPTER 9

Joe Danton was alone with his memories. Rummaging through them as if they were historical documents. Folding and unfolding them. He found one of the biggest memories of his life and unfolded it.

Three. Seven. Eleven. Seventeen. Nineteen. Twenty-three. The numbers ran through Joe's mind. They weren't bringing him any comfort.

Warm, dense air began to surround him. Again, no comfort was being brought. An eerie calm settled, and static ran through the atmosphere. A giant oak tree took centre stage, and a sickening smell of death filtered through Joe's nostrils.

Twenty years had passed since the numbers had first come and gone. The first time, they took his parents. What did they want this time? He certainly found out what the numbers wanted. They wanted the girl.

Memories. Not always the gilded moments you hoped they would be.

The bright balloons and colorful streamers were plastered against the smooth brick walls. The happy, charged laughter of the kids filled the air. Charged, because today, their mommies and daddies would be joining them at the happy place. Coming to see their work and their crafts and their drawings. Coming to see *them*.

Joe winced as this movie replayed.

He could see himself entering the brick building. This wasn't only Parent's Day, this was validation day for Joe Danton.

Joe had survived the loss of his parents, survived the foster care years and survived the awkward torture of high school. 'Homeless Joe' they called him, in the high school hallways. It wasn't enough he had lost his parents, his home and his grandparents. The teenagers decided to amp up his loss with their own form of torture. Thanks for the character build.

Homeless Joe was no more. Homeless Joe was gone forever. Over the past two decades, Joe had moved many times around the country. He had plenty of opportunity to re-make himself into anything he wanted to be. Some things had worked out. Some things hadn't. It was a big country with many, many possibilities. There were as many opportunities as there were pitfalls. Joe had already endured a lifetime of pitfalls. It was time for something good.

So here he was, operating his own business, making a living, and most importantly, *he was watching the kids.*

Who would have thought?

No more Crazy Joe either, those troubles were also buried deep in his past. No more *anything* he used to be. Grade six would always haunt him. The spinning. The lights. The bad grass. The numbers. The behavioral specialist. The awful pills making him sick. Then mom and dad were gone. Not a good year at all.

Joe Danton was a true survivor. He rebuilt his world. He found his beautiful soul mate and life partner. He could not have done any of this without Marie. She was amazing. She loved Joe, and god, did Joe love her. They both adored the kids. The awful kicker was Marie unable to have kids of her own. A crushing defeat she carried. Crushed, because she knew her Joey and his love for kids.

Together, they chose this path. If they couldn't have any of their own, perhaps they would be able to help others. So, here they were, the two of them, on validation day. Joe and Marie Danton had arrived. Business was booming, the waiting list was long, their reputations were growing, their young clientele was happy and the parents were thrilled.

Joe and Marie knew they had chosen the correct path. They were good with the kids. They could mentor these kids and shepherd them to a better future. In reality, they could line these kids up and pipe them anywhere they wanted. The kids trusted them. Completely. The kids would follow. Joe would never be a dad to any of them, but he could support them, nurture them, and watch out for them. Because the damn numbers were back. The numbers were everywhere.

The memory tape skipped ahead.

Joe was outside in the green, green yard. The giant oak was stretching to the heavens, strong, powerful and everlasting. A sentry, a rock of ages. The oak was as eternal as any living thing could be on this planet.

The sun was blazing in the bright blue sky. What a sight this late in the year. What, a spectacular day. The way Joe felt right now, every day could be validation day.

Joe was aware of the warm solar rays lighting up the morning, a perfect accompaniment to this Parent's Day. Why then did he remember lifting his face to the sun, closing his eyes, his wonderful Marie at his side, and feeling no warmth and no comfort? He remembered the three seagulls, wheeling through the sky, buffeted by the wind. The kids so busy, so active, then it was lunch time, then right back outside to take full advantage of the glorious day.

Joe fully and cleanly stepped back inside the memory.

1987. The ninth month. The eleventh day.

An implausible void filled the backyard. Everything went still. Static ran through the air. The smell of death rose from the earth. Unexpectedly, the heat drained out of the sky. A large cloud began to pass across the sun. The cloud was thick and ponderous. Sinister, swirling, soot filled and alive. Everything began to lose color.

Joe froze.

His whole being began to tingle.

Something was………

It was happening! Right now!

He hurriedly looked around. Grasping for clues, summoning his wits and his strength.

Where?

What?

Why?

How?

More clouds rushed in. Joining, congregating, ink black and foreboding. Day suddenly became night. Streetlights clicked on up and down the block. The clicks were extremely loud, as if the lights were begging for enough juice to fight back against the dark.

Joe heard the faint sound of police sirens. A mild thumping arose in the far away sky. Some sort of rescue operation had been mounted. The temperature dropped so fast Joe could see his breath. Mist and fog began to shroud the backyard. He placed all of his sensors on high alert.

Be ready Joey!

Watch behind you.

Watch right on your shoulder.

They were coming.

They were coming for her.

Damn!

Too late!

They were here!

Move now Joey! Move!

Get to her!

Protect her!

The blast of white light. Paralyzing any response. The white light went out. Sheer blackness. More mist and fog. Choking the backyard.

Joe recovered quickly. He could barely see.

There!

Movement!

He counted fast.

His mind spit out the numbers.

One.

Two.

Three.

Four.

Five.

Because there were five of them.

This had nothing to do with the old sequence of numbers, back in his grade six days.

CHAPTER 10

Tom carefully watched the ripples. They seemed to be in a holding pattern. This was a good thing. Keep them steady and calm. Don't get them riled up. Tom could hear the factory thumping away. The never ending sound reverberated through the ground. Reverberated through the pond even. Producing a secondary set of ripples. Ever since he was a kid, the factory had blasted away. The factory was one thing you could count on in Jamestown. Jobs, jobs and more jobs. Dependable jobs. Life time jobs. Wages. Pensions. Health benefits. Vacation pay. Spending. Good times.

Yes, the factory was Jamestown.

Why was the factory thumping? Hadn't the place closed down last year?

Sure it had.

Or was it the year before? Or three years ago? Or a decade ago?

Tom couldn't keep track anymore. Fog and rust and dust clogged his brain. Current events and time were becoming non-entities in his life.

Tom drew again from his flask. As he did, he kept his eyes peeled for the next damn bullet train. Thinking about the bullet train allowed the factory situation to drift out of his mind. His 'intelligent thought' retention skills were getting weaker every day.

Tom was staring hard, alert and watching. Wait a minute. Wait *one* minute. The railroad tracks. Where were they? The tracks were gone.

When had they pulled the tracks out of Jamestown? There it was, the time thing again. Tick tock. Where was the clock?

A small headache was growing at the base of Tom's skull. There was something wrong here. Bullet trains. What about the bullet trains? He was no dummy. Bullet trains had not even been invented yet. So what the hell was going on? How could time shift so crazily? How could time, once such an important part of his daily life, be marginalized so badly?

Time to get up in the morning. Time to go to work. Time to leave work for home. Time to go grocery shopping. Time for the pickup football game. Time for breakfast. Time for supper. Time for the Super Bowl. Time for bed. Time to set the time.

Time had becoming fingernail dirt for Tom Forbes.

Time for Parent's Day at the Busy Bee.

The first wave hit high on his rubber boots.

Tom switched his attention from the missing train tracks to the water surrounding him. Not so bad yet. The water was still mostly travelling in ripples. All around, the water was definitely heading towards him. He was the center of attention in this game. What Tom needed to do was extricate himself from this mess and get to his Jeep. The Jeep was within reach, all shiny emerald green. He had left the windows down and could see the child carrier behind the front passenger seat.

A second wave sloshed up against his boots. All of the ripples had turned into waves, small but still harmless looking.

Tom guzzled the rest of his flask and fired the empty bottle at the next wave approaching. The wave broke and whimpered away. The headache stepped up a notch as the bottle did its job on the wave. Tom figured he needed many, many more bottles to empty and toss at these waves. If he was going to win. He looked back to the Jeep. A worn, red toy lay in the child carrier, tossed in haphazardly, or left behind. He had not seen it there a moment ago.

The next wave breached his rubber boots, sending water inside. Both of his feet were soaked. Tom reached inside his jacket pocket and pulled out the vial.

The vial was 'the next level'.

This was the same vial from the Indian Sports Bar. From 1987. He kept refilling it, year after year after year. He didn't know why, he just did.

Tom sprinkled a touch of powder on the back of his hand, bent his head down and snorted. The headache ramped up immediately, and the waves grew. Both entities seemed to realize a defense mechanism had been triggered, so they flew into attack mode. The first of the cavalry would be coming. In fact, the cavalry was thirty seconds away. Tom held his hands to his ears, closed his eyes and endured the throbbing in his skull. The waves were above his knees, soaking his pant legs with warm water. Not cold ice water from a melting skating rink. Warm, soggy water.

Tommy, why aren't you simply walking out of the pond to the dry security of your Jeep?

Good question.

The better answer is coming, in a second. The cavalry arrived first. The headache began to abate and the waves returned to below boot level. Tom sighed. Much better. He looked again at his Jeep. It wasn't gleaming emerald green anymore. It was plain green. Dusty, sand whipped and dirty. The windows were still open.

Tom caught and held his breath.

His little girl was sitting in the child carrier!

Waving one hand at him, clutching the red stuffed elephant in the other!

There she was!

What a picture!

His beautiful little girl, smiling and waving.

At him.

As if, he was the best damned father in the world. Giving her the best childhood possible. He would always be there for her when she fell, or got sick, or when she just needed her dad.

He would be there, for any reason.

Any reason at all.

How long did he have her?

He did not know. He never knew.

A second?

Four seconds?

Ten, if he was lucky?

To answer the earlier question, Tom inched towards the Jeep. Towards his little girl. The Jeep stuttered in his vision. Sort of a bad vertical adjustment on the old television set. Tiffany stuttered and faded with the Jeep.

God no!

Tom backed up slightly. The picture sharpened again. She came back. He grabbed a deep breath.

What the hell should he do? What? How was he going to get to her? Tom tried once more.

He had to. It was his little girl. His angel. His life. His *everything*.

This time, it was a full step towards the Jeep.

The vertical hiccups went crazy. The Jeep vanished; he could no longer see his Tiffany. Panicked, Tom retreated immediately. The Jeep and his girl came back. He could even hear her giggle.

There, question answered. There was no way for Tom Forbes to get to the Jeep.

Another wave breached his boots. The water poured in and Tom knew the cavalry was gone. He had made the mistake of trying to leave the water and move towards the Jeep. Towards his little girl. Now he was in the penalty box. The headache was back. Marching upward. Growing in fortitude.

A rogue wave crashed against Tom, hitting him right at his belt.

Jesus!

Where the hell did that one come from?

The ocean around him was getting angry. The ocean around him was saying 'Enough of this bullshit, it is time'.

Fuck you, Tom thought.

He pulled the vial back out. Dumped the rest of the powder on his hand. Shit, a lot of powder right there. For sure.

Too bad. He needed it. Did he ever.

Tom sucked the white poison deep into his nostrils. Licked the rest across his tongue. Straight away, his tongue went numb. The headache and the waves both reacted as expected. They leapt into action. He thought his head would blast right off his shoulders. The water reached for his chest and neck. Clawing and grasping. Tom glanced once more at the Jeep. His little girl was standing beside the green machine. Clutching the red stuffed elephant. Waving her tiny little hand.

The Jeep was parked on the railway tracks.

Holy Jesus in heaven!

The railway tracks were back!

This time, Tom heard the bullet train. Of course he did. This is the way the game played out. The train was coming. Hard and fast. Much too fast for a large population center. Far too dangerous. An accident, waiting to happen.

In the beginning, a giant mallet swung from the heavens, obliterating his little girl. Totally ridiculous and dream-like, but with devastating consequences. As the years went by, the mallet faded, giving way to falling buildings. Yes, Tom and his little girl walking into a building in New York City or Chicago. A tall, tall building. Tom holding the door for his princess. The eighty-two story monster collapsing right on the spot. Turning his girl to dust. Tom unhurt, because he had stepped back on the sidewalk to pull the door open. A true gentleman. A father.

Now, it was all about the bullet train, with intermittent visits from the giant mallet and the falling building. Over the next years, Tom had no idea what would bring the pain.

And guess what?

Tom would not be able to save her, regardless of what brought the pain.

Every single day for the last three years of his life, or the last five years, or ten years, or whatever time had passed, Tom had failed. Christ, he couldn't even remember how long she had been gone. Didn't matter. Eight years or eight days, it was still the same. Raw. Unbelievably raw.

Tom was supposed to be at the Busy Bee at 2:00 p.m. on September 11th, 1987.

A simple task, wasn't it? Be there for your daughter's big day.

Did you not have enough notice?

Did you not remember how to get there?

Was your fancy Jeep not running?

Tsk. Tsk. Stupid man.

Tiffy disappeared at 2:00 p.m. sharp. Tom had been sound asleep at his office desk at 2:00 p.m. The possible concussion from the falling trophy. The six aspirins ingested later. The coffee whiskey combo. Had all added up to a major systems breakdown.

The system was still broken.

Only worse.

Much worse.

Despite the booze and the drugs and his attempts to soften the hurt, his brain kept reminding him over and over, and over again, of his failure. He was truly a weak man. He needed help. Desperately.

Thank Christ, help was coming.

Tom's personal powdered white cavalry was mere seconds away. He could hear them approaching. The galloping across the hard ground, the sloshing as they hit the water. Good thing too. The waves were crashing over his shoulders, threatening to drown him in the ocean of despair.

Tom lay back in the warm, warm water. He thought he saw a flash of his beautiful Karen wading towards him, wearing her teeny, tiny white bikini. Was he seeing a cactus tree? Or a palm tree?

Puffs of white cloud drifted by. Tom felt so unbelievably tired. The Jeep was gone, the bullet train had passed. His little girl was still gone. Tom was in a warm cocoon, protected and closeted. The cocoon was collapsing, almost suffocating him. Sweltering him. Barely allowing him to breath. Barely allowing him to live. Any second now, he would hear her voice, calling to him from another world.

This was as good as it got for Mr. Tom Forbes.

For Tom Forbes, it would be 1987.

Forever.

CHAPTER 11

Five of them all right. Coming out of the mist.

Strangely, none of the kids were frightened of the mist. To their young minds, the mist resembled something out of a fairy tale. A Disney show. Magical. So soft and gentle, and swirling, and pretty and white. Peaceful and pure and beautiful.

Two of the intruders went for Tiffany Forbes. They were extremely organized, and definitely, they were targeting the little girl. Marie was already moving. She was quick of thought, and fast of feet. Marie moved to intercept.

The collision was ferocious.

The collision was fatal.

Fatal for Marie.

Joe was right on his wife's heels. He was only one step behind. The one step might as well have been a mile. The one step made him the last one to the party. Joe charged into the mist, desperately trying to see what evil lay ahead. The mist and the smoke were so thick. Overpowering and enveloping. The intruders were fast and they were strong. Joe had never experienced an opponent as powerful or as brutal as this.

In the blink of an eye, it was over.

Marie was sprawled on the ground. On fire. Burning up. Critical. She was not going to make it. Tiffany was gone with her abductors. Joe was left empty handed, with nothing. He had lost. He had failed Marie. He had failed the little girl. The police sirens had died. The thumping in the sky was gone. There was no help coming. There was nothing.

Darkness fell.

Joe had been savagely beaten. How many bones had they broken? His fingers and hands, his arms, his jaw, his ribs, all battered. His eyes were swollen shut. The pain at his throat was gruesome, a brand of pain he had never experienced before. By rights, he should be dead. He really should be. However, Joe was a warrior. He would rejoin this battle. First, what he needed was a medical miracle. Or two. Or six. He was so badly wounded. He needed to heal. He needed to rest.

If only he could make it to the……

Joe fell into the darkness.

Time frames.

People.

Places.

Things.

They all became very jumbled after this.

One thing was crystal clear. The numbers had come and gone, again. The numbers had left devastation in their wake. Not only was the little girl taken. Marie was dead. Both he and Tom Forbes, were ruined. A neighborhood, a community, hell, the entire city was destroyed. The ripple effect spread far and wide. Many, many lives would be altered and shattered.

It would take time, and a monumental effort, but Joe Danton would fight back. He would return. This was all so wrong. God willing, he would return one day and make it right.

Memories.

Weren't they wonderful?

CHAPTER 12

THE MIST HAD BEEN SO WELCOMING TO THE CHILD. IT WAS SOFT AND magical. Yes, run into the mist and play. You could play forever in the mist, and the mist played back with you. The mist was smart and funny and always knew what game you wanted to play. The mist was truly, *interactive*.

However, there were no 'things' in the mist. There were no swings or teeter totters or plastic toys or black and white dotted soccer balls. Tiffany could still see those things in the backyard. She could see them but she could not quite get to them. She was unable to touch them, or pick them up. They were always out of reach. Why? She didn't know. How could she? She was not even two years old.

Tiffany could see her mommy and her daddy. She could see her granny and her grandpa. She could see them all, but she couldn't touch them. Or talk to them. And they wouldn't talk to her. They wouldn't hear her.

Why?

Why didn't they talk to her?

Why did they keep doing their chores, walking right past her?

Why?

Couldn't they see her? Couldn't they?

She was *right here!*

Calling. Begging. Crying.

Mommy and daddy and gramps and the neighbors kept on going about their business.

Pretending she wasn't even there.

Why would they do this to her?

What had she done?

Did this ever hurt. It hurt her bad. She so wanted to hug her mommy. She wanted her big, strong daddy to pick her up and squeeze her tight.

Please. Somebody. I am right here!

Nothing.

From nobody.

Nothing.

Tiffany would walk down the narrow hallway, turn into her room and find the furthest, deepest, back corner.

And she would cry.

As the days passed, mommy and daddy began to fade away. To the little girl, this was terrifying. She was so, so scared. She needed her mommy and daddy. So bad. The days became weeks. She hardly saw mommy and daddy anymore. The little girl cried, and trembled and despaired. The weeks became months. The toys in the backyard faded away. The sweet smells of the flowers were no more. She couldn't feel things she touched. The months became years. The sounds of birds chirping in the trees, of leaves rustling on their branches, and the cars driving past, faded away.

Even the colors were gone. The sky was gray. The grass was gray. Her clothes were gray. Her favorite elephant was gray. She so missed the glorious red fur of her only friend.

Tiffany was spending all of her days wandering around in the mist.

Searching. Searching.

At night, she returned to her room.

To cry.

The mist was no longer welcoming. It was no longer fun to be here. It was a place of great nothing. Other kids and people were wandering around as well. So lost. So sad. So defeated. They didn't seem to be trying to find a way out. They had given in and given up, and were attempting to live their lives as they had before. They were stuck in this empty place of nothing. Not the place they should be.

Not the place *anybody* should be.

All the little girl could do was to continue with her search. There had to be a doorway out of here.

She really, really wanted to go home.
She *had* to go home.
She called for her daddy.
Every, single day.
Daddy *had* to hear her.
If daddy heard, he would come.
Yes he would.
Because daddies did things for their little girls.
Daddies came to their little girls.
To save them.
Save them from the great, big, nothing.
The years were fast running away on the little girl, turning into decades.

As the years became decades, the little girl survived in this static world of nothing.

She would be two years old, forever.

CHAPTER 13

Kingman, Arizona. Present Day.

The sun was stalled directly over Coasters Trailer Park. The temperature was climbing into the hundreds. A stiff desert wind blew sheets of fire through the air, kicking up burning sand in its wake. The flimsy trailers rocked on block foundations. Heat waves rose off silver tin bodies, shimmering skyward. A few scrub cacti provided meager vegetation in the bleak park. It was high noon in the desert.

In one of the tin boxes, Tom Forbes lay on a filthy, single wide mattress, in a somewhat altered state. He thought he was sleeping, but he couldn't be sure. Live snapshots of his life before kept popping up in front of him. Was he seeing these snapshots in his mind, or was he actually seeing them with his eyes? Again, Tom couldn't be sure. These snapshots reminded him of those hand held slide boxes from the early seventies. A one inch by six inch set of pictures. Insert first picture in view box. Look at picture through view finder. Slide the knob and the next picture appears in the window. Hold the box up to the sun or aim it at a bright light to enjoy the full effect.

The snapshots he was seeing were quite vivid, therefore he couldn't be sleeping. Or, he could be sleeping and dreaming. Or, he could be awake and hallucinating. Or, he could be awake and playing with an actual slide box. Or none of the above was happening. Or all of the above was happening. Or something not yet named was happening. It was all so confusing to Tom. Which is why he was so tired when he woke up, and even more tired when he went to sleep.

Tom sensed the pounding before the sound filtered through to his brain. It was an irritating, annoying sensation, pushing the snapshots out of the way. The pounding began to seep up his ear canals, making contact with his eardrums. Sending a synapse to his brain core. Finally coming to rest deep in his skull, bringing the pain. Tom cracked his eyes a slit, aiming towards the clock radio. The red numbers 12:01 glowed through the murky trailer. Was it afternoon or midnight? He wasn't sure. Did it matter? Not on Tom's schedule.

An empty syringe and a half filled whiskey magnum sat on the table beside the clock radio. Another syringe was visible on the floor beside the bed. The fusty air in his trailer reeked of stale liquor, sweaty flesh, dirty laundry and urine. Tom was soaked right through his clothes. His little window air conditioner had shut down again. It was a hundred and fifty degrees in his coffin.

The pounding came again, this time louder, clashing with his mental and physical distress. Tom looked towards the door. The flimsy aluminum shook with the pounding.

"What?" he managed.

The door shot open. A blazing, white light screamed on in, blinding Tom. The light sent his skull into a new dimension of pain. Hot sand came with the wind, rattling through the trailer. A dark figure stepped into the light. Tom shaded his eyes and squinted to see who the hell was bothering him.

"Tom Forbes?"

The voice rang an ancient bell, buried deep in Tom's remaining brain cells. The hairs immediately stood on his forearms. Tom's entire body tensed. He pushed himself up to a sitting position, the bed creaking under the shifting of his weight. This maneuver sent a wave of nausea sloshing against his brain. Tom held tight to the bed, staring at his visitor, ready to puke his guts right out.

The figure moved in a few steps, the wind slamming the door shut behind him. Dead silence. Pure blackness. Seconds ticked by. The usual murkiness returned. Tom squinted hard, forcing more visual adjustment. Then his eyes began to open.

Wide.

Wider.

Widest.

It could not be!

Not after all this time!

"Looks as if you've seen a ghost," his visitor stated.

Tom Forbes was speechless.

Joe.

Fucking.

Danton.

Are you kidding me?

Tom managed to stagger to his feet. The booze, the drugs, the nausea, everything. He didn't know if this was a bad trip, or a desert illusion.

"What the hell? You bastard! What did you do with her?"

Tom took a step toward his uninvited visitor. He was prepared to kill the man. Or vision. Or hell spirit, or whatever it was standing before him. Strangle the bastard with his bare hands. Tear his bloody head off.

"Tom, Tom. Listen to me."

Tom moved another step closer, staggered, but held himself upright. A small miracle, considering how hammered he was.

The visitor raised his hands to calm Tom.

The raised hand bit was not going to work on Tom Forbes.

"Tom," the visitor said. "I know where she is."

That worked.

Did it ever.

Tom stopped in his tracks.

"What?"

Tom was incredulous.

He was *dead* stopped in his tracks.

Feet frozen to the floor.

What had Danton said? He knows where she is?

Impossible.

Or was it?

"You know where she is?" Tom tried.

"Yes. Yes I do," the visitor answered.

Tom tried to get his brain to digest this. His brain unfortunately, was barely functioning. His brain was allowing breathing and sweating and pissing and drinking and spitting and farting and crapping. His brain was allowing some sight and some hearing. His brain was allowing some basic arithmetic and speech. Not much else.

"Tom. I know where she is. She is alive."

Tom's brain allowed those words in.

She is alive.

What exactly did those words mean?

SHE. IS. ALIVE.

What year is it now?

Numbers swirled around in Tom's mind.

2011? 2012? 2013?

He wasn't sure. The basic arithmetic allowed for a twenty-five or twenty-six year time frame. She would be what, twenty-seven years old? Thirty years old? His Tiffy?

Tiffy was *alive*?

Joe Danton was suddenly, right in front of Tom. Tom shuddered. He had not even seen the man move.

What the hell was he, some kind of ghost?

Both of Joe's hands were on Tom's shoulders.

Touching.

Joe Danton, was touching him.

Tom felt something exchange between them. Or almost exchange between them. It was as if the drugs in his system were acting as a barrier, preventing the energy or the evil spewing out of Joe Danton from entering his body.

Joe Danton spoke again. He seemed to be able to read Tom's mind.

"Yes she is Tom. She is alive. Get yourself together. It is time for us to go home. It is time for *you* to go home."

Tom tried to pull a thought process out of his brain.

Going home.

What did 'going home' mean?

What was home? Ohio? Jamestown?

They were going to find her? His little girl? Alive? After all these years?

This was too unbelievable, too insane. But, what else was there? If there was even the *slightest* chance. And what did this Joe Danton really know? What?

Tom had to see how this journey into insanity was going to play out. Unlike the past twenty-five years, at least he wouldn't be going alone. Tom had a million questions for Joe Danton, or whoever or whatever this was, standing in his trailer.

Joe held up one hand to cease the questions before they could start.

"We need to go. We need to go now. Time is of the essence."

Tom thought hard. It hurt his brain to do so. How could his little girl still be alive? She vanished completely, all those years ago. Not a single trace. The cops, the state police, even the FBI could not help. Tom could not help. Daddy could not help. He had let her down. Daddy had failed.

"What do you need to pack?" Joe interrupted.

Pack? Pack what? What did he have to pack? Tom had nothing. She was alive? He was so confused now.

"Not much. Not much at all," he was able to answer.

"Let's roll then. I will be outside."

Joe opened the flimsy door allowing the searing white light back in. Tom covered his eyes until the door banged shut. He stripped his wet clothes and dressed. Numbly, he jammed a few pieces of underwear, a few loose socks, a sweater and a jacket into a duffle bag. Tom went to his tiny bathroom, closing the door behind him. He filled his shaving kit, but it wasn't shaving gear. He couldn't even remember where his shaving stuff was. The kit served other purposes now.

Tom looked at the dirty, streaked mirror. What a colossal mess. He saw a man with matted, wild hair and a three week growth of stubble. He saw yellowed teeth and inflamed gums. He saw sunken eyes and a bloated, jowly face. Where there was no facial hair, the jowly face was covered with grayish, tired skin. Wow, he looked to be about seventy-five years old. Tom splashed cool water on his face, and then put his mouth under the tap to drink. The booze, the drugs and the heat had combined to purge most fluids from his rotting carcass.

Tom had been confined to his bed for the past three days, riding the latest wave. As a result, he was under-nourished but not particularly hungry. Dehydrated, but not overly thirsty. His system had been working hard through his latest binge. Trying to push the poison out. Trying to figure out if it should be hungry or thirsty or neither. His system was fighting a losing battle. Unfortunately, two and a half decades of poisonous residuals were firmly ensconced in Tom's blood cells, liver and brain. One last look in the mirror. Pretty sad. This was as good as it got.

Tom exited his dark trailer, finding blinding sunshine waiting for him. The wind threw hot sand against his face, stinging his skin. Tumbleweeds and garbage blew past. There was such a lovely ambience in this trailer park. Tom realized he didn't even have a key to lock his trailer door. He had no idea where it might be. Didn't matter, there was nothing in the trailer. There was about as much nothing in the trailer as there was in him.

Tom looked to see what form of transport his guest had arrived in. Joe Danton was staring off into the distance, looking towards the east, a duffle bag at his feet in the dirt. Of course, there was no vehicle waiting. No taxicab, or truck or chariot or spaceship or helicopter. Why would there be? Joe Danton had appeared. Beamed in. Formed out of thin air.

In all actuality, Joe Danton was probably a total figment of Tom's imagination. Another Mr. Snuffleupagus, the adult version, for druggies. This was probably another bad trip full of juicy, real life details and impossible situations. Or bad dreams, such as tumbling down an endless set of stairs. Or having snakes crawling out of your pant legs forever. Tom couldn't be bothered thinking about Joe Danton and his magical arrival, or even asking about it. He was going with the flow. What choice did he have? Was there any way to turn off a bad dream? Of course not. Nor was there any way to bring a bad trip to a happy ending.

Tom's trusty old Jeep Cherokee would take him to Ohio. He supposed. If Ohio was where they were actually going. For real. As in the real world. As in, not lying on his filthy bed in his steaming trailer, imagining all of this. Magically, the keys to the Jeep were crusted in the bottom of his pants pocket.

There was one benefit to living in the desert. The Cherokee had no rust on it, and had hardly been used. In fact, it had less than twenty thousand miles on the odometer. Jamestown, Ohio to Kingman, Arizona. Plus a couple miles every two weeks to the dealers. The odd trip to the grocery store. Don't forget the Bottle Stop. If Tom could be bothered to clean her up, she would be a nice looking vehicle. He remembered when the Jeep was brand new. So proud, driving her off the lot. Emerald green. The sparkly finish. The slick, black knobby tires. The new car smell. Sure beat the smell coming off him now.

Tom was in no condition to drive, so he dug the keys out of his pocket and tossed them to Joe Danton. The spooky man could drive. The two of them got in the Jeep.

Would he find what he had *stopped* looking for, somewhere along this journey?

Would he find his precious little girl?

Think about it idiot. No you won't. Because the search is long over. Finished. Closed. An unsolved cold case. Because she is dead, a sad little skeleton. A pile of bones and dust.

Even if she was alive, she wouldn't be little anymore, would she?

If we are playing the alive game, how about this? She would have no clue as to who in the hell you are because she hasn't seen you in twenty-five years.

You don't have to worry though, because there is no way she is alive and well, is there?

Because this is another bull crap hallucination and you have finally, totally, lost your mind.

Joe Danton? The bastard deserved to be dead. Deserves to be dead. Soon, he would be. If Tom had his way.

If any of this was even real.

Pretty damn confusing stuff.

Yes, the drug abuse had been a wonderful choice.

Joe fired up the Jeep and put the truck in gear. 1987, here we come. Back to the Future Part Six, Tom figured. Michael J. Fox and Christopher Lloyd. Tom figured some more. He came to a conclusion. Yes, he does look like Christopher Lloyd. Christopher Lloyd, at age eighty.

Off they went, the vehicle's tires kicking up dust and litter. Joe grabbed a pair of sunglasses off the dashboard. Tom grabbed a pair as well. Tom the druggy always had plenty of sunglasses in his Jeep. The eyes had to be covered. To hide the mystery and the abuse, and to protect the skull from the intensity of the desert sun. The two men were sad interpretations of Keanu Reeves.

The sun was pounding down mercilessly. Hell on earth the desert was. Tom looked out the window as they drove away. Man, this trailer park was really a dump. A few hundred beat up trailers sitting on concrete blocks. Crappy cars, the odd swing set, zero landscaping, plenty of garbage and broken junk. They drove past the one and only tree in the park, a scrubby looking stump holding a scrubby looking bird. The bird was ugly, black and pointy beaked. The bird stared at Tom as the Jeep passed by. A line of communication opened up between the two species.

The bird said, 'You are one sad, pathetic creature. Hard to believe you are at the top of the food chain. Time for you to die, you worthless piece of shit'.

Tom answered back, 'Oh yeah? Same to you, you ugly old bitch'.

Great.

Now he was talking to birds through ESP, or the Vulcan Mind Meld, or a stupid Ouija board. Black birds spoke English? Who knew? Tom shook his head at his own idiocy, then sat back and watched as the desert sailed by.

The barren, unforgiving desert had been a perfect fit with Tom's mindset. He couldn't think of a better place to be tortured these past two decades. The desert was harsh, it held no beauty and it held no hope. It was a land of bare survivability and ugly black birds.

The old, no longer glittering, plain dark green Jeep turned off a dusty trail and hit the interstate. Then roared up to speed and began to devour the asphalt miles. This vehicle was an old friend. It had been with Tom since his days in Ohio. Officially, the journey into madness had begun. This segment, anyway. Tom's journey into madness had started a long, long time ago.

CHAPTER 14

THREE HOURS AND TWENTY-SIX MINUTES LATER, A SMALL RED LIGHT began to blink. The light was in a darkened basement room beneath Central Hardware, in White River, Idaho. This basement space is not an inventory office or a lunch area for Central Hardware employees. It isn't a storage room or a furnace room or an electrical room. It isn't a room for warehouse boys and cashiers to grope each other in.

The room is an old rural monitoring office run by the FBI. There are only half a dozen of these offices remaining in the unpopulated middle of the country. The others are in Iowa, Montana, the Dakotas and Wyoming. All of these offices are located on second floors or in basements. Nondescript is the name of the game. The offices are only manned part time and are less than a year from being mothballed. They are from a time before computers and cell phones and instant everything.

The blinking red light is situated on a wall map of the United States of America. An ancient GPS tracker beacon has been activated. This means a motor vehicle of interest has been moved beyond the allotted two hundred mile home base radius. Time capsule photography over the next four days would show the blinking red light tracing a path out of the Arizona desert, heading in a northeast direction.

A more reasonable explanation for this light being activated?

An electrical malfunction of some sort, because these beacons are no longer in use. This is dinosaur technology from the seventies and eighties.

These last six rural monitoring stations had been caught in the 2007 budget reallocation. Resources were being pushed fervently towards the southern border, the airports and Homeland Security. The great middle states were not considered prime terrorist targets. They were probably the whitest places on earth. Anybody with brown skin or a deep suntan, who was not Mexican labor, would stand out in Idaho, Utah or Montana. Immediately, the brown skinned ones would come under suspicion or surveillance.

It was a Thursday afternoon, and nobody would be in this undermanned office until Monday. The red light blinked in the empty darkness, as rural folk bought rakes and leaf blowers and enviro friendly paper bags upstairs on the main floor.

CHAPTER 15

Monday morning, an urgent call was placed from the basement monitoring station in White River, Idaho, to 935 Pennsylvania Avenue in Washington, D.C. Because of the time difference, the call arrived in Washington after eleven a.m. The young agent placing the call was at a loss. A red tracker beacon, of which he had no record and almost no understanding of, was blinking. The beacon was moving across the country with nearly a four day head start on them. The young agent had been working in this office for three years and a tracker beacon had never been activated before. The wall map was simply a relic from the past, an amusing piece of art décor. Quickly forgotten, treated as detritus on a bulletin board. It had meant diddly squat to the new generation of feds working there.

Not any more.

Malfunction or not, this call had to be made.

Protocol demanded it.

The call was bumped up the ladder from the main switchboard, landing on the sixth floor. Cold Case Operations Chief Jack Ramsey reached for the phone. Jack Ramsey was sixty-one years old. Four years away from retirement. When he hit sixty-five years of age, Jack would have forty years of service under his belt. This meant the golden goose was waiting for him. A plump, full pension with juicy benefits. Jack had risen as far as he would go. He was one floor below the penthouse in the gleaming seven story building. The new FBI was not his game. Because of his inability to adapt, Jack had hit his glass ceiling. This was fine with him. A man has got to know his limitations. Dirty Harry had said so.

As Cold Case Operations Chief, Jack was in charge of thousands of dead files. Cold Case was an unimportant assignment for an old man playing out the string. This was fine by Jack. He was not a politician. He was an agent. Shit, his boss was only thirty-seven years old, very wet and very green. His boss possessed tons of schooling and Academy training, but zero street credibility. The man had no battle scars and had experienced no real crime fighting in his young career.

It was all about image projection, and budgets, and spreadsheets, and profiling, and electronic wire tapping, and computer interception, and a lot of other crap Jack either didn't understand or didn't care about. Don't forget politics. Politics was huge in the Bureau these days.

Since the call from Idaho was about old technology, it automatically went to the old guy. Jack Ramsey answered the call. The veteran lawman knew immediately what this was. The red beacon was early generation technology, and had been phased out a long time ago. Since ninety-eight per cent of the Bureau operatives had been replaced over the past fifteen years, Jack was one of the few people left who knew what this was.

Who had the Bureau been watching in Arizona? Way back in the eighties?

Jack was intrigued. He knew there was nothing on the computers pertaining to these beacons. The beacons were too old. This system had been killed around 1990, after everything had been transferred to the Next Gen system. Like all electronic crap, the Next Gen system faded into history. Today, the feds used satellite GPS and Google EarthView Watch and all kinds of other high tech stuff. The FBI could now sit in a Starbuck's coffee shop and run observation on suspects from hand held devices, two thousand miles away.

Jack thought some more. This had to be a malfunction, if anything. Or electronic noise. Didn't matter. Follow through on it. Make sure. CYA. Cover your ass. Page one; line one, in the new FBI handbook. Yes, the house could be on fire, but make sure you have done the paperwork. The towers could be collapsing, but make sure you have done the paperwork. Make sure you follow the chain of command. Make sure you put in all the correct requests. To the correct departments. In triplicate. With a hard drive back up. While the house burns to the ground. Don't arrest or shoot anybody. Because arresting and shooting means even more procedural problems and more paperwork. CYA indeed.

Jack took the elevator down to sublevel six in the basement file storage catacombs. The Archives level. The Archives was a massive storeroom facility. Aisle upon aisle upon aisle, stretching across ten football fields. Among other skills, the Bureau was good at collecting information. Good information, bad information and useless information. Pages and pages and reams of information. The computer age had not cut back on paper use; in fact, it had increased paper use tenfold. More trees were falling than ever before, because the computer age let everyone know everyone else's business. So, everything had to be catalogued, filed, and of course, backed up, just in case.

A clerk searched the database for the old beacons. Only one beacon from the eighties had not been retrieved. The beacon was attached to a closed case file. The file had long ago been placed in storage. The clerk searched his locator screen for the aisle and correct storage bunk. Then he hopped aboard an electric cart and went racing off into the maze.

Jack drank coffee as he waited. A voice inside him, some long crafted instinct, told him something was up. The eighties. Arizona. An ancient tracker beacon. What could it be? Jack sensed this might be more than a simple malfunction.

Ten minutes later, the clerk returned, dusty cardboard jacket in hand. Jack signed the file out and went back up to his office.

He began to sift through the paperwork. The first six pages pertained to jurisdiction, chain of command and procedure. Jack shook his head. Even back then, the FBI was churning out the paperwork. Finally, on page seven, the actual case began.

The case was vaguely familiar. A kidnapping in Jamestown, Ohio. A little girl was taken. The date? September 11, 1987. Jack thought to himself, was September 11 always going to be infamous? It certainly looked as if it would be. In fact, maybe September 11 was a bad day, a high crime day, an alignment of the criminal element and the sun and the moon and the stars. Maybe it always had been a bad day. We didn't notice it. Until the *big* September 11. Now we know.

Perhaps when Jack was retired, he would research this theory. Conceivably write a book if it proved out. Go on a speaking tour. Not a bad idea.

Get your tired old ass out of the clouds. Back to the business at hand, Mr. Ramsey.

Jack read on. The Cleveland Field Office held jurisdiction in the kidnapping. The big four, the father, the mother and the day care operators went under immediate suspicion. The father and mother had air tight alibis. The day care operator quickly became the prime suspect, because he went missing with the little girl. Indeed, the missing day care operator using the alias of Mr. Joe Danton was front and center, *the* person of greatest interest. The day care operator's wife, Marie Danton was killed the same day in a bizarre accident. Even more bizarre was the fact neither Joe nor Marie Danton's identities could be established. They had appeared in Jamestown as if out of thin air. When it came to a past paper trail, the man and his wife were ghosts.

There were no other suspects or leads, no witnesses, no clues and no motive. A child had been snatched from a day care center in broad daylight, during business hours. Plenty of people were around, kids and workers, but nobody saw. Nobody saw *anything*. This wasn't the story you read in the paper where so and so has vanished. Jack Ramsey had been a cop for too long. Nobody vanished. The vanished were sometimes hiding of their own volition, or being kept away from family and friends by a nutcase, but mostly, they were dead. Murdered in some horrific way. The idiotic media loved to use the term 'vanished'. It was more mysterious, and probably helped sell their newspapers and TV shows.

Back to the file.

The FBI was called in when the local cops decided interstate transport of the kidnapped child was a distinct possibility. With the big six lane highway so close, and the Canadian border not far away, it was the right call to make. Troopers shut down the I90 and set up roadblocks on the state routes. The border crossings were sealed. Nothing got through and nothing turned up.

Jack continued reading the paperwork. This was one strange case. The day care operator never resurfaced. Similar to his past ghostly footprints, Joe Danton's identity trail into the future ran stone cold. In this case, the child was gone forever. This time, truly vanished. The parents crumbled and split. The day care center shut down. The city died. The second last page of the file had been stamped in bold red letters.

Unsolved: Closed.

Jack turned to the last page of the file. There it was. The early, cutting edge technology, a GPS beacon, had been requested, and attached to the father's vehicle. The father's home base was Kingman, Arizona.

Wow.

A long way from Ohio, Jack mused.

Jack looked to the bottom of the page.

Who had requested this beacon? Which retired FBI relic?

The beacon had been requested by………..wait a second.

There was a number in the place where a name should be.

Strange.

A number? Some sort of code?

Jack picked up the papers. Looked closer. Harder. Thinking. It took a few seconds, and then Jack remembered what this meant. No name. Only a number. The number *was* a code. A code for a nameless agent.

Shit.

Anxiety rose in Jack Ramsey.

Carl Franklin Horner. The man without a name.

"Carl Horner," Jack said aloud.

He winced. Looked around his office. Simply hearing this name had such an effect on people within the Bureau. The man was a legend. The coldest man Jack Ramsey had ever met. Freaky, scary cold. Dead, in fact. If eyes were the window to the soul, Carl Horner had no soul. Carl Horner's eyes were gray, cold, cruel and devoid of humanity. The man was a machine. Relentless, ruthless, detailed and intelligent. Horner had tracked, run down and executed many of America's worst nightmares. His targets included mobsters, bikers, drug dealers, serial killers, terrorists and foreign agents. Anyone who threatened America. Little did Joe Public know how many judge and jury free cases had been closed.

Permanently.

By Carl Franklin Horner.

Jack Ramsey and Carl Horner entered the Academy training program together. 1977. Jack was four years older than Carl. They graduated together and took different career paths inside the Bureau. Jack lost touch with Carl, although he had heard the rumors. The FBI had a Black Dog, but never was a name officially attached. Nobody was stupid enough, or had the guts to attach a name. Jack did not see or officially hear of Carl Horner again, until 1984.

The hot August summer of 1984. Jack had tracked longtime serial killer Dean Perron from New York City across the country to Missoula, Montana. Perron was wanted for an extensive series of rapes and murders in the Big Apple and Jersey. The dreadful crimes were committed against young boys and girls. Committed against children. Perron had posed as a school teacher to position himself as an authority figure. He was good. He was very good. Perron was a chameleon with many personas and disguises. He created cleverly forged documentation backing up his accreditations. New York City was huge. Perron was able to avoid the authorities and remain active for a long time. Three long years of mayhem and terror. Probably longer, because Jack wasn't sure they had found all of the victims.

Dean Perron was a clever bastard. He was a teacher. He was too successful. Perron's body count was the beginning of his end. So many bodies were being found. Jack's task force was able to cut chunks out of New York City and Perron's work field became too narrow. He turned rabbit and ran for home. They always ran for home.

Jack's team had the Perron family under complete wraps. The sick bastard was inside the family home with his parents. Plans of action were being considered. Draw the parents out. Draw Perron out. Storm the house. Tear gas the house. Arrest, trial and conviction, and then let him rot in jail for the rest of his life. Or, leave him for about ten seconds in genpop. Probably the best course of action.

Carl Horner arrived on the scene. He unfolded himself out of an unmarked black Chevy Impala. Walked up to Jack and showed no inkling they knew each other, let alone they had ever crossed paths. Horner threw down paperwork giving him full charge of the case. A case Jack had poured three long years of time, overtime, sweat and resources into. Jack was floored. He stared at the paperwork in utter disbelief as Horner broke through the ranks of law enforcement. Horner marched up the front sidewalk towards the house as Jack recovered and began his move. Horner simply lifted his leather gloved hand to Jack, to back the hell off.

Horner was now on the veranda.

Three steps and crash!

Horner kicked the front door right off its hinges. In the blink of an eye, an eighteen inch defender ripped out from under his long coat. The Perron family sat startled at their kitchen table. Jack made it to the empty doorway in time to see the first blast from the defender take Perron senior out of his chair. Senior flew back, crumpling against the wall, blood pouring from holes in his shoulder. The second blast slammed into Dean Perron's left thigh, dropping him on the ragged linoleum floor. Perron's mother screamed and clutched at her bosom with one hand. The other hand reached towards her husband, then her son, not sure where her pity should go. Horner looked right into the woman's soul and shook his head. Her pity was going nowhere. The scream died in her throat. Both of her hands now clasped at her ample chest.

Horner stepped over the prone child rapist. Jack Ramsey was now in the house, weapon drawn. Jack could see the look on Perron's face. A look of shock at being hit, then a look of anger at being stopped. Being stopped from his true joy and passion. The children. His children. He had so much more to teach them. His mission was not finished.

Perron's face began to twist, almost a smile. No, he assuredly was not yet done. This situation was temporary, a stutter in time. Someday, society would pronounce him rehabilitated, he was such a clever man, and he would be set free. Free to resume his teachings. Free to enlighten the children. Free to punish those bad children who did not readily accept his lessons. Yes, while incarcerated, he would find religion or Buddhism or some other bullshit. He would repent, emerge from his stained self as a new butterfly, and be released back into the world. He would be the rare success story in prison rehabilitation.

A grimace replaced the smile on Perron's face; the steel pellets had severely damaged his flesh. Perron was angry now, angry at this stupid law enforcement hero who had so badly injured him. Disfigured him. Crippled him. He looked up at the lawman. Perron was not happy with what he saw.

Horner stared down at the rapist. The worthless piece of human garbage. Horner took one hand off the shotgun. Reached deep inside his coat and pulled out photographs. Horner dropped the photos, one at a time, down on Perron.

One, two, three pictures.

Four. Five pictures.

Pictures of children.

Seven, eight, nine pictures.

Boys and girls.

Ten. Eleven. Twelve.

Smiling, happy children.

Fifteen, sixteen, seventeen pictures.

All smiling and all happy kids. Before Perron had taken them. Before the torture. Before the violation. Before the teachings. Before the murder.

Carl Horner did not utter a single word. An understanding passed from Horner to Perron. A look of bewilderment, morphing into pure terror, crossed Dean Perron's face. Twisting his features, grotesquely.

Picture number twenty-two landed on Perron's chest. The final picture. Another smiling child. The last smiling child. A dead child.

Jack Ramsey reached for his handcuffs and was about to step forward. It was time to collar this creep.

When the shotgun barked!

Barked a second time!

Barked a third time!

Dean Perron was executed. Blown to bits. Head. Chest. Back to the head. One, two, three. No chance of medical repair. No surgery techniques known to man could fix him.

Horner walked over to the distressed, badly wounded father. Reached down and pulled a handgun from the back of the wounded man's pants. How did Horner know the old man was packing? Is that why Horner shot him first? How could he know? Horner had zero case intelligence, and had not received a briefing from Jack's team.

Horner straightened, moved the barrel over the old man's chest. He pulled the trigger. Blood, vertebrae and innards blew out the father's back. Execution number two. Such a good father, packing a pistol to protect his only son. Not any more. Perron's mother was desperately clutching at her own heart. She was moving to cardiac arrest. She would not make it. Execution number three was seconds away.

It was done. The New York School Murder Case, was closed.

Horner walked out of the house, got in the unmarked and drove off into the black night. Jack Ramsey was stunned.

No arrest would be made. No incarceration. No press. No trial. No asshole defense lawyers. No technicalities. No plea bargains. No judge and jury. No sentencing. No million dollar expense to house this prick for the rest of his life. No shrinks, trying to figure out why. No bleeding hearts telling us how poor parenting or the wrong cafeteria food or some other simple factor was responsible for Perron's choices. No, there would be nothing. Indeed, this case was closed. It had been wrapped up nice and tight. Justice served up, American West style.

There was one less piece of crap on the planet.

There was one less predator on the planet.

The kids were a little safer.

And the rumors were true.

The FBI had a Black Dog.

A Black Dog. A lone wolf.

Off the record.

Nameless.

Only a number.

Right off the grid.

With Carl Horner, right off the reservation.

The Black Dog answered to one man only. The director of the FBI. The FBI had its own psychopath, trained and licensed to kill.

The bad guys would never anticipate what wickedness was coming their way.

Christ, even the good guys were terrified of Horner.

Jesus, all right.

Jack Ramsey sucked in a deep breath. With shaking hands he set the papers down on his desk. This was a memory Jack did not need to rehash. He steadied his hands and calmed himself. Easy Jack, easy.

He thought long and hard. Why would Carl Horner be involved in a kidnapping, in Ohio? Why indeed? This was not his specialty. Little was known about Horner's training within the Bureau. Even less was known about the man himself, or the motivation which allowed him to become a killing machine. One thing was sure. Jack Ramsey knew full well of the legend. The legend saying Carl Horner had never left a case unfinished. He had closed the book on each and every one of his assignments.

Except. Possibly this one?

Was this a bureaucratic mix-up and the case *had* been successfully closed and not updated? Was the case updated and misfiled, now sitting on the wrong shelf downstairs in the enormous storage room? Or, was the case a victim of the paperwork-to-digital transformation procedure which had messed up so many of the old files?

Jack sat back in his chair. Thinking. Was there one open case remaining? Was there? An open case would explain the unrecovered beacon. Horner must have concluded this person out in the hot desert, Mr. Tom Forbes, needed watching. Jack moved to his computer. He shifted through the screens to access the Arizona Department of Motor Vehicles. Jack glanced down at the file, searching for the Jeep registration. He typed in numbers, and waited for a response.

What were the chances?

Hold the bloody phone!

The vehicle was *still* registered to Mr. Tom A. Forbes, of Kingman, Arizona. Formerly of Jamestown, Ohio. Jack had a hard time believing Mr. Forbes had not driven from the desert in his Jeep, in over twenty years. He had a harder time believing Mr. Forbes still owned the same vehicle. Surely by now, Forbes would have traded the Jeep in on a newer model, or sold it outright. Had Forbes sold the Jeep illegally and someone else was driving it now? Perhaps one of those Mexican laborers? This didn't make any sense either, because a new buyer would have driven the Jeep more than two hundred miles from Kingman.

Was this a case of very old information not being kept up to date? Or a better explanation, a malfunctioning beacon? Triggered by what? Who knows with this old tech stuff. A seismic event? Failed circuitry? Radio frequency interference? These were better explanations, because anything else was so damn improbable.

Except.

Except for Carl Horner's involvement.

Jack rifled through a few more screens. Very little from the eighties had made it to the data base. Mostly summaries and statistics. For an old guy, Jack was pretty adept at the keyboard. He hammered away, shifting screens, searching. Finally, he pushed away from the computer. As best as he could tell, the case had never been solved.

So. What was the executioner doing on a child kidnapping case?

Protocol required definite steps which had to be followed when a beacon was activated. No matter how old the beacon was. Step one was the greenhorn in Idaho making the call to Jack. Step two was Jack's move. The original crime scene was in the jurisdiction of the Cleveland field office. Jack should be on the line to Cleveland. Should have been on the line to Cleveland twenty minutes ago. Cleveland would determine if this was part of a real case, or simply an errant, malfunctioning beacon. If it was a real case, a surveillance team would probably acquire the vehicle and tail it for the rest of its journey. A second team would be prepped and sent to Jamestown. Jack figured it was pretty clear Jamestown was the destination.

Yes, calling the Cleveland office right now would be proper procedure.

Jack moved back to his computer and accessed Horner's file. Where was the big man now? Jack knew Carl Horner had retired a few years ago. After a shootout gone wrong. There must be a forwarding address. Bingo. There it was. Horner was at Echo Lake in Saskatchewan. Echo Lake was an abandoned FBI safe house way up in the Canadian northlands. Why would the man be in a former safe house? No phone was listed. Figures. There was an Email address. Thank goodness for technology. Out of respect, and perhaps, out of fear, Jack began to type. He finished.

The message was ready.

The message was waiting.

Jack Ramsey asked himself once more.

What was Carl Horner doing in Jamestown?

A small child had been taken. This did not involve a terrorist, or a mafia hit man, or a renegade biker, or a drug dealer. It was a small child from a small town. Then again, Jack had never gotten an answer as to why Carl Horner was allowed to erase Dean Perron from the face of the earth. Dean Perron was not a terrorist, or a mafia hit man, or a renegade biker, but he was a serial killer. A killer of children. Why was the Black Dog in Montana on that hot august night in 1984? What was the Black Dog doing in Jamestown? Maybe there was a common denominator. Maybe it was the children. Dean Perron had kidnapped, raped and murdered children. Jamestown involved a kidnapped child.

Were the children the connection?

Jack inhaled once, and slowly let out his breath. He was tingling all over. This was the true Carl Horner effect. Christ. The guy was thousands of miles away, and retired, and he could still elicit this effect. Okay then, okay. Jack nodded to himself, trying to calm his nerves. He drummed the desk top with his fingers, thinking. He knew in his heart the decision was already made. So much for protocol. So much for the CYA rule. This day, there would be no call to Cleveland. If this blew up in his face, retirement would be moved up for Jack. Possibly even today, he mused.

Jack remembered the paperwork Carl Horner had thrown down to take charge of the Dean Perron case. The instructions ordered Field Agent Jack Ramsey to show no one else, to speak of it to no one else, and to personally destroy said paperwork, completely. Signed and stamped by the FBI Director himself.

The signature on the paperwork was enough for Jack Ramsey. Very few men were this close to the Director of the FBI.

Carl. Franklin. Horner.

Again, Jack glanced around his office.

He hit the send icon.

CHAPTER 16

CARL HORNER WAS SITTING OUTSIDE ON THE WOODEN VERANDA, working his favorite pipe. The old rocking chair beneath him creaked with age as he moved it back and forth. Carl inhaled from the pipe, holding the smoke deep in his lungs. This was the only way the tobacco blend would work its magic. Carl had finished a four hour stint chopping wood out in the bush. It was time to relax. Tomorrow, he would start hauling the cords in. The freezing cold of winter was on its way.

The silence of the early evening was deafening. The water below him was as still as glass. Not a needle moved on the thick pine trees. The start of fall was upon the land. The black flies were gone. The mosquito hordes were gone. The biting no-see-ums were gone. These nights at Echo Lake were magical. Soothing. Quiet. If only he could get rid of the constant buzz inside his head.

Carl was approaching the end of his third year of retirement. A somewhat forced retirement. He had been moved away to this lake, way up in the boonies of northern Canada. This used to be the FBI's remotest safe house on the continent. Echo Lake had been a perfect spot for people entering the witness protection program. Access was by chopper or by foot, across hundreds of acres of rugged forest land claimed by the militant Saguenay First Nation. The FBI gave the property to Carl as a retirement present. Let the noise, the press, the media frenzy die down. Relax, and recover. Let it go.

Carl spent his first winters cutting wood, trying to produce enough fire logs to keep up to the fearsome cold. The nights of January and February saw temperatures drop forty degrees below the freezing mark. Carl snow shoed and hiked. He tracked the forest animals. Only tracked them. His killing days were over.

Despite being fifty-seven years old, Carl was in remarkable condition. At six foot four, he carried a solid two hundred and forty pounds. His step was light, his thickening midsection had disappeared with the manual labor, and his back pains were gone. The scorching summer sun had bleached his hair white, and leathered his skin a deep, reddish brown. The right ear continued to bother him. The constant buzzing and the stabbing pains were his lifelong reminder of a deal gone terribly sour.

The position, the authority and the guns were gone. Finally, the mindset was softening. While he was working, nothing had bothered him. However, the first year of retirement had been tough. The adrenaline of the hunt, the electricity, the juice, had all been turned off. He was now an old car battery. He was drained. Carl had plenty of time to reconcile his actions. The rights, the wrongs and the whys. The sobering facts began to wear away at him. He had executed *so* many people.

The pleading, the crying, yes, even bad guys cried when it was their time, the gunshots, the blood, the carnage. The death. Carl brought death. He had scoured so much worthless garbage from the face of the earth. Hundreds of executions, by gun and by his bare hands. All fully sanctioned by his government.

He had held the power and he used it.

Why?

Why was it so easy for him?

Indeed, Carl thought he might go crazy during his first year of retirement. All alone. Thinking so much. Carl had always been a loner. Except, he had always been busy in mind and body. Now, he was busy only in body. His mind was free to wander. To question. To account.

How could he ever forget the career ending disaster? The tractor-trailer, jack knifing and then blasting through the guard rail. Careening off the cliff. Sailing. Sailing down. A giant wounded bird, heading for a crash landing. The firestorm following the impact with the unforgiving ground. The innocent deaths in the hiking preserve down below. The charred, unrecognizable victims. The dead children. The shootout. The blast ripping off his ear. All part of the living nightmare.

For sure, year one alone in the bush, with the memories, had been tough. Carl decided he best knuckle down and pull himself together. The punishing physical work required to survive in the northlands, and his return to nature, proved to be remarkable therapy.

Carl took another drag on the pipe. This was good stuff. He bought his tobacco from the Saguenay natives. It was a powerful elixir. It dulled the pain in his head and helped gear him down. Truly, Carl was losing his edge. He smiled at this thought. Carl had spent thirty-three years honing his edge. Finally, it was starting to slip away. He no longer needed the edge. He was no longer playing the game.

The game of life and death.

A beeping noise interrupted the tranquility. Carl rubbed his ear to clear the buzzing. This usually allowed him about a second of relief. A second was all he needed. The beeping was coming from inside the cabin. The noise was vaguely familiar, but he couldn't quite place it.

Carl rose from his rocker, pulled open the screen door and entered the cabin. He possessed very few instruments capable of making such a sound. One of them was the solar generator powering his lights and satellite computer. Carl knelt down and looked under his desk. He checked to see if the generator was the source of the beeping. The generator was nearly full, the result of another strong sun day. It wasn't the generator. He stood and tapped the computer keyboard, bringing light to the screen. The Email envelope was flashing. The beeping was explained. Carl was still having trouble locating certain sound tones with one good ear, and one damaged ear.

Carl had not received an Email in over six months. He sparingly used his computer, mostly looking up birds, animal tracks and berry bushes he came across. Carl was fast becoming an expert on northern Canadian flora and fauna. Occasionally, he would play some on-line poker and read the news. His computer usage was very limited.

Carl removed his jacket and hung it on the back of the desk chair. A fire crackled in the stone corner fireplace. A massive German shepherd was stretched out in front of the hearth, sound asleep. Carl sat down and opened the Email.

He read the file.
Stopped himself.
Reread the file.
Closed the Email.
Stopped again.
Carl sat back in his chair.
Stopped, once more.
Unbelievable.
He was now at a full dead stop. His body and mind both.
Barely breathing.
Now thinking.

After everything Carl had seen and done in his life, he *still* had the capacity to be surprised.

How implausible. After all this time, twenty-six long years, the rabbit was on the run.

Heading for home.

They always went home, didn't they?

It was instinct, it was nature.

Home.

Home was a return to the days of simplicity, to the days of innocence. Before the bad shit had taken over. Home was mommy and daddy, and familiarity and comfort, and the perception of safety. Warmth and nourishment and sanctuary.

Carl had reached into many a sanctuary to obliterate the bad people. Yes he had.

But stop.

This, was *really* it.

This, the only unsolved case of his career.

Carl put his brain to work, reeling back through the past. He returned to the eighties, to Jamestown, Ohio. This was the only case in his lengthy career he could not bring home. Although it was not officially his case, it became his case when he stuck his nose in, and it stayed his case because of the victim. Granted, the case was stone cold by the time he got involved. He had been far too late to make a difference. He wasn't sure he could *have* made a difference, even if he had been at ground zero, on that September day.

Carl stood and went to his bookshelf. He picked a volume from the wall and opened the cover.

There it was.

The picture.

Her picture.

Faded.

Waiting.

The little girl, not even two years old, smiling at him.

Captured and frozen in some bizarre world, forever and ever.

With those haunting eyes.

She had a name. Yes, she did. Tiffany. Tiffany Amber Forbes. She had a name, but she had no peace. Carl had been unable to bring her peace. He had been unable to protect her. Or her memory.

The girl's radiant smile seemed to bring life to the worn photo. With the life came the reality of the awful defeat.

However.

With this new bit of information, possibly, there was a chance.

Something was happening out there. The FBI tracker could sense it. Instinctively, Carl sniffed at the air. Took in a deep breath. He was an animal, using all of his senses. The slightest footfall. A twig being brushed. A breath being exhaled in the forest. Something was moving.

Something was moving in the sick, sick place called Jamestown.

Was it finally time for Carl to bring the little girl home?

His rested, rejuvenated body began to tingle. The juices cultivated from thirty-three years of hard service began to flow back from hibernation. Carl placed the picture face up on his kitchen table. He walked to the screen door, pushed it open and stepped back out onto the wooden veranda.

Carl looked to the sky. It was awe-inspiring. So clear and so pure. Cloudless and still. Darkness was beginning to fall down. The first white stars were appearing in the heavens. The last red streaks of the sun were fading in the western horizon, somewhere over the stiff backbone ranges of British Columbia. Carl let his eyes drift down to the lake. Not a single ripple or blemish tarnished the water's surface. The majestic, soaring pine trees surrounding the lake did not budge a needle. Carl was looking at a perfect snapshot. A true freeze frame. It all looked so serene and so ideal.

Eerily serene, and eerily ideal.

It wasn't. No, it definitely wasn't. Not even the natives who had lived on this land their entire lives could sense the approaching storm.

Carl could.

Because he, Carl Franklin Horner, was the storm.

A powerful rage was incubating.

The eyes of his humanity began to flicker.

The peaceful, tranquil landscape of Echo Lake slipped away.

The Black Dog was emerging from three long years of hibernation.

Cold. Angry. Vengeful.

She was calling.

CHAPTER 17

This was the strangest road trip Tom had ever been on. The two travelers hit truck stops, gas stations, convenience shops, diners and for Tommy, liquor stores. They stayed in forgettable cheap motels. Or possibly, they slept in the Jeep. Tom couldn't be sure. Things were really this bad. After twenty-five years of abuse, his brain had fallen into a dreadful state of decrepitude.

The terrain outside the Jeep windows had purposefully morphed from flat beige desert nothingness and talking black birds, to elevations and incredible mountains. Then to rolling plains and corn and cattle. Now it was hills and trees, forests and green. The Jeep cruised through small cities and bypassed large cities. The temperature cooled down noticeably. The sun rose and the sun set. They kept driving. The sun rose and set again. Tom went from bottle to syringe to sleep, to stupefaction. He shot up in bathroom stalls and puked in rest area toilet bowls. His stash was going fast. He would have to up the booze until he found an eastern dealer.

What great habits he had picked up in his life.

What a champion he had become.

There would be no giant cherry wood trophies handed out for this behavior.

The endless miles crawled past. The grass medians and concrete barricades and white painted lines stretched on forever. Curving, meandering, rising and falling. The white painted lines were mesmerizing, continuously unfolding from an endless reel of white lines.

The Jeep seemed to be running on autopilot. From time to time, Tom could swear the driver's seat was empty. These were probably the times when Tommy himself was playing sky pilot, riding the wave of drug induced madness, searching for the damn bullet train. Ready to plug it with a couple of heat seekers. Before it could run through a population center and obliterate a green Jeep. And a small passenger. The bullet train had been with him for a long, long time.

As had the little voice and the ocean of despair. These, along with the skull ripping headaches, were Tom's main, prime time companions. The ghost known as Joe Danton was a new arrival on the scene. A new character in the twisted, diseased mind of Tom Forbes. Probably taking over from the bullet train.

Most of the time, Tom did see Joe Danton in the driver's seat. Though not as bad as Tom, Joe Danton had still aged unfavorably, adding many extra years to his appearance. He had the same long hair Tom remembered, in the same pony tail, but now showing plenty of gray. Joe's beard was much thinner, and his eyes were tired.

As the hundreds and hundreds of miles slipped past, Tom realized the two of them had barely spoken. This Joe Danton character, or apparition, or whatever it was, offered nothing to Tom. There were no questions, no answers, and no conversation. Tom desperately wanted answers about his little girl, but felt it was better not to ask. In his messed up mind, he figured if he started asking real questions, this whole mirage might disappear and he would be right back in his boiling tin coffin. Back in his tin coffin without hope.

While they weren't conversing with one another, Joe Danton was certainly conversing with himself. Tom couldn't be sure, but Joe seemed to be doing a lot of mumbling, and calculating, and discussing. As if he was recollecting and putting together some great story. Yet, Joe was recollecting and putting together this great story in a language which made little sense to Tom.

What the hell was up with this guy?

What *was* his story?

Something was definitely off with Danton, but of course, Tom was approaching this from a fairly handicapped perspective. Stoned and nearly brain dead himself. Joe was lost in his thoughts, whatever those thoughts were. Good old Tom Forbes was lost in his substance abuse. Tom had to wonder if he was riding with the devil himself, or with his savior.

Was this the man who had really taken his little girl?

Did this man know where she was?

Could this man possibly bring her back?

Jesus. What nonsense. What utter bullshit.

What is wrong with you, Tommy?

How could anybody bring her back, after all these years?

Go stand in the ocean of despair and wait for her. Better chance that will work.

Was this what happened when you ingested too many drugs? Had he crossed a mental deterioration rubicon, and was he too, lost forever? Unable to discern reality from fiction?

It was a crazy trip with a crazy man.

This had fast become two mutes on a journey to nowhere.

The trip had begun as a blur.

Tom was sure it would end as a blur.

CHAPTER 18

Carl Horner tried to get comfortable in the 737 jet. He stretched his legs under the seat in front of him. Not good. His size thirteens wouldn't fit. Carl hated flying. Airplanes were never designed to accommodate people his size.

The Northeast Air jet was twenty minutes out of Buffalo Niagara International and was now at cruising altitude. A scattering of passengers was spread throughout the cabin. Not a popular flight, Buffalo to Cleveland. Not a surprise. One decaying metropolis to another.

This had been a long day for Carl. It started with the four a.m. chopper ride out of the bush to Prince Albert. A six passenger Cessna took him over to Regina. A small jet flew him off the great prairies and into the big city of Toronto. An airport taxi got Carl as far as the Peace Bridge. A thirty minute crap fest was held at the border crossing. Good old Homeland Security. Yes, let's hassle retired FBI agents, what a great idea.

Finally, he made it to the Buffalo Airport and began a two hour wait for this flight. Carl yawned. He was tired. The cabin air was warm, the engines hummed. The constant buzz continued in his ear. The cabin illumination was dimmed for the duration of the flight. A handful of reading lamps snapped on. The dimming of the cabin lights sent a signal to Carl's eyelids. The eyelids understood, and began to slide shut.

Sleep would be welcome.

It was not to be.

A dreadful scraping sound, hard metal against pavement, rattled through Carl. Finger nails on a chalkboard, times fifty. Could anything be more annoying? Especially when you were trying to sleep?

Out of nowhere, a preposterous, enormous, black mechanical thing appeared.

What on earth was this?

Was it walking?

What?

Yes, it was walking. Out of the cockpit area at the front of the plane, working its way down the narrow aisle. Every seat it brushed against blew up in stuffing. In revulsion, passengers leaned as far away from the aisle as possible.

What the hell was happening?

Carl couldn't even begin to understand what he was looking at. This was some sort of, creature thing?

Carl blinked his eyes hard.

He had to be dreaming!

Hallucinating!

He blinked some more.

The herbal pipe tobacco he had been smoking for three years? Could it be?

As the thing got closer, Carl felt every nerve in his body responding. Every one of his FBI trained sensors screamed, EXTREME DANGER!

Thirty-three years of experience blared at him, PREPARE TO REACT!

Carl had never seen such a horrific looking creature in his life. What was it? The creature had a large cylindrical torso, with metallic arms and legs. Its head was mostly teeth, with spit drooling from razor sharp fangs. For only the second time in his life, Carl began to tremble.

Tremble with fear.

The creature was getting closer. Closer. The creature grew in stature, the top of it now scraping the ceiling of the plane, its shoulders banging against the overhead compartments. As the creature drew nearer, Carl was being reduced in stature, in size, even in age. This was incredulous. He was now a small child, quivering, with teeth chattering, but otherwise, he had been stricken with immobility.

His legs and his arms were dead to him. The legendary Black Dog, the FBI man of action, was utterly frozen in place.

The creature began to evolve, now resembling less of a machine, and more of a human.

Carl stared.

How preposterous was this?

The creature was now a large, loud, putrid, awful man. Six foot eight, three hundred and fifty hard pounds. The black darkness of the creature stayed with the man, manifesting itself as rage. A rage Carl could not comprehend. The rage was powerful. Overwhelming. Suffocating.

Carl could see down the aisle past the creature. A broken form lying between the fading airplane seats. It wasn't a fellow passenger. Or a flight attendant. Carl knew it was his protector. Defeated. The only person capable of saving Carl from this creature.

Carl was alone now, the creature nearly upon him.

Flashing teeth.

Snarling.

Screaming.

Swearing.

Carl was suffering the thrashing, breaking evil pouring from the creature. He could smell the overpowering reek of sour liquor and body effluent. Try as he might, Carl could not break the fear controlling him, enveloping him. Because his protector was dead, and soon, he would also be dead. He did not want to die. He was a child.

The child had to fight back. Had to. Carl felt something in his hand. Something solid. Something sending a tiny quiver of strength up his thin arm and into his small chest. A bright light. Hope. Carl looked down at his hand. His hand was so young looking. So small and smooth and delicate. It was a child's hand.

How?

In the child's hand was the power. The awful power. The power surged through both of his arms and demanded a reaction.

Demanded ACTION.

Still trembling, Carl did what he had done so many, many times in his long professional career. He was able to raise the solid steel eighteen inch barrel. Tuck the wooden stock in against his shoulder. Nice and tight. Ready for the kickback. Grip the weapon. Grip it hard. Take aim.

Keep your eye on the prize, his daddy always said. Keep your eye, on the prize.

In that second, the world stopped.

How on earth did Carl, his dead protector, this horrible monster, and this sleek killing weapon end up on a Northeast Air flight? In the darkening night sky between Buffalo and Cleveland?

There was no possible answer to this question.

How could there be?

Carl's heart was thudding away, filled with such an incredible fear. He could hear every single thud. In *both* of his ears. Even the damaged one. Carl had endured three long years of buzzing in his damaged ear. Now, the buzzing was gone. Completely. The damaged ear was healed. Or more improbably, it had not *yet* been injured. Because he was only a kid. Not an adult. Not all grown up and grizzled and retired in the northern bush lands.

The creature was frozen in place, in the throes of its final assault, mere inches in front of Carl.

What on earth? What was happening here?

No time.

The world re-started. The creature leapt.

Carl fired.

The kickback from the shotgun blast sent him crashing through two rows of seats. The ball shot tore apart the creature's chest, puncturing its heart in forty places. Disbelieving, clutching at its chest, watching blood drip through talon-like yellowed fingers, the creature turned its ugly head toward Carl, and died.

Turbulence rocked the small jet.

Sweet Jesus!

Carl sat bolt upright in his seat.

Sweating.

Where the hell did that come from?

As quickly as it came, the dream was gone. Carl looked around the plane. It was exactly the same as when he got on. A scattering of passengers. A flight attendant handing out peanuts and pretzels. Cabin lights set on dim. A smattering of reading lamps glowing.

It was only a dream. A dream. Not real. Fluff into the atmosphere.

Carl began to calm himself.

He rang the flight attendant for water.

The dream was indeed insane, but it was also a revelation. A revelation which left Carl with one feeling. Anger. Anger at those who bullied the weak. Anger at the bastards who took advantage of those who were smaller, or gentler, or trusting. Anger at those who preyed upon the innocent. Especially the innocent kids. The innocent kid in the picture, folded in the pages of a book. A book from his bookshelf. From his cabin. A picture he now carried with him.

The picture from the broken glass frame.

Anger all right. Not at all dissimilar from the rage feeding the horrible black beast of his dream. Not dissimilar at all.

Anger.

This anger made Carl Horner everything he was. This anger made Carl Horner, the Protector. He knew this already, deep down inside. He knew his role. The FBI tests, the training he received. The missions he acted upon. The scores he settled. The garbage he took out. The lives he saved by doing his job. Yes, he was the Protector.

Except.

Except for the little girl.

Tiffany Amber.

He had not been able to protect her.

This fact was about to change.

He could feel it.

CHAPTER 19

To the best of Tom's recollection, the sun had set four times since the trip began.

Or was it six times?

Or ten times?

Or was he still in his bed in the tin trailer?

How could he be sure of anything?

He had no idea what day it was, what month it was, and wasn't sure what year it was. It didn't really matter. In Arizona, it was one endless summer. Some months were hotter than others. Mostly though, it was sunny and hot every day, dark and cooler every night.

While Tom owned a television set running off a neighbor's splitter, he rarely watched the news or anything remotely intelligent. He did not subscribe to any papers, he didn't read magazines, and he didn't listen to the radio. He had never owned anything connected to the web. He was clueless regarding time, information, world events, local events, anything, and everything. He had not advanced his knowledge level since community college, and was sure the drug abuse had cost him most of his intelligent brain cells. Over the last two decades, he had truly become, a stupid man.

Tom was pretty sure four sunsets had passed. Sounded good. The four passing sunsets meant four days had also expired. He could still do the simple math. The four days of driving matching the four sunsets meant this mindless journey had to be coming to an end. Even a fantasy flight had to come to an end, right Tommy?

He felt it first.

The dampness.

Something he had not experienced in a long, long time. The dampness began to settle into his bones. His internal feral sensor was signaling, telling him he was nearly home. Tom could make out the vast dark expanse of Lake Erie along the north side of the interstate. The traffic was heavy. Big trucks, lots of them, and many cars, all heading somewhere. Probably heading home.

The last green exit board for Jamestown came towards him on the right. The listed amenities once available in the city were patched over with green paint. The newer green paint was not quite the same shade as the original. Tom could see bits of those amenities left over on the sign. There were ghostly images for hospital, telephone, food and lodging. Apparently these services were no longer available. Even the population line had been patched over. The state highway crews were erasing Jamestown from the map.

Interesting.

Or not.

Who cared?

Not Tom Forbes. There was nothing here for him. This place was the past. The awful past. Skating rinks and falling buildings and bullet trains.

Tom sipped the last drops from his current bottle of choice. The sun was slipping down once again; the weak daylight would soon be absorbed in shadow. The dirty, green Jeep pulled off the interstate at the Jamestown turnoff, as a few sloppy wet snowflakes began to fall. The wipers were flipped on. The dampness chilled Tom to his very soul. He was missing the dry desert already.

The exit ramp led them along into yesterday.

The Jeep cycled down off the interstate. Traffic on the Jamestown cloverleaf was non-existent. Theirs was the only moving vehicle. No one else was pulling off the interstate. No one else was cycling to get onto the interstate.

Weird.

The traffic had been steady on the big highway; noisy, thick, plenty of cars and trucks blasting past, and now, nothing.

Suddenly it was eerie quiet.

Tom Forbes was home.

They drove off the cloverleaf onto the main drag, onto the start of the once proud Miracle Mile. The Miracle Mile was totally devoid of moving traffic. Even more disturbing, the Miracle Mile was totally devoid of pedestrians.

The road was potholed, the curbs were all broken.

Hydro wires were missing from the tall poles. No. That wasn't quite right. The hydro wires were indeed missing. So were the poles. The tall poles had been chain sawed right down to the ground and removed. Some of the poles had been axed and removed. Dead stubs of these former hydro poles protruded anywhere from a few inches to a few feet out of the sidewalks.

What on earth had happened here?

Stripped down, derelict vehicles dotted the angled parking slots. The vehicles were graffiti covered, with tires missing, axles missing, windows shattered and hoods missing.

Tom rubbed at his eyes. Made sure he was awake. This was unbelievable.

Were they even in Jamestown?

Or some third world country?

Or on a movie set?

Boarded up storefronts and smashed out streetlights lined the sidewalks on both sides of the Miracle Mile. Tom could only shake his head as he took in the sad state of these once striking buildings.

He scanned up from the retail street level. The second, third and fourth floor windows were mostly boarded up or dark. A few flickering lights illuminated a handful of the openings. It appeared to be lantern or candle power. Tom could see hydro wires torn, hanging from the buildings, connected to nothing. Still, there were no pedestrians. They had yet to see a moving vehicle, human being, cat, dog, sparrow or squirrel in this disarray posing as downtown Jamestown.

They drove on, forging deeper into the old business district. Tom saw up ahead the beginning of the famous Food Row. The Eggstop, Wendy's, Johnny's Diner, McDonalds, Tasty Freeze, Taco Shoppe, Dairy Queen,

Bonanza, Burger King, Red Barn, Ponderosa. All closed. Windows boarded up or blown in. The iconic brand signage was mostly trashed. Graffiti was sprayed all over. Bricks had been torn out of walls. Chunks of roofing were missing completely.

Tom could only stare at the carnage, dumfounded.

The sun peeked through the clouds, a last gasp before nighttime took hold. Through the splattering wet snow, beams of light slanted across the Miracle Mile in front of the Jeep, hitting square on the food row buildings. Tom was working his brain, trying to come to some conclusion about what had happened here. He was not having any success, and he certainly wasn't prepared for what he saw next.

Suddenly, the restaurants filled up, packed with diners and kids and parents!

Finally!

People.

Live people.

Tom felt a little better.

The people were sitting at tables or lined up at the order counter. Eating, drinking and socializing. All normal behavior. Where did these people come from, so out of the blue? A Star Trek moment for sure. Beam us all in, Scotty. Beam us up to deck seven for our supper.

Tom couldn't remember burgers and fries on the Star Trek menu.

Almost funny, then suddenly not.

Tom gulped at air.

Wait a damn second!

These weren't real people, were they Tommy?

Tom squinted his eyes, staring hard.

Holy shit!

What the fuck were they?

They looked..........moving skeletons.

Or radiation burn victims.

Filthy ragged clothes. Diseased, haggard and desperate creatures.

Not human, were they?

Not of *this* world.

The sun beams vanished, as did the diners.

The restaurants were empty again. In another moment, the Jeep was past the dead food stores.

Tom looked at Joe. Joe looked right back at Tom. Joe kind of nodded.

"I saw that," Joe mumbled.

Confirmation.

Yes indeed, they had both seen it.

How disturbing, even to Tom, on so many levels. It was bad enough to have experienced those *things*, or whatever they were, but what he the druggie had seen, Joe the loony had also seen. So it was real. At least on some level, or in some dimension. Oh boy Tom thought, what could possibly come next?

A really disturbing thought ran through his drug mussed brain. He hoped to God his little girl wasn't here. Not with whatever those things were. Totally impossible, right? Those skeletal things were part of a bad trip, an accumulation of after effects from the many trips he had taken in the past twenty-five years. Nothing more. They weren't real.

Right?

No way was his Tiffy here.

Existing with those............things.

Except.

Where had he seen this before?

Where?

Something was vaguely familiar about this. A long corridor. A long, dark corridor. With open doorways. Tom skating. Skating fast. Down the corridor. With deep rooms behind the doorways.

What else?

Something was in those deep rooms?

Yes.

People of some kind. Sick people. People who didn't look right. And a giant mirror full of sharp glass.

Snap. The thought simply faded away.

Tom struggled to get it back.

Nothing.

Faded and gone.

Drugs.

Not the wisest choice to have made when you actually needed to use your brain.

The tour continued through the dead city. Four desolate blocks past the once famous food row, a partially lit marquee sign announced Champ's Chicken and Bar. The Jeep pulled into an empty stall in a mostly empty parking lot. Three other vehicles were in the lot, but it was hard to tell if any of them were operational. The wet snow was dropping faster, pooling water in yet more potholes. It surprised Tom to see Champ's was still in business. The only open establishment they had come across, thus far.

Champ's was once an important part of his social life. The ultra cool, fifties style diner had been a throwback, even in the seventies. As a teenager, the T-Man was the cock of the walk. Sports hero, heart throb, superstar, future college boy, future pro. Tom held court at Champs every Friday night. The greasy chicken and fries, the fancy juke box, the tight dance floor, the long bar, the spinning stools, the romantic booths. Everyone who wanted to be someone came to the restaurant to rub shoulders with the T-man and his boys. Once upon a time.

Tom and Joe got out of the Jeep.

Closed the doors.

Mostly quiet.

There were no street sounds. No sounds of walking feet or shuffling pedestrians. No sounds of voices laughing or shouting, or yapping on cell phones. There were no people sounds at all.

There were no traffic sounds either. No horns honking or engines working or tires bumping over asphalt. No buses or trucks whooshing past.

There were no city sounds at all. No trains blaring or factories belching. No police sirens or dogs barking. The only sound was a muffled diesel motor running somewhere behind the restaurant. The sensation outside the Jeep was one of emptiness.

Emptiness, but watchfulness.

They approached the front door of the diner and paused. Were there actually going to be real people inside? Or more of the things they had seen in the Food Row?

They hoped it would be the former.

The travelers entered the dingy restaurant. The first thing Tom saw was the juke box. He had memories of this particular juke box. He sure did. They turned right and grabbed a booth near the kitchen. For quick service. Joe sat down on a ripped vinyl bench with foam padding spilling out. Tom took a chair opposite, and carefully sat. The chair looked ready to splinter and fall away. They rested their elbows on a carved up, defaced wooden table top. Burnt out light fixtures and water spotting dotted the ceiling. The carpet was bare and worn. The wallpaper was peeling and stained. The place smelled of mold and old, and backed up sewage and rot.

So appetizing.

What a dump.

The only other customers were a group of teenagers sitting at the opposite end of the restaurant. Where the T-man used to sit. His spot. The little bastards. A cloud of cigarette smoke hung over their table, framing animated conversation. What smoking bylaws? The teenagers looked real enough. Tom didn't figure skeleton creatures would smoke, or would be so loud and obnoxious. Tom heard an exaggerated belch, some swearing and forced giggling. Man, what he could have taught these punks about being cool.

Joe ordered two dinner specials from a tired looking, overweight waitress. Her size made her real enough. She looked to be about five foot two inches tall, and the same across the beam. She had to be a live human, because Tom had never seen a fat skeleton.

Tom ordered a bottle of beer. No, make it two bottles of beer. From the Champ's waitress there were no hellos, no welcomes and no smiles, only service, straight up.

The food came pronto, the service was speedy. The food steamed off the plates, a microwave muddle of heavily salted, preserved mush, with melting Styrofoam container smell mixed in. Both men were ravished, they ate quickly. Tom could not remember his last meal. Once in a while he did get the munchies. Something about the drug abuse, and the sleeping, and the doing nothing, and the miniscule metabolism, and the not eating for three or four days.

Joe pushed his plate back first.

Tom looked across at Joe, raising an eyebrow, the old 'what now' expression. Tom figured Joe Danton had spent three or four whole days silently preparing what he was about to say. After watching Joe incoherently babbling to himself in the Jeep, Tom hoped it would at least be in English. Fire away, buddy. Make it good.

Joe began.

"Tom, I spent a lot of time in the hospital. Things happened to me there, especially when I was recovering. Drugs, treatments, therapies. I have a problem with timelines. There is a whole stretch of my life I can't remember."

Tom sort of smiled to himself. It was not a smile of joy or happiness. It was more a smile of twisted irony. Mr. Joe Danton thinks he's messed up? Can Danton even contemplate what Tommy boy had done to his brain during the last two and a half decades?

"Here goes. I remember being outside with the kids. A fall day. A strange day. It was so warm and sunny. The sky was blue. An Indian summer day. It was a big event for the kids."

This memory was still sharp for Tom.

"It was Parent's Day," Tom interjected. "Parents Day."

Despite the effort to blunt the memories, they were still there. So fresh, after all these years. Still, so damn raw. Immediately, Tom felt the despair rolling towards him. The ripples of darkness and despair, his old friends. Lapping away at first, calm little eddies approaching. The despair would grow in strength and speed and darkness. The despair would develop as dark waves, and then finally, a tsunami of black. Tom would drown, one more time. Let's not even think of the falling buildings, or the giant mallet, or the streaking bullet train. Or the little voice from some other world.

"Right," Joe continued.

"Parent's Day. There was a blinding flash of light. A lightening strike. Against the back fence. A fire started. Smoke began to roll out from the fence and then across the grass. Wispy smoke, then really thick smoke. The fence was on fire, and the grass was on fire. It must have been four or five guys, yes, it was five guys coming out of nowhere. I don't know if they climbed over the fence or what. They were wearing hoods or robes. It was so bizarre. They were looking at all the kids, and they grabbed your daughter. I remember the way they looked at her. They selected her. Pre-planned. A military operation. Quickly, they began to......"

"Began to what?" Tom asked, shaky and bracing, waiting for more waves.

"They began to fade away. I know it sounds crazy. They went towards the fence and disappeared into the smoke. Did they go back over the fence? I don't know. I must have been in shock. Marie was closest to these guys. She ran into the smoke, chasing after them. I ran after her. The only thing I found was Marie. Lying on the ground. It was horrible."

Joe stalled, weakening.

In a small voice, "She was burnt to death."

Joe stopped.

"My Marie............"

Tom had never given two thoughts as to the death of Marie Danton. He always thought of her as an accomplice, somehow involved in his little girl's disappearance, so whatever, it was good she was dead. Tom was one hundred per cent sure Joe had taken his Tiffany. The rationale being, Joe was gone and Tiffy was gone. They had gone together. Marie was Joe's wife, so Marie was somehow responsible or culpable or had to have known *something*.

Because Tiffy did not go of her own free will. She wouldn't have. She couldn't have. She was a two year old child. With parents who loved her to death. She went of Joe's will. The death of Marie made zero sense at the time. The death of Marie had always made zero sense. So Tom forgot about Marie, he couldn't care less about her. Tom blamed Joe Danton one hundred per cent for his little girl's disappearance.

End of story. The bastard.

As he looked across the small table at Joe, Tom could see the man was crushed. Or a great actor. Or a great hologram. Or a ghost. Or a figment of a drug addled imagination. Since Tom was going with whatever was happening here, he kept Joe out of those last categories. For now, Tom would leave Joe in the 'man' category. Yes, Joe the human.

Deep, deep down, Tom didn't believe Joe the human was acting. Because Tom knew grief extremely well. Yes he did. He was a learned scholar of grief. A master. He certainly grieved his little girl. Every, every day. He grieved losing his beautiful Karen, and his life before, even his mortgaged house and boring job, and all of his buddies and his home town.

The grief Tom carried for Tiffany was a more punishing variety.

Because he didn't know what happened to her. He didn't know where she was.

For damn sure, Tom Forbes understood true grief.

True grief is what he was seeing in Joe Danton.

For the first time, Tom understood the loss of Marie was as devastating to Joe as the loss of his Tiffy was to him. This threw a new light on the entire episode of his little girl's disappearance. Tom felt the game was beginning to change.

Joe wiped his eyes with his fingers and took a deep breath.

"But, we are here for Tiffany."

Hearing her name from another person's mouth was enough to release the next waves of despair. The waves began to reach for Tom. Tears welled behind his eyes. He crunched back the tears. Tom was not going to open the dam because he might not be able to get it closed again. He was amazed the tears could still form. He had to be cried out by now. Cried out a thousand times over. He knew he never, never would be. Never released from his prison. Ever. Tom had failed his little girl. He did not protect her.

With the waves of despair, came the headache.

Pounding, pounding.

Throbbing.

Reverberating.

Joe leaned across the table. Took another deep breath. Found some new resolve.

"This is where it gets really bizarre."

Tom raised his eyes.

Skeleton things eating at McDonalds? Now that was bizarre.

Marie murdered, and possibly not an accomplice? Also bizarre.

The downtown of Jamestown devastated by some unknown force? Really bizarre.

Tiffany here, with these creature things? He didn't want to think too hard about this, but also bizarre.

Tom here, with Joe Danton, the taker of his child, eating dinner at the same table? Bizarre.

Tom in Jamestown, and not in the desert?

Shit.
What could be any more bizarre than this?

CHAPTER 20

"A SECOND BLINDING FLASH OF LIGHT HIT. WHEN THE SMOKE CLEARED, it was nighttime. Nighttime, Tom. I was in a downtown back alley. Not here. I was in a back alley somewhere in Cleveland. Ninety-five miles away. Dirty, filthy, bloodied. Pretty much beaten and left for dead. Broken arms, crushed fingers, broken jaw, slashed across the throat."

Joe pulled his shirt collar down to show Tom the ugly, still fresh scar. The scar ran from Joe's right collarbone, across his neck, and up to his left ear. Tom winced. It was horrible. What on earth? Tom had not discerned the scar while they were in the Jeep. The beard provided some cover, and the scar was most noticeable on the left side of Joe's face, away from Tom's passenger seat point of view.

"Jesus," Tom said, reaching inside his jacket for the headache pills.

Tom had not yet caught the time travel implication of Joe's statement. Attacked in Jamestown, found in Cleveland. No, Tom was all eyes and thoughts on the scar. The scar looked as if it still hurt. Twenty-five years later, with pain. Joe was lucky his head hadn't rolled off. American Jihad.

This story was getting to be too much. Tom uncapped the three hundred pill bottle and spilled white tablets into his hand. He gulped about eight of them, with the beer chaser.

The teenagers were up and about the jukebox, pushing and slapping, yelling in loud, exaggerated, moronic tones. Coins were slid into the machine, clinking loudly through the money slide. Buttons were punched. An idiotic argument broke out over which songs to play.

Joe continued.

"I had no identification with me, and couldn't speak or write. I was picked up as a homeless person and taken to emergency. They cleaned me up, stitched me up. Set my bones. Shaved my hair and beard. I lost forty pounds eating through intravenous tubes and straws. Then I was shipped to the big house in Cleveland, the Mental Institute."

Joe paused, as if straining to remember.

"Tom, your daughter disappeared in 1987. I was picked up in the back alley, in the year 2000."

Tom's jaw nearly hit the table. He was stunned, and a little more than confused.

Had he heard this right?

2000?

Now he caught the time travel double whammy.

Jamestown to Cleveland, *and* 1987 to 2000.

"What?" Tom asked, not quite comprehending. Actually, not comprehending at all.

The lights began to flicker in the restaurant, as if they were not being powered by continuous electricity. Tom felt a panic attack, then small chills, and then he thought he heard whispers. He looked to the booths around him. There was nobody else in the restaurant. It was them and the stupid teenagers and the squat waitress. Why did it feel so full?

"The year 2000, Tom. *Thirteen* years later. Thirteen years of my life I don't remember. Thirteen years of my life I cannot account for."

Tom rubbed his temples and looked at Joe. Across the small table. This was a bad trip. Tom the druggie and Joe the lunatic in a faceoff. Tom could see the years had taken their toll on Joe. While Tom figured he looked a good seventy-five or eighty years old, Joe wasn't too far behind. What the hell was this travel and missing years bullshit?

More importantly, what about his Tiffany?

She and Joe disappeared together that day. Now, Joe was back. Should Tiffany not be back as well? Tom would give the lunatic another few minutes to finish his stupid, fucking story. If the story didn't get better or proceed towards a favorable ending, Tom would have to do something. Something severe.

The jukebox music seemed awfully loud. It was the new shit, the urban shit, the horrible, thumping rap. The owners must have updated the music list from Seger and Madonna and U2. The only updates this decrepit place had seen. The beat helped punctuate Tom's headache. He looked over towards the teenagers. They seemed to fade in and out of his vision, in sync with the lights dimming and flickering. Similar to the things they had seen in the Food Row stores.

Joe carried on.

"They could not identify me in any way, shape or form. They ran me through DMV, IRS, Military Records and Social Services. Nothing. I was a John Doe. The local cops checked missing persons and matched me up with some guy who had walked out of the mental hospital years before. They gave me his name and closed the case. They had wasted enough resources on me. Who cared about another homeless bum? The treatments I got, the medication they put in me, were not mine; they were for the guy I replaced. I was starting to go crazy in there."

Starting?

Jesus.

Full fledged crazy is more like it, Tom surmised.

Time travel? What could be crazier than time travel?

The beer bottle was empty. Both beer bottles were empty. When had he consumed the second beer? Tom was now working a small whiskey jar. Pulling the jar out, sneaky, taking a sip, then slipping the bottle away. Did it really matter in this dump? Tom pulled the flask back out, sipped again, then set it down on the table. The waves of despair relented somewhat. The booze was beating them back, as much as was possible.

Joe soldiered on.

"The story gets crazier. I met a priest inside."

Great, Tom thought. Let's add some religion to the mix. Religion was always welcome. And to boot, let's make it a priest from a nuthouse. Who else can we bring into this tale? Captain Kangaroo? The Friendly Giant? Mr. Rogers? Tickle Me Elmo?

"The priest was committed in 1999. He was already in when I got there. He desperately feared for his life. In fact, the priest was petrified. He said some cult was gunning for him. The priest had been some big shot author who had cracked under the glory of success. He was a shrink's dream. A master of conspiracy theories. Honest to God, I really believed this guy was nuts, but somehow, he knew stuff."

"Really," Tom said aloud.

Let's summarize, he thought to himself. A religious nutcase, talking conspiracy, with another nutcase, in a loony bin. Wow. Must have been incredibly productive.

"What stuff did the priest know?" Tom asked, riding along.

"When I told him what I had experienced in Jamestown, he nearly fell out of his chair. The priest pulled out a file full of newspaper clippings. Kidnappings, sabotage and horrific violence, all seemingly unconnected. Random acts. According to the priest, the clippings all had one thing in common. Somewhere in the picture, either on the clothing, or spray painted on a wall, or tattooed on a perpetrator, or as a symbol left behind, was the same thing. A ragged lightening bolt. Nobody but the priest could see these bolts. *I* could see the bolts. The shrinks in the mental institute said he was crazy. They said I was crazy. The priest was convinced......"

Tom held up his hand.

Joe stopped.

Something in this drivel had shaken Tom to his core.

"What did you say?"

"I said, the priest was convinced...."

"Before that. Did you say a lightening bolt?"

Joe nodded.

Tom's guts hit the floor.

Chills flew up and down his spine.

He sat upright.

His mind reversed.

Suddenly, this was no children's/nutcase/religious fairy tale. Twenty-five plus years of drinking, drug abuse, headaches, guilt trips, suicide plans, personal destruction, it all raced backwards. It came to a screeching halt in the backyard of the day care. On the charred plank fence.

There it was.

Plain as day.

Except.

Except nobody saw it. Not Karen. Not any of the cops. Nobody. Nobody but him.

"Tom? Tom, what is it?" Joe asked.

"The fence at the day care. In the backyard. There was a lightening bolt burnt into the fence. Nobody else could see it. Only me. I thought I was in shock, hallucinating."

Joe reached inside his jacket. He unfolded a sheet of paper.

"The priest had this clipping in his file."

Joe handed the paper to Tom. It was a photocopy from the Jamestown Evening Tribune. Tom read the caption under the picture. The crime was pegged as a kidnapping/murder. The photograph showed a tarp covering a body. Marie's body. Behind the body was the plank fence.

Holy shit.

There it was.

Unmistakable.

Tom could see the lightening bolt charred into the wooden fence.

"One more thing," Joe said. "The guy who grabbed Tiffany? His wrist was tattooed with the same thing. The lightening bolt. I saw the lightening bolt on him."

The temperature suddenly dropped in the restaurant. The light fixture above their booth swirled, moved by an unseen force. More whispers slipped through the restaurant, from the ceiling, out of the walls, up from the dirty, worn carpet. It was as if the restaurant was full of diners, or had been, and they had left, but their impressions or life forces remained behind. Or perhaps, the restaurant was right now, full of those skeletal freak things. Tom's head was pounding. The waves were sloshing at him again. Something was definitely whispering at him. The restaurant was either full, or it wasn't.

Which was it?

Let's not try to think too hard, Tommy.

No, let's not think of the skeletal things at all. They couldn't be real. So let's get back to Joe Danton's tale. Something that *could* be real.

Right.

Joe Danton was weaving a gigantic tale, which Tom could never hope to dream up. Or even hallucinate, during one of his binges. However, the tale was doing something. The tale was growing in relevance. Up until this moment, twenty-five years after the fact, Tom was convinced Joe and Marie were totally culpable in his little girl's disappearance. It happened at their day care. On their watch. With kids and employees all over the place. But no witnesses? To a child abduction? From their own backyard?

Impossible.

Had Joe and Marie prearranged with, or abetted the hooded people who took Tiffany?

No, Joe Danton had taken Tiffany. This is why they both disappeared at the exact, same, time.

Yes, Marie was deader than dead. Why? Why was Marie dead?

Were the cop's first theory of Joe and Marie working as a team, wrong?

It had always been wrong, hadn't it?

If the cops had been so wrong about Marie, were they also wrong about Joe?

Was *he* wrong about Joe?

Was he?

So far tonight, Joe's stories were the stories of an insane person. An insane person who admitted he came from a loony bin. Who thinks he had beamed himself from Jamestown to Cleveland. Who had forgotten thirteen years of his life. Honestly, the guy had probably been in a coma, or drugged, or electric shocked, or cattle prodded up the ass for those thirteen years. His entire story, every utterance out of his mouth, should be considered crapshit.

But here came the damn relevance.

The lightening bolt on the fence. The lightening bolt *had* been there. It *had* been real. The lightening bolt was from before the abuse. From his other life. Tom had seen it way back then. Clear as day. Damn straight he had seen it. He was seeing it now, clearly, in the old newspaper clipping right in front of him. Joe could see it in the newspaper clipping. Nobody else had seen see the lightening bolt on the fence. So the two of them, he and Joe, now shared something else besides the skeletons in the Food Row.

The relevance was indeed growing.

A sliver of light suddenly pierced the darkness of Tom's being. The sliver of light meant there was a sliver of hope.

Tom reached across the table, knocking his beer bottles over. He grabbed Joe by the jacket collar, pulling him up out of his seat, shoving him back against the wall.

"These bastards have her? Who are these people? How do we get her back?"

The table of teenagers quieted, staring at the confrontation. The rap music continued to thump.

"Tom, Tom. Easy."

"Did you take her? Did you? Who the *fuck* took her?"

Joe put his hands on Tom's. Tom felt a remarkable strength and calmness in Joe's touch.

Joe looked into Tom's eyes, more, right into Tom's soul.

"Good god no. I did not take her. I did not. How could....?"

Tom could see the pain in Joe. The overwhelming disbelief. How could Tom have *ever* thought such a thing? Joe was wounded. Crushed.

Or again, a damn fine actor?

Joe said, "I was supposed to watch over her. I was supposed to protect her. I am so sorry Tom. I failed. I failed Tiffany."

Tom felt............he wasn't sure *what* he felt.

Could he have been wrong, all of these years? Was he that messed up? Was Joe Danton for real?

Or was Joe Danton the biggest con man on the face of the earth?

Was all of this a figment of Tom's dying brain?

Synapses firing feverishly and randomly?

Damaged and shorted by cocaine and heroin and alcohol abuse?

This cheap dinner table, and this restaurant, and this micro waved food, and the skeleton people, and the horrible rap music, was any of this real?

Tom looked at Joe, releasing the grip on his jacket and stepping back.

"Joe, where is she?"

"She's right here Tom. In Jamestown."

Tom was at a loss. Another bomb had just gone off.

"What?" he stammered.

Joe nodded slowly.

"She is here. She never left."

Tom tried to recover.

She never left?

Tiffany? Tiffany is in Jamestown?

In a long dark room?

All this time?

Good Christ.

He was in the desert, Karen was gone to the east coast, and Tiffany was still here?

Calling for him?

Calling for her daddy?

Where or how could this make any sense?

"She never left?" Tom mumbled.

"That's right Tom. She's here. In this sick, dangerous place. We *will* find her. I promise. Tomorrow. We start tomorrow. Tonight, first we need to get some rest. I need to think. You need to think. You need to really open up your mind and go back to the day. All the way back. With clear and true honesty. You are the key to all of this, Tom. You will decide whether we find her or not."

Tom thought about Joe's words.

Open his mind? To what?

The drugs had already performed the can opener of all time on his mind. He couldn't open it any fucking further.

He was the key? How could he be the key to this? How could he be the key to anything, anymore?

He was a pathetic mess. A piece of shit, drug abuser.

Decide about what? How could he decide anything?

He knew nothing about his little girl's disappearance. He only knew she was gone. He also knew *he* was gone. Gone, gone, gone. Around the bend. Off the deep end. Over the cuckoo's nest. Off of his rocker. Marble hunting. Searching for cards to fill up his deck. Take your pick.

Joe dug in his pocket and pulled out his wallet. He dropped a twenty on the table. Twenty bucks for two beers and two microwave dinners. Tipping not required. Not in this dump.

They made their way towards the exit. Tom stopped in front of the jukebox. He stared at the flashing neon lights and the faded chrome buttons. Some chick was wailing something about 'a good feeling'. What did this bitch know about anything?

Tom rubbed his temples with both of his hands. His head was making ready for lift off. Tiffy was here? All this time? In Jamestown? *He* was the key to finding her? How the hell was he supposed to think about all of this? Especially with this wall of thudding noise?

Tom couldn't take anymore of the pounding crap. There was no way he would ever be able to walk out of his ocean of despair, but this little truth didn't prevent him from bashing this infernal music machine to bits. Then he would bash the little bastards who had turned the bloody thing on. Tom's eyes swam out of focus. He leaned on the machine to steady himself. The rap became a dull roar, before it began to soften. Suddenly, silence.

There it was.

Tom heard the tiny cry.

"Daaaaaaaaaaaaaaaa................."

The voice of an angel.

His angel.

Calling to him.

Calling for him.

So lonely. So scared. So lost.

So overcome.

The little voice was cut short.

As it had been everyday for as long as he could remember.

Christ!

A hot knife skewered his guts.

Tom cringed, physically absorbing the non-existent blow.

His eyes cleared and sharpened on the gaudy lights. The knife was withdrawn. The wall of noise pretending to be music rushed in and filled his ears.

'Good feeling'?

I will show you a fucking good feeling. Tom stepped back and kicked the machine as hard as he could.

The music stopped.

There was golden silence.

Interrupted by, "Hey man!"

Tom turned on the group of teenagers. What a bunch of little pricks. Ear rings. Nose rings. Eyebrow rings. Tongue rings. Forehead rings. Shit rings, probably. Colored hair. Filthy baggy clothes. Tom stared at the group. His look of personal misery and near insanity kept the kids glued to their seats.

The light fixture above their table buzzed and brightened. Tom focused on one kid, who had lightening bolts shaved into both sides of his head. Tom stared so hard he was sure he could see right through the kid's skin and flesh, right down to the bare skull. He started toward the kid when he felt Joe's hand on his shoulder.

"Not now, Tom. Not here."

Joe pulled Tom back, Tom unwilling to give up his eye lock on the kid's skull. Finally, Tom relented. The kid's flesh and skin returned. The light fixture above the teenagers' table dimmed. Definitely, this was another one of those freaks.

"Tom. Let's go."

Tom turned and together they walked single file towards the dumpy waitress. Her big fat ass was jutting across most of the aisle. Five and a half foot wide aisle, five foot wide ass. Tom thought for sure they would bang into her; they would have to if she didn't move.

She didn't move, and Tom watched as Joe passed on through. As if she wasn't even there.

Tom did the same.

A weird feeling, for sure.

Maybe, she wasn't there.

The waitress didn't smile; say thank you or even goodbye.

CHAPTER 21

Carl Horner drove on through the evening. The wet snow had started to fall as soon as he departed the Cleveland airport in his four door rental. His windshield wipers slapped the wet flakes away. He had taken the largest vehicle they had in the fleet so he would be comfortable. He needed legroom and he definitely needed comfort because he sensed some stakeout duty would be required.

The interstate traffic was steady, evening rush hour was on. Buffalo, New York to Erie, Pennsylvania to Cleveland to Toledo to Detroit to Chicago, this was still a busy traffic corridor. Mostly a conduit, as the vehicles were all in transit. A highway full of steel, plastic and rubber was heading west, and it was as equally thick heading east. Topping sixty-five miles an hour, the opposing vehicles were separated by eight modest inches of concrete median. The inside lane was packed with tractor trailers. The behemoths were spilling over to the middle lane as well. The odd cowboy was blowing by in the fast lane.

Carl had dreadful memories of a particular tractor trailer. A smashed guardrail. His ear bursting into fire. No need to go there. Those were not hidden memories. Those were crystal clear memories.

What about the new memories?

The ones coming to him on the airplane? Then fading away?

What were those all about?

There was no time for further thought, because out of the dark, the exit sign for Jamestown appeared. It was time to put the game face on. On the exit sign, Carl saw the amenities once offered up by the city had been scrubbed out. Even the population tally was covered. Twenty minutes on his cabin computer had told him why.

Jamestown, Ohio had been settled by strong pioneers, carved right out of the countryside. Homesteads were built, a forge was built, then small enterprises, then bigger factories. Then more homes, and churches, trade markets, repair shops, schools and amenities. Growth, prosperity, synergy. Then, the eighties arrived. Outsourcing. Corporate relocation. Free trade. Soaring stock prices. Closing factories. Job losses. The toxic lands. The government housing experiment. One failure after another. The outmigration of the people.

Jamestown officially went bankrupt in 2002. In 2003, the city lost its incorporation status. In 2006, the city was sold out of bankruptcy to a numbered company. Jamestown was now private property, which meant Jamestown was probably lawless. Carl doubted very much if the absentee owners were providing any level of security.

There were no longer municipal crews working on road repair, garbage pickup or snow removal. Ohio Power and Light no longer serviced the city, nor did Erie Water or Northern Gas. The last census in 2004 put the population at nine hundred and twenty-four people. A far cry from the sixty-eight thousand plus back in the heyday. Today, it was probably much less than the nine hundred and twenty-four.

From prosperity to poverty, everything was in reverse. Deteriorating at an unheard of pace. Moving into the future on the time clock, but moving into the past on the development clock. No identity. No structure. No rules. No nothing. Carl was anticipating a totally unpredictable situation. He was heading into undiscovered country, so to speak, an adventurer moving backwards through a wormhole of some kind.

Perfect.

Worked for him.

Carl felt the buzz begin. He simmered it down, it was way too early. Being out of the game for so long, the buzz, the adrenaline rush, could potentially hurt him as much as help him. Carl had lived with the adrenaline rush his entire career, and then he had quit cold turkey.

The adrenaline rush could be as dangerous as a gun. Carl had to be very careful. Twenty-six long years had passed since the crime occurred. This would take thought, patience and planning. This might take something he had never used before.

He had to bring this little girl home.

He had to.

This was it.

One shot.

Carl signaled into the furthest right lane, finding a gap between the glowing big rigs. He exited the busy interstate. The traffic, the bustle and the noise immediately faded as Carl clover-leafed away from the highway. By the time he was off the exit ramp, the traffic and the noise had disappeared completely.

Carl rolled onto the main drag. He could see no one. No traffic, no pedestrians. No life. This was uncanny. There were hardly any lights on in any of the buildings. The lights he saw were flickering; they had to be candle or kerosene.

Carl wasn't prepared for the deterioration and destruction. Both sides of the main drag looked rioted out.

Welcome to Judgment Day.

Carl drove on, deeper into the dead city. There were still no moving vehicles and not a single pedestrian. McDonalds was closed. Burger King was closed. Red Barn was closed. Ace Hardware was closed. Ohio Financial was closed. Wells Fargo Bank was closed. K-Mart was closed. The U.S. Post Office was closed. These businesses were not only closed and out of operation. They were shuttered, boarded up, smashed in, pulled apart, torched or in some state of forced demolition and decay.

Carl did see a Seven Eleven looking as if it might be open for business. A few wavering lights burned behind plate glass windows covered in metal cages. The famous brand sign out front had been patched and taped back together numerous times. There were no cars in the parking lot and no folks lined up at the counter. This was not the same as every other Seven Eleven Carl had seen, busy, busy, busy. This one was dead, dead and dead.

Carl drove on.

In these conditions, it should be pretty easy to find his prey. His prey might be the only thing exuding life in this urban graveyard. There were no streetlights on or traffic lights working or even hydro wires strung up high along the roads. Garbage was piled up everywhere. Garbage was strewn across the road and sidewalks. Garbage was stuck in fences and underneath the vehicles lying in ruins at the sides of the road. Everything was faded or filthy. Everything was abandoned.

Jamestown was truly, a ghost town.

Up ahead, Carl saw the flickering light of a palm tree. How ridiculously out of place in this dead city. The sign above the palm tree was mostly busted out. The only letters remaining were GO IN. The 'something or other' Inn, Carl deduced. Very cute. 'Go in'.

The adrenaline buzz shot through him again. Carl already knew what he was going to find in the parking lot. A filthy green Jeep from the great western desert. The Jeep he had personally attached a GPS beacon to, a long time ago.

This case was no longer *Unsolved: Closed*.

This case was wide open.

CHAPTER 22

The air outside helped some. It was better than the smoky, musty, sewage smelling diner. However, the air outside was damp and unpleasantly cold. The air outside, still reeked of sewage.

Back in the Jeep, Joe and Tom drove another six dark, desolate blocks and found a few lights flickering inside the Flamingo Inn. The two story building looked nearly abandoned. There were no other cars in the parking lot. Not a big surprise. The lot was badly potholed and in desperate need of repair. At the front entrance, a partially lit neon palm tree buzzed with inconsistent power, welcoming the travelers.

They exited the Jeep and walked toward the motel office.

Right away, Tom could hear the sound of a diesel motor, same as at the restaurant. The racket was coming from somewhere behind the squalid building. Tom's brain finally put it together. The chopped down hydro poles, the missing power lines, and the sheared bits of wire dangling from the taller buildings. No electricity service. Therefore, gas or diesel generators supplied the juice.

Why not?

Jamestown was already heading back to the Stone Age. Tom recalled George Bush or Bill Clinton or somebody threatening to bomb Pakistan back to the Stone Age. Already happening right here in your own country, Mr. President.

Tom pulled opened the office door and they walked into the entrance foyer of the old Flamingo. Cheap paneling lined the walls. Worn tiles covered the floor. Tom hit the service bell on the manager's desk. A shuffling sound, then heavy steps brought the innkeeper out of the back room.

Good grief.

Tom was staring at Benny the Innkeeper. Benny looked at his guests, narrowed his eyes, and settled on Tom. The old fool sensed a familiarity, but could not make a connection. Benny gave up and grunted toward the register, their cue to sign in. The innkeeper tapped the price sign on the wall behind him, grunting again. The going rate was now forty bucks a night. Tom wondered if the old fart had forgotten how to speak. Benny had never been the sharpest knife in the drawer.

Tom remembered spending time at the Flamingo. Not clear memories, but he knew this foyer, he knew old Benny, and he knew the basic rooms offered as accommodation. Usually, an hour was plenty of accommodation. Back in the day, you could get an overnight room for ten bucks. Or, the hourly rate, which most of the studs chose, a 'buck a fuck' they called it. Two studs to a room, two lucky girls with them. Two dollars plus tip. The customers were on the honor system to make the beds and tidy up for the next occupants. You really didn't want to book one of these rooms for an overnight stay.

Joe fished in his pocket for his wallet and more cash, found two twenties and placed them on the counter. The old man stared at the bills. Salivating. Tom figured customers and cash were pretty damn scarce at the Flamingo Inn.

Age had not been kind to the innkeeper. Benny was grossly overweight and terribly bloated out of proportion. He could have been a reject from the Biggest Loser. He must have weighed four hundred pounds. The pounds were consistent with malleable blubber. His wife beater was blemished a filthy yellow. His belly rested on a thick belt adorned with a huge, silver, dinner plate buckle. The buckle portrayed two screaming eagles clawing at a whimpering Arab. The belt held up a very large pair of patched trousers.

Scraggly wisps of hair remained on Benny's enormous, balding head. A few blackened teeth were held by rotting gums. Skin hung from his upper arms, once large, hard and proud. Now the arms were giant, soft and old woman-like. The boat anchor tattoo on the right bicep was contorted to some awful configuration. The USMC lettering below the boat anchor was no longer legible English. A Chesterfield cigarette was burning down between fat, stained fingers. Non-smoking rules obviously did not apply in Jamestown.

Benny had once been a local legend. A big, tough, ex-marine, the king of the bar scene. Not any more. The king was old, ugly and mute, a nasty tub of smelly fecal matter. Even in this lobby, Tom smelled shit. Christ, everything in Jamestown smelled of sewage.

Tom could see a newer tattoo on Benny's furry forearm. Tom peered through his bleary eyes. The tattoo resembled the awful lightening bolt, but he couldn't be sure. Benny dropped the room key on the table and scooped up the cash. Tom was about to pick up the key, when he reached across the desk and grabbed Benny's forearm. Benny grunted in surprise. Tom yanked Benny's arm forward and looked closer. What the hell was on his arm? He still couldn't tell.

"Tom. Let him go," Joe intervened.

Tom released Benny's arm. Benny grunted, flipped a stubby middle finger at his guests, and shuffled into the back room. He clutched the forty dollars as if it were gold.

Back outside the motel office, Joe walked with Tom past three boarded up units to their room. Tom keyed the door and went in. He felt along the wall and flipped the light switch. A ceiling bulb alleviated the darkness, but only slightly. Joe walked over to a night table and switched on a lamp. The darkness lightened a little more. A cheap partition wall separated the two beds. A privacy wall. For privacy during the sex act. A neat touch, courtesy of the Flamingo Inn. Tom heaved his duffle bag onto the second bed. Dust rose off the top blanket. Joe turned on a third light. All three lights flickered in weak brightness. Definitely, generator power.

"How does it feel to be home?" Joe asked.

Tom stopped.

"Shit. This place stopped being home a long time ago."

The two men sat down in folding metal chairs, across a cheap, battered card table. Tom put a new bottle on the table, along with the aspirin container. He could tell Joe was itching to tell the rest of his story. The rest of his incredible, nonsensical, but possibly true, fairy tale.

CHAPTER 23

"Back at the diner, I was telling you about the priest, the conspiracy guy. The priest was convinced that the end of the world was being manufactured by this gang, or group, or cult. Upon his release from the mental institution, the priest was going to expose the group. He said he had evidence, details of their operation, the whole nine yards. He was going to blow the lid off. On the day the priest was released, he was killed."

"Killed?" Tom blurted.

He stopped himself again.

Jesus.

Could this Joe Danton ever tell stories. Amazing stories.

Once more Tom asked himself, how might any of this be true?

Joe went on.

"The priest was shot to death. Shot as he was walking down the hallway to freedom. I had just said goodbye to him. In the day room. The visitor's room. The gunman was waiting in the hallway, dressed in doctor whites. The gunman was then shot by security. The security guard was advancing when the wounded gunman committed suicide by detonating a grenade. He blew half the hospital floor away."

Once more, Joe had managed to gain Tom's full attention with his telling. His spectacular, wild story. Converted to a movie, the stars would have to be a drugged out Johnny Depp from Fear and Loathing, and the nutcase Woody Harrelson from Defendor. The priest could be played by the Shining's Jack Nicholson. Perfect.

"About two months after this, they let me out. It was right before Christmas. I came back to Jamestown. The city had changed. Changed is not really the word for it. The city had died. The big steel factory was long closed. The downtown was shuttered. The arena was barricaded. Homes were boarded up. A neutron bomb might as well have hit the place, taking all the people out. I went to the library, one of the few places still open. I found a microfiche and went back through the old newspapers to September 12, 1987. The day after."

What next thought Tom?

Where was this story going?

He sipped from his whiskey bottle, as a baby would sip from a formula bottle. Sipping for comfort. For satisfaction. For something to do. Sipping out of habit. When he wasn't sipping, he was holding the bottle. Close.

Joe kept talking.

"I was shocked. I was the prime suspect in Tiffany's kidnapping. I was also wanted for Marie's murder."

Joe paused.

"My Marie......................"

Joe ran a hand across his eyes. He soldiered on.

"The local cops had called in the FBI. The FBI shut down the interstate and the Canadian border. Road blocks and checkpoints went up for hundreds of miles around Jamestown. The FBI dug deep. They said Joe Danton was an alias. An alias so cleverly constructed, the real man was untraceable. They said Marie Danton was also an alias, and what a bastard I must have been to murder my accomplice. The day care closed down the day Tiffany disappeared, never to re-open. The evil had been released in Jamestown, and everything began to die. Tom, the whole city began to die."

Tom thought about the skeleton people. The punk with the lightening bolts shaved into his skull. The fat assed waitress who's ass wasn't really there.

The bloody whispering.

The small motel room was getting colder.

Tom got up to check the wall thermostat. He wondered how much heat they would get with the place running on a generator. Wet snow splattered against the flimsy single pane window. He pushed the ratty curtain aside and looked out at the dreary view. The snow was beginning to carpet the vacant parking lot, covering over the man made decay and imperfections. Good old Mother Nature was trumping us once again. Tom had to admit, it looked so peaceful.

A car was slowing on the main drag.

The first moving vehicle he had seen in Jamestown this day.

Tom noticed the headlights were off. The car looked to be a cop car, or maybe a rental. The dark four door sedan turned into the parking lot and stopped in front of the motel office. A large man wearing a black trench coat and a cowboy hat got out. A ping of familiarity ran through Tom.

The stranger walked into the office, and a moment later, was back outside. The man glanced toward Tom's room and returned to the car. Tom dropped the curtain back. The ping of familiarity had dissolved in his swampy mind, sinking below the murk. Tom watched as the sedan reversed carefully across the cratered lot and parked. Exhaust fumes evaporated in the air behind the car. Tom felt the temperature drop even further. He checked the hot water radiator with his hands for warmth.

The story of Joe continued.

"The priest talked about the end of days. It wouldn't be the biblical version of fire and brimstone, the four horsemen and all. The end of days would not be so spectacular, and it would not happen overnight. It would be a long, unstoppable, insidious process. It would start in villages and small towns and spread to large cities, and would grow, resembling a cancer. The cancer would multiply and infect the next towns over and continue multiplying across the countries, and around the globe."

"Jamestown seemed to fit the bill. The complete destruction of a once proud, honest, hard working, God fearing society. In 1989, the big factory was hit hard by foreign dumping and global competition. Union wages were too high to compete in the brave new world, said the capitalists and the free trade lobby. The United Steelworkers came to Jamestown to save one of the biggest remaining factories in America. A line was drawn in the sand at Jamestown. No more factory closures. No more outsourcing. No more sending our living wage jobs out of the country."

"A massive lockdown crippled the city. These guys picketed everything. Grocery stores. The downtown businesses. The swimming pool, the fire station, the library, the police station, the hospital, the schools, the churches. The lockdown pitted longtime neighbors against each other. Everyone was forced to take a side. Everything shut down. Suddenly, nobody was working. A Cleveland street gang was brought in to add muscle. The gang brought a flood of cheap drugs to a once clean city. The idle townsfolk became instant customers."

Joe coughed, got up from his chair and went into the bathroom. He returned with a glass of water, and sat back down. He was about to drink when Tom stepped over to the table and stopped him. Both men looked at the glass. The water was filthy. Joe went back to the bathroom and ran the water longer. Same result. More filthy liquid. Joe passed on the water.

"I remember the County sheriff we had, back in '87. Sure could have used him when all of this crap started."

Tom was back at the window, watching the parking lot. The memory ping again.

"I remember him too, a big guy, a cowboy from out west. An ex-Ranger or something. Whatever happened to him? Why wasn't he there?"

Even as he asked, Tom was recollecting.

Then recoiling.

Holy shit.

The sheriff had died in a car accident, responding to the kidnapping call.

At the day care.

Good Christ. This would never end, for a lot of people.

"Unreal," was all Tom could offer.

Joe continued.

"The factory shipped all of their manufacturing equipment down south. The Union lost the biggest fight in their history. They did not have the power to stop corporate and political America from moving to the cheap labor pool down in Mexico."

Tom took one more look.

The car was still there, idling, doing nothing.

Tom sat down as Joe continued with the history lesson.

"The situation when the factory closed was untenable. The morning it shuttered, sixty per cent of the jobs in Jamestown evaporated. The same day, property values fell in half. A few weeks later, they found toxic waste underneath the new high school. A week later, underneath the new subdivision. The railway right of way behind the day care was next. The toxic crap was everywhere. Property values dropped to zero. Everybody lost their equity, their futures, everything they had worked all of their lives for. They took a hit where it hurt the most. In the money belt. Theft, vandalism, assault, murder, even suicides became common. Total anarchy took over. The good people moved out in droves, walking away from their worthless homes. The state began to use the abandoned homes to house welfare recipients, parolees, all of society's unfortunate."

"After I was released, I picked up the priest's cause. I spent two years searching for evidence of this cult. Newspapers, internet, TV footage. I found so many of the acts of violence and mayhem were being manufactured. I believe the incidents were being used to divide and conquer, the oldest military strategy in history. Divide the people. Weaken the people. Defeat the people. The violence was being played all over the media. People would be frightened into their homes, stay in their own countries. They would lose faith in their fellow citizens, and the authorities' ability to protect them. Think about the Newton shootings and the shock to our school system. Even bigger, think about 911 and how the world reacted. Twelve years later, we are still dying over it, paying for it, and reeling from it."

Tom sipped from his bottle as he listened.

"The new world of the internet would divide and isolate the people even further. Shopping from home. Working from home. Entertainment at home. Never going out. All the while, being bombarded with the violence, and fear and gambling and pornography. The loss of human dignity and respect would speed up the downfall of society. People would lose their ability to interact with one another. People would not care for one another. People would begin to lose their humanity. I mean, whoever thought going to high school would become a game of life and death? Grab your backpack and make sure you are wearing running shoes. Set your cell phone on '911 standby' and have a good day."

Tom had seen something on his little television about school shootings. He remembered his own high school years as being pretty good. Yeah, those years were really cool. He had been the king of the high school court. Now these little bastards were shooting each other? Why? Were the classes that bad? Did the teachers suck? Were the students pathetic little shits who needed guns to do their talking?

"Jamestown is a perfect example of crash and burn. On a small scale. Look at Cincinnati and Cleveland and Baltimore and Newark and Detroit. Those are large scale implosions. Fancy splashes of money for stadiums and towers or casinos, but the majority of the people are living in grinding poverty. There are hundreds of thousands of empty homes in these cities, and the death spiral continues unabated."

This was getting to be too much for Tom to digest. He possessed only highlight reel information regarding the state of the nation. He figured what he saw on the intermittent newscasts was exploitation reporting. This is why he watched them so infrequently. He didn't need the world's crap piled on top of his own.

And what crap it was. The jam packed, overfilled prisons. The teenage gangsters murdering each other in the big cities. The record unemployment. The empty, rotting subdivisions. The collapsing health care system. The Arabs or the Koreans trying to set off bombs. The grinding poverty of the new middle class. The thousands and thousands of incapacitated war veterans. The incalculable debt of the nation. The millions of illegal immigrants. The blind ignorance of the leadership. Scary stuff, if this was happening on a country wide scale.

Tom stopped sipping and drank liberally from his bottle. He knew next to nothing about this internet phenomenon, but he could understand how one stop everything from the convenience of your abode could not be a good thing. He was not too drunk or stoned to realize he was *the* prime example of this isolation. He had isolated himself for more than twenty-five years and had contributed exactly nothing to the human condition.

Joe was talking again.

"This plot to disrupt civilization can be traced back to the 70's. Probably even earlier. I am not a researcher. I tried to map out locations and chart incidents for the past forty years. What I see is a pretty methodical and frightening scenario being played out. One glaring piece is missing. I don't know who is doing it, who is responsible. The priest claimed he knew, but he did not tell me anything, nor did he have any notes or writings on the subject. He said it was too dangerous, it was his burden to carry. He was right about the danger. Dead right."

Joe exhaled.

Tom figured the end of the story must be near.

"The priest once thought that major events or triggers might be involved in this world collapse. The millennium was a possible date for a major event. The millennium came and went. Nothing happened. 911 came and went. 911 was a really big event. Everybody agrees 911 was a direct attack against the west. It had nothing to do with this cult. The Mayan 2012 date came and went. Again, nothing happened. So, it is not a date thing, but more a marathon of destruction, with no timeline and no deadline. I think there's a lot more coming down the pipe and nobody is even remotely prepared for it."

This was a great deal for Tom to absorb. Now he knew why Joe had been mumbling so much on the car ride. This was a big story to prepare. A never ending story.

What about his little girl?

How was this story going to tie in to his little girl?

Why was there a car idling in the parking lot? *This* parking lot of all places?

Why would anybody be out there, on such a dreadful night, in such a dreadful town?

The city was so bloody dead. Nothing was moving, nothing was happening. Did the damn bullet trains still run through Jamestown? The trains might still pass through, on their way to a better place. If a better place existed. Tom wasn't so sure of this any more. Because regardless of where on this earth he slept, or ate, or breathed, or shit, there really could be no 'better' place.

Joe forged on.

"These guys are so secretive, so disciplined. Always, when an investigation gets close, the trail either goes cold, the witnesses die, or the perpetrators commit suicide. These few perps who were nearly captured were covered in napalm grease. They torched themselves rather than being taken. No fingerprints, no identification, nothing. These people were nobody. They were ghosts. How to you track down and fight nobody? I know they are driving Homeland Security absolutely crazy."

Ah, the 'C' word again.

Crazy.

Three or four days of driving. Crazy. Skeleton things eating in the fast food joints. Crazy. Finding his long lost daughter. Crazy. The dead city of Jamestown. Crazy. Joe Danton and his story. Crazy. Tom Forbes and his brain. Crazy.

"I took my findings to the Cleveland office of the FBI. Post 9/11. Al Qaeda. Timothy McVeigh. The White Militias. Conspiracy. The feds were open to any and all possible threats. I was able to present my information. One agent in particular showed an interest in my story. A real big guy. He reminded me of our Jamestown sheriff. He was on some sort of task force, investigating missing kids. The agent was curious as to why I knew so much about Jamestown. Of course, I could not use Joe Danton as my name, because Joe was still wanted for kidnapping. I did not want to open that can of worms in the office of the FBI. Apparently, this agent went to Jamestown and looked around. I believe he uncovered something. He called me late one night and said he may have some information regarding the missing children of Jamestown. Apparently, Tiffany was the first of many to disappear."

Tom moved to the edge of his chair.

"What? What did he have?" Tom asked, ever and falsely hopeful.

"He said he had found something. I should meet him, and then the line went dead."

Tom sat with his mouth open. The line went dead? That was it? The line went dead?

The waves were rolling in, higher and higher.

"I heard nothing more from the agent. I phoned the Bureau the next day. They said the agent had reported in. He had found nothing. Since the guy was near the end of his career, he had taken retirement. I asked for a forwarding address or phone number, but such information was confidential. It was over. The FBI signed off."

Tom could only shake his head.

Slowly.

The line went dead. The guy retired. The FBI signed off.

This was not the ending he was hoping for. He pretty much spit it out.

"A great big story, but really, more of nothing. Twenty-five years of nothing. And now, add another day to the twenty-five years of nothing."

Joe was looking at a man in despair. A beaten man. A man who had lost everything and was reminded of it, every single day of his life. Any sliver of hope Tom Forbes may have possessed, was fast fading to black.

"Tom. Listen to me. The FBI agent found something. Something right here in this town. I truly believe it. That's why I came to get you. To bring you home. To help you get her back. The priest in the institution convinced me of one thing. To have faith. Not only faith. Unwavering faith. Something I know you haven't had in a long, long time."

Amen on that one, Tom said to himself.

The line went dead. The FBI signed off.

Everybody signed off.

The whole fucking world signed off.

He, Tom Forbes, had signed off.

Now we are talking about faith?

Faith?

Really?

What a joke.

CHAPTER 24

Tom had almost, but not quite, tuned Joe out. There really was nothing more he needed to hear, was there? All this talk, this great elaborate story, had produced absolutely nothing. No hope. No information. No Tiffany. Nothing.

Joe was talking, again. Jesus, wasn't he finished yet?

"The strange thing is, my meeting with the feds had been going so well, until I brought up the lightening bolts. I had highlighted them in each picture. Circled them, drew arrows at them. Guess what? Nobody else in the room could see them. Nobody. Which means, *not everybody* can see what is right in front of them. In fact, most people can't. The priest, and you, and I, we aren't special in any way. We have no magic powers. Other than the ability to see what is really there."

"The feds, they mostly thought I was cracked. My prior credentials from the big house didn't help. They grilled me about all kinds of things. Asked me about Jamestown. They asked no further questions about my findings. When all was said and done, I believe they were simply hoping for information, or even a confession, so they could clear a crime from their cold case."

Tom looked at Joe.

"Information? Confession? About what?"

Joe looked right back at Tom.

"About Tiffany."

Tom tried to think. A confession *might* be in order, Mr. Danton. Because regardless of what you have said so far in this gigantic, fantasy story, one fact still stands above all else.

Tiffany left. And you left.

Together.

On the same day. At the same time. From the same backyard.

Now, you are back, and she isn't.

The waves were angry, thrashing at Tom and growing in height. The headache was pounding. The reverberations had started up once more, throbbing his skull from the inside out. Good times all around. Tom was in far too much pain to deal with Joe Danton. As much as Tom wanted to believe in this crazy story, and in Marie's awful death, and in the fall of the entire city, and in the skeleton people, well, things were not making any sense. Certainly not tonight.

"Look Tom. What happened on that September day was catastrophic. We are both connected to it. I was right there at the day care when Tiffany was taken. *Right there,* Tom. I failed you and her both. Because of my failure, something very unpleasant happened to me, and I ended up in an institution. I met this priest and made a connection with him. The clippings he showed me. He understood the lightening bolts. The connection with the priest involved your little girl. I finally tracked you to Arizona, it sure wasn't easy, and here we are. I lost thirteen years of my life to who knows what. You, you lost twenty-five years. Marie. Marie paid with her life. At least Marie had *some* time. Poor Tiffany. My god, she lost everything. She was only two years old."

This was tough, even for Joe to spit out. More so than he expected.

Memories.

Rehashed.

Rehashed and stirring, clinging to a speck of life.

Embers in a dying fire.

Which they were, Joe and Tom both. Not much more than embers from their past.

Joe reached across, putting his hand on Tom's shoulder.

"Something surreal, something unbelievable happened. Tom, it is *still* happening. You know it. I know it. It is all around us. There is something really, really wrong with this place. We can both feel it. Tomorrow, a new day starts, for both of us. We have to believe in ourselves. You have to believe in *yourself*. Because there is nothing else, and no one else. I don't know what will happen tomorrow, or even what we are supposed to do. But something is going to happen. We have to find a way inside this dimension or whatever you want to call it. We will find a way in. We will find our answers. I believe it. You have to believe it too."

Tom digested this as best as he could. None of what Joe was saying made any sense. Any sense at all. Nor should it. At the same time, it all made sense. It was all crazy enough to make sense. There was something terribly wrong with Jamestown. Even Tom grasped this fact. There was something going on here, below the surface of what he considered normal. Normal, before the drugs took over his life.

Tom was one empty soul. The belief and faith parts weren't going to work for him. There was nothing left in this world he could believe in. Or have faith in. Tom reached for another blast from the bottle, his automatic response to everything.

Joe picked the bottle up first.

"What happened to you Tom? How did you fall so far?"

Tom had not spoken about it since he left Jamestown. To anybody. Twenty-five years? He had not held a job, nor made friends nor had any interest in companionship. He was the Isolation Man. Other than his suppliers, and some faceless women, there was nobody. The interactions with his suppliers and the women were brief ones, regarding price and amount.

So why not.

Let her rip.

Time to share.

"After Tiffy, I did fall. Straight down. Hard. I am still falling, but not as fast. It's as if I am almost at the bottom. Who am I kidding? I am at the bottom. I blame myself for having her in the day care. I blame myself for not being there. On so many levels."

Tom was impressed, and a little frightened at how clear his memories could suddenly be. Christ, he was right back at the Busy Bee, slowly reversing out the door, waving at his little girl. Joe Danton was holding her tight. Joe Danton, the Pied Piper of kids. Tiffy, was clinging to her red elephant, staring at her daddy.

"I remember when I was leaving. She was waving. Her mouth and her face were smiling at me, but her eyes were speaking volumes. I read her eyes, then dismissed what they were saying. What were they saying Joe? What? Her eyes were so.….I don't know if sad is the word. It was as if she could see something approaching. Something inevitable. Something unstoppable. Shit. I don't know what the hell I am talking about."

Tom needed his bottle.

Joe was still holding it.

Tom sucked in a deep breath and soldiered on.

"I blame myself for not finding her. I blamed the cops for not being able to do anything. I blamed Karen for everything. Nobody just disappears. Not the way Tiffy did. I stuck around for a year. The cops, the FBI, I hired a private detective, two private detectives, a third private detective, and they all found nothing. Not a single, solitary clue as to where she went."

Tom looked in Joe's eyes.

"And you. I wanted to kill you. I still do. I don't know why I haven't done it already. You were with her, in the backyard, at the day care. All this time, I believed you took her. You come to me with this story. This magical, fantastic, world ending story. If you are still here, she should still be here. But you are here, and she is not. My brain is so fried, some of what you are saying actually makes sense."

Joe put the bottle down.

A stiff wind rattled the loose window glass. The lights flickered in the room.

Tom snatched the bottle up.

"Karen blamed me as much as I blamed her. I hated her for playing the blame game. I hated me for playing the blame game. We fought. We couldn't even begin to get past it. Everything in this town reminded me of Tiffy. Everyone I saw reminded me of her. At first, they said how sorry they were. Then they stopped. At some undefined moment, life goes on. Life moves forward. It's what humans do. People didn't know what to say anymore, so they said nothing. Even avoided me. The avoidance was enough, because them saying nothing, was them saying volumes. Do you *know* what they were saying? Where the FUCK is your little girl?"

Another drink to cap those waves. To maintain the headache.

"Finally, I had to get away. I drove and drove. Ended up in Arizona. The heat felt good. I sat in the sun and fried myself. I thought it was cathartic. It was, for a while. The booze, the drugs, I was just starting. The first visit to the Sports Bar in Cleveland. What an idiot. Those first snorts of the magic powder. Amazing stuff. The powder, I could get used to. A nice buzz. A nice reward for a good week's work. I started hard on the stuff after Tiffy. It cleared my brain of everything. Wiped my slate clean. Not for long. Tiny little cracks let her back in. The cracks grew wider because the pain of losing her kept growing. Then the questions came. Big, and hard and fast. The questions which have no answers. The questions which *can never* be answered."

Tom stopped. The questions. The horror of the damn questions.

Here we go again.

Mr. Forbes, we have some questions for you.

How many times had Tom heard this stupid fucking line? From the police and law enforcement agencies, even from his own private investigators. From his wife and his friends and relatives. From everybody in the whole damn world. Yes. Everybody had questions for Tom. Tom had no answers for them. None at all.

Tom did have questions of his own.

Well then, Mr. Cop and Mr. FBI man and all of you inept, useless officials, I have some questions of my own.

What have you done to find my little girl?

What clues have you found?

What procedures and protocol are you following to ensure her safe return?

When can I expect her safe return?

Joe Danton you bastard, when I find you, I will have some questions for you.

God in heaven, if you are up there, if you truly exist, man, do I have some questions for you. The first question being *why*?

And the worst set of questions?

Were the ones Tom saved for himself.

The questions he couldn't share with another soul in this world.

Was Tiffany alive? Rhetorical, but necessary and ever hopeful.

Was she dead? The practical and realistic question.

Had she been hurt?
Had she suffered horribly?
Had she been *molested*?
Had she been *raped*?
Had she been *cut up to pieces*?
How scared had she been?
Did she cry out for me? For her daddy?
Did she cry out for Karen?
Did she?
We didn't come, did we?
WE DIDN'T COME.
Why her?
She was just a little kid.
A small, two year old, baby girl.
Free and innocent.
She had done no wrong on this earth.
To nothing and to nobody.
Tom gripped his skull.
He was failing fast.
Damn the fucking questions.

CHAPTER 25

Tom tried to push past the questions.

"The pain grew, pounding in my head. Like it is pounding right now. I upped the booze and drugs. Anything to lessen the pain. Then the despair began to roll in. I went to even higher levels of abuse. It does give some relief, but I know the next day will always be worse. I've lost the will to live, even the will to die. I've contemplated suicide, but I can't even get my shit together to off myself."

A sudden gust of wind blew against the motel. The lights flickered once again, and went out. Tom stood and walked over to the window. He looked outside. The night of the living dead. The power was out all down the motel. The generator must have been shut down, or it ran out of fuel.

On the road, none of the remaining metal streetlights were operational, and all of the businesses were long ago boarded up. The dark sedan was still parked at the back edge of the lot, idling as the thick wet flakes fell. Tom sat again, wondering who could be out there on such a rotten night. It was one of many questions racing around in his sick, diseased mind. Yes, another god damned question, with no bloody answer.

"Joe? What did they do to Tiffany? Why did they take her?"

Joe took a deep breath. Exhaled. He wasn't quite sure how to respond, but he had to.

"The priest said there were people among us who could see through the smoke screens, charades and cover-ups. People who could see this cult or group for what they were. People who could see even more than he could see, or you could see, or I could see. People who could see past the lightening bolts. These people were the biggest threat to the cult or the gang or whatever it is. They had to be eliminated. Murdered, or locked up, or simply destroyed. Or taken away."

The old motel creaked and groaned, pushed by the strong wind. Joe was looking down now. Shaking his head slowly.

"Tom, I am just going to tell you. I believe I found evidence; some people were used as sacrifices. The youngest people. So many kids were taken in the last few years of the eighties. Missing and gone forever. In fact, the data is no longer available. The Orange Alert program has helped bring awareness to the problem, but still, so many kids are missing. Those kids taken in the eighties, well……never mind. We can talk about that later."

A slow moving hammer connected with Tom's skull. Slow, because the booze was dulling whatever faculties he had left.

"Jesus H. Christ. A sacrifice? Are you serious?"

This was something he really, really didn't need to hear. Never mind digest. His two year old baby girl, a sacrifice? Tom placed his hands on his head and squeezed. His brain was about to explode.

"I am sorry, Tom. I am so sorry for all of this. I wish I could have done more."

Joe rose from his chair and made his way around the partition.

"Remember Tom. She is here. I feel it. I *know* it. Have faith. Unwavering faith. We have to believe. You have to believe. This has been wrong for far too long. Twenty-six years of wrong. Right now, we might as well try and get some rest because tomorrow is our day. Tomorrow we take everything back. I need you big time on this."

There was only one way Tom would get any relief tonight. He wasn't going to wait for the god damn bullet train to reappear and run through his world. He knew the speeding demon was out there, waiting, waiting. Waiting to make its grand re-entrance. The bullet train, plus the voice, plus the black waves, plus the Joe Danton apparition were going to make for one powerful performance.

Tom's head was ready to detonate, bursting with the day's experiences and tomorrow's possibilities.

What possibilities? Really.

What bloody possibilities?

The possibilities for tomorrow were the same as they were for last week, and for last month and for the last decade. The possibilities for tomorrow consisted of drinking, drug abuse, pain, vomiting, sleeping, hallucinating, sweating, a skull pounding headache and a swim in the ocean of despair.

And the voice.

Welcome to tomorrow.

Can't hardly wait.

It was time for a massive preemptive strike. Obliterate those rushing waves. Derail the speeding train. Stand the skyscraper back up. Turn the giant mallet into a harmless pile of wood dust. Remember what your coach said? Way back in college? Offence is the best defense? It was time for some offence. At the least, he would offend his veins, and his bloodstream and his cranial matter. And hopefully, the waves and the bullet train from hell.

Tom slowly shook his head.

Really? Deal with this? Kidnapping? The end of the world? The loony bin? Child sacrifices? Faith? Tom rummaged through his duffle bag and found his shaving kit. Inside the shaving kit was the only thing remotely resembling faith. Through the darkness, he fumbled his way to the bathroom and closed the door. Using his cigarette lighter for illumination, he laid out the tools of the trade.

He twisted the surgical cord around his bicep, tapping at the ravaged vein. How many more shots could he endure before a full system collapse ensued? He had to be near the end of this road as well. The sliver of steel penetrated the ugly blue vein. Tom blasted home the juice. The last shot from his stash. He unwrapped the cord, and instantly felt the headache ramp up and the waves cresting over his head, trying to outrun the cavalry. Tom was holding his breath so he wouldn't drown. Holding the sink so he wouldn't topple. This was the good stuff, because ten seconds after, the flush began. He didn't have long to go.

The headache softened. The dark waves quickly ebbed; he was back floating in the desert. Cacti. The warm air. Lazy birds. Palm trees. A beautiful lady in a white bikini. The sun drying out his mortal soul.

Tom dropped the needle onto the sink ledge as tiny black spots began to dot his vision. The happy spots, he called them. A misnomer of sorts. Because nothing could make him happy. Relief was a better word, a more realistic word.

Tom staggered out of the bathroom towards the bed. An enveloping warmth was chasing the chill of the room away. The pressure in his skull eased. Tom floated the last few steps to the bed. He turned and sat down. He was surrounded by a soft cushion of warm air.

Relaxing. Relaxing. So warm.

Finally, something resembling peace.

He lay back on the bed as his vision began to fade.

Almost there, Tommy.

Almost there.

Let everything go.

Atta boy.

Find your peace.

Go with it.

Slide on into the peace.

Embrace it.

"*Daaaaaaaaaaaaaaaaaaaaaaddy*..............."

Damn!

If he didn't hear that!

Too real!

Absolutely!

Tom staggered to his feet. He was frantic.

It was her! It was!

This time, daddy was coming!

Daddy would forge through hell itself to find his little girl!

Tom took a mighty step forward, and crashed to the floor.

★★★★★

Joe lifted Tom on to the bed. The man was out cold. Joe layered dusty blankets over his fallen comrade. Tom Forbes was one tortured soul. He was completely unarmed; fighting demons he had no chance of beating.

Joe had felt the defeat many times in his own life. Insurmountable odds. Unassailable situations. Something had kept him going, kept him fighting. Victory was never guaranteed. Each side had victories, and each side had defeats. The battle continued, as it had since the beginning of man's time here. As it would, until the end of man's time. Tomorrow, he would try to arm Tom Forbes. Tom Forbes would soon be joining the fight of his life.

Joe stretched out on his own bed, resting his head against the lumpy pillows. He knew trying for sleep was pointless. So, he once again hit the rewind button, and then the play button, to try to make sense of his own mind. A frivolous exercise he repeated on a nightly basis. Where had he been after the kidnapping?

Brief, white flashes in his eyes.

Where had he been for those thirteen years?

Was he really Joe Danton, or was he a nut job from the Cleveland Crazy House?

More white flashes.

The lush, green backyard of the day care. The mighty brown oak tree. Fully leafed, beginning to turn fall shades. Magnificent. The kids running and shouting as kids do. Playful, happy, excited. So innocent. So free. So safe. Colorful toys everywhere. The big teeter totter. The swing set. Laughter. Joy. Energy. Playtime at its best. The sun shining so bright. The sky so blue. Smog free sky. Indian summer. A magical day.

A hiccup in the movie.

The tape breaks.

The tape is trimmed with scissors and spliced back together.

The tape stutters and begins to play again.

The sky has turned to black.

What is crawling on the nape of your neck, Joey?

Who, or *what*, is standing so close to you?

A nightlight is burning behind the day care. The numbers are everywhere. A brilliant flash comes from the sky. There is a brief fire, and smoke is everywhere. Marie is down. Marie is down. She is fatally wounded, burnt horribly. Joe, you cannot help her. Tiffany is being taken. Men in hoods are everywhere. They are bad men. Joe, this is the fight of your life. You have to stop them. This is why you are here. There are far too many of them. They are fast and powerful. They overwhelm you, they are a tidal wave hitting your bamboo shack on the beach. You are in the filthy alleyway, barely clinging to life. Your injuries are near critical. The complete breakdown of your mission has occurred. You have lost.

A long pause..........

Was this what happened?

To him?

Or to someone else?

Had he read about this case in the papers?

On an old microfiche machine in a county library?

Did he tour the sight later?

Over and over again?

Did he become the site, become the character?

Had he spent years putting together this little story?

The hooded men and the lightening strike? The mist and the smoke?

Had he ingratiated himself into the role of Joe Danton?

Was he the Method Actor of all time?

Anything was possible in this world.

The movie ran on in Joe's mind.

A shovel.

Orange flames.

Jungle foliage.

Musket fire.

A child's shoe.

A mushroom cloud.

The thundering sky.

A tranquil lake.

Grade six. The bad numbers.

The white flashes continued, as did the flickering images.

The occupants of room 113 at the Flamingo Inn were lost in themselves. They were oblivious to the gusting wind and the heavy, wet snow. The generator was off, and the room was getting colder.

The room was still being watched from outside.

CHAPTER 26

After his apprenticeship with the Bureau, rookie Agent Carl Horner was challenged by a wide variety of field assignments. Because of his remarkable psyche test scores, the Bureau wanted to see exactly where his talents lay. These talents were quickly noticed and aggressively exploited. Carl was moved to advanced training programs within the FBI, and even outside the FBI, with Army Special Forces. By 1982, Carl was 'off the books' and had begun exterminating threats to the nation. He would continue to do so for the next twenty-eight years.

His connection with the children started in 1984 when he wrapped the Dean Perron serial child killing case from New York and New Jersey. Perron murdered children. Raped them first. Boys and girls. It didn't matter. The guy was evil. The guy was a genius. If he was captured, he would figure out the system, become the system and beat the system. When Perron was back in society, his rampage would continue on a faster and more devastating trajectory. More children would be needlessly put in harm's way. Not going to happen. There was only one way to prevent it. Everyone in American law enforcement looked at Perron through the same eyes. Everyone in law enforcement was handicapped by the justice system.

Almost everyone.

Carl received a green light from the Director, and he acted upon it. One of the New York City victims was a distant relative of the Director.

Not distant enough, for Dean Perron. Carl was thrilled to take this predator down.

In 1985, Carl wasted the Detroit Strangler, another psychotic child killer. Fourteen kids murdered in a dirty basement, then planted in a back garden.

In 1986, Carl said goodnight to the Travelling Gypsies. The husband and wife team were taking 'lost' children from theme parks across the nation. Twenty-seven kids in all.

In 1987, Carl caught up with Suspect Zero, the long distance trucker who was stealing kids from the poorest sections of the poorest cities. Luring them with money and toys and bicycles. Then dragging them across the country to be used at his whim. In the custom designed torture chamber behind his tractor cab. Then dumping the bodies thousands of miles away from where he had taken them. Completely baffling authorities. The sick bastard.

There was more eradication of this predator species as his career progressed. Somewhere along his journey, Carl became extremely attuned to anything concerning the children. After wasting the piece of shit called Dean Perron, Carl so wanted to be involved in these cases. He wanted to protect the little ones. The Bureau had stumbled upon Carl's sweet spot and began feeding him information regarding these predatory perverts. After reviewing the paperwork, the anger would rise, the death mask would be put on, and Carl would request the green light from the Director.

In late 1989, while briefly attached as an advisor to the Missing Children Task Force, Carl had partnered up with the agent who had worked the unsolved kidnapping in Jamestown. The agent had been rattled at how short his findings were. The little girl simply vanished without a trace. Or not so simply. Not a single clue had been found by local or state police. Impossibly, there were no eyewitnesses, and no prints, no DNA, no forensics, nothing. By the time the FBI got there, the crime scene was already cold. The day care director vanished at the same time, he was a ghost.

This case was wrapped in so much mystery. Rock solid alibis were in place for the parents. There was no motive. There had never been a child abducted in the history of Jamestown. Child snatching went on all the time, but it was usually done by a vindictive spouse, by a predator, or for profit. Mommy and daddy Forbes seemed to be getting along, but daddy was dipping into dangerous territory.

So how did the little girl fit in?

What about the missing day care operator? How could anyone completely vanish and leave his dead wife behind?

The distressed agent Carl teamed with ended up going to his retirement, silently haunted by the missing child.

The agent's distressed anxiety transferred to Carl. Something about the case screamed for him. It was the little girl screaming. He could sense it. When Carl was handed the photograph, well, the deal was sealed. The photograph taken from the father's office, taken from a gold picture frame with broken glass. Carl went to Jamestown, and poked around. He visited the closed day care center and the former Forbes home. He drove past the shuttered factory and watched the continued migration out of the city.

His main observation was the continuing decline of the American Empire. If the boomtowns were failing, the whole nation was in trouble. It was an insidious trouble. The economic disease was spreading slowly, but surely. Carl figured it would manifest itself as a full blown disaster in about twenty years. We were a super rich country, but we continued to over-spend on everything, especially gambling, alcohol and the new unstoppable vice, drugs. Three items with a combined return to the purchaser of absolutely nothing.

Tons of money out, nothing in return. Talk about bad investing.

What generation decided a mountain of personal debt was the way to go? To buy our cars and televisions and toys? Eventually, somebody would have to pay the bill. America was still the wealthiest nation on the planet, and would be able to gloss over these poor choices for a few more decades. The wake up call would be coming. When it did, the call would drive hard, a hammer crushing a glass house. As a nation, we were stealing when we should have been buying.

Beyond the economic mess, there was something else wrong with Jamestown. Carl felt it all around him. A current of some sort. Stronger in some places. Especially strong around the burnt fence behind the day care, and in front of the closed factory gates. Carl figured the current might be even stronger, deep in the bowels of the dead factory.

Something was going on which Carl could not quite grasp. Something not tangible, not measurable and not calculable. Carl could sense it, but not see it or hear it or touch it. Definitely, this 'something' had a lot to do with the missing girl. The eerie sickness was strengthening with the failing economic situation of the city.

After 9/11, Carl was in Cleveland and took a detour, making his second trip to Jamestown. Twelve years had elapsed since his first visit. What a disaster lay before him. Everything was closed or closing. The vandals had hit hard. It appeared as if the jails had emptied out into Jamestown. Cars were burning in the streets, gangs of punks roamed and the few law abiding citizens Carl saw looked terrified. The law of the jungle ruled. Police cruisers were parked at street corners, watching but doing nothing. The National Guard would be called in before the year ended.

The supernatural feeling Carl had picked up on during his first visit was much more powerful. For sure, something strange and dangerous was afoot in this decaying town. Whatever it was, it continued to be out of his reach, strengthening and growing, as Jamestown withered and died.

Carl flicked on the dome light of his rental, holding up the picture of Tiffany Amber Forbes.

The picture looked tiny in his large callused hand.

What was it with Jamestown and this little girl?

The picture had come from the father's office. Oddly, the glass protecting the picture had been badly cracked. Carl remembered this tiny detail. Coincidence? Maybe not. The glass and the frame served to protect a picture. When the glass cracked and the elements were allowed in, the picture was no longer protected. The same fate suffered by the beautiful little girl, who had also not been protected. Throughout the rest of his career Carl could never completely shake this missing child. For some reason, she stuck to him. He didn't mind. Carl felt as long as she stuck to him, she would be okay. He could not explain this rationale. It just was.

No, this one single case in Carl's peculiar, varied career had stumped him. The answer was always out of his grasp. Another dimension was involved. Perhaps, not another dimension, but something else had been at play. A skill set he had not yet learned might be required to crack this case.

Perhaps he was too old, and too dumb.

Perhaps, he was only, a shooter.

Still holding the picture, Carl looked through his windshield at the dark motel.

He thought about the man inside room 113. For a good twenty-five years, Tom Forbes had been drinking and drugging himself from one day to the next. As an only child, he was living off and wasting a substantial inheritance left by his parents. Tom Forbes could very well be shouldering an enormous load of grief Carl couldn't hope to comprehend. Grief could be a tough emotion to deal with.

At the beginning of his career, the death of a fellow agent had devastated a young Carl Horner. The blame game. What should I have done differently? What do I tell his wife and kids? Then came the dead perpetrators. Those people didn't matter, because they didn't count. Then a second dead agent. The grief was not as severe. The misfortune, the death, was an occupational risk. More dead perpetrators followed. Again, nobody cared. When Carl became a solo act, there were no more dead agents. However, the dead bad guys continued to pile up. Quickly.

As time wore on, death became part of his job. Now, after three years of retirement in the northlands, the shield of indifference had begun to fail him. Death was not part of his psyche any longer.

Death was what it was……death.

Death was not a name to be ticked off a hit list, not a number to be notched in a record book. Death was the end of someone's one and only chance at existence. One single chance, in forever, to live. Forget about religion and the hereafter. Those were things *nobody* knew about. Nobody. All we had, was what was right in front of us. Right now. Period.

In his career, Carl dealt exclusively with those bastards who had forsaken their right to live.

Not a problem.

But a child?

A child who had not lived to be two years old?

Carl could both appreciate and respect, the loss of a child would be something else indeed.

Something devastating.

Something both emotionally and physically crippling.

Carl flicked off the dome light. The wipers flapped intermittently, set on slow. The heater was set on low, keeping the damp chill at bay. The gas tank showed over three quarters full. He was good for night, right here in this car. The night was dark. There was nothing happening out there. Nothing at all. Carl tucked the picture away. Back to Mr. Forbes.

The cop ingrained in Carl left one other door open. Because, if it wasn't a load of grief Forbes was dealing with, then what was it?

Mr. Forbes' substance abuse could be an attempt to erase or hide powerful memories from his decaying brain cells. Important, life changing memories. Even quite possibly, burying his past deeds. There was usually a strong emotional prompt which set one down the path of hard drug abuse. The death of someone close, abuse, rape, bullying, financial trouble, human failure, depression. Guilt.

Yes, guilt was a huge trigger.

What are you hiding, Mr. Tom Forbes?

Are you guilty?

Of what?

Does it have something to do with your missing child?

Does it?

The Bureau watched the Forbes family for a year and a half. There was nothing. The old man moved to the desert. The wife took a new job on the east coast and eventually remarried. The case was transferred to the unsolved file. Carl had gone with his gut those long years ago, making the trip to Arizona, planting the GPS beacon on the fancy Jeep.

How utterly impossible could it be that Mr. Tom Forbes was still driving the same vehicle?

How even more impossible could it be, that Mr. Tom Forbes had *never* driven his Jeep from the desert in all of these years?

Forget about the impossibilities.

Concentrate on the facts.

The perpetrator had to have been someone familiar with the operation of the day care. Hours of service, routines, responsibilities, and so on. The perpetrator was on the day care property, giving him access to the child. The perpetrator managed to isolate the little girl from a group of staff members and children numbering over thirty. All of this suggested familiarity between the perpetrator and the day care, and between the perpetrator and the little girl. The only potential witness was Marie Danton. She interfered and was killed. Or, she recognized the perpetrator and was killed. Or, she was betrayed by her accomplice and was killed to tie up the only loose end.

Really, only two people fit the bill. The mysterious person calling himself Joe Danton was one.

The other?

The other was Mr. Tom Forbes.

Daddy.

Yes, daddy was a possibility.

Carl never discounted a suspect on the basis of an alibi. Never. He didn't give two shits about Tom Forbes' alibi from the fateful September day.

Why would Tom Forbes kidnap his own child?

Good question.

Carl Horner could give you twenty answers as to why someone would do something so heinous. These twenty answers would make your guts twist. These twenty answers would make you question your belief in the human condition. Shake you to your foundation. By the time you were at reason six, you might not make it back.

Twenty horrific reasons why parents took their own children. Carl had seen them all in his career.

So yes, daddy was a possibility.

Now, after twenty-six years, the rabbit was back in town.

Home.

Was Tom Forbes ready to give up the ghost?

★★★★★

Carl fiddled with the fan control, sending heat up to the front glass. Snow fell against the windshield, melting on contact. The wipers cleared the wide expanse of window. Carl watched the shabby motel. The strong wind seemed to be rocking the old building, threatening to pick it up and toss it away. In this town, anything was a possibility. The motel was in complete darkness. Carl looked past it as far as he could see in both directions. Everything was dark. The hydro electricity was long gone.

As was the water service. Carl had seen the city water tower when he rolled in off the interstate. The big tank and steel girder tower had toppled to the ground, resembling a crashed spaceship. How that had happened, he couldn't even begin to guess. So there was no piped in water, and therefore, no sewer service. There was no natural gas, or internet, or land line telephone.

Carl reached in his pocket and checked his pay-as-you-go cell. Bought for this mission. Carl didn't know what he would use it for. He sure as hell wouldn't be calling for backup. Anyhow, there was no signal, which meant there were no cell towers either. No city work crews, no garbage pickup, no hospital and no EMT service. No law enforcement. There was nothing. It was the year 2013 and the few stragglers left behind were using candles to light their little hovels. Jamestown was indeed heading back to the Stone Age.

Dust to dust.

Carl had not pulled stakeout duty in a long time. It was not much fun. Not unless he was going to pull the trigger and remove some more garbage from the world. Carl's head buzzed on the right side. He was tired. It had been one long day of flying and waiting. Carl looked at the clock on the dashboard. It took forever for the minutes to change. Nothing was happening in the motel. The druggie was pacing and sitting and standing, and going nowhere.

At least Carl could stretch his legs out. He sure couldn't on the damn airplane. He unbuttoned his long car coat and shook out his arms. Carl felt warm. He let go a mighty yawn, and began to nod off, as he had on the plane ride in from Buffalo.

The night deepened.

Suddenly!

The horrible creature from the 737 was back!

Right in front of his windshield.

Carl stared.

He was not frightened this time, but fascinated. He was not frightened because it was him staring, him sitting in the car, Big Carl. The six foot four killing machine.

This thing in front of the windshield was no mechanical creature.

This thing....was his father.

No way old man, you worthless piece of crap. You don't scare me. Not any more. Carl watched the little boy struggle to raise the shotgun. The gun looked enormous. Carl stared into the little boy's face. The face showed determination, strength, fear and sadness. The gun was up. Tucked under his small shoulder, as good old daddy had taught him. The gun was pointed, right at daddy.

Daddy was drunk and angry, and now something else had entered the equation. Something brand new. Something dire. This time, daddy had done a very, very bad thing. He had gone one step too far, and he knew it. For a brief second, daddy felt his own mortality. Even with the alcohol coursing through his bloodstream, making him a big, powerful machine, daddy knew he wasn't bulletproof. Not from the thing pointing right at him.

A brilliant flash, Carl winced, waiting for the sound to echo through the car, but there was none.

It was over.

The creature was dead. Daddy, was dead.

Carl's protector, was also dead.

It had taken forty-nine hard years of living, for the revelation to break through.

Here it was.

Signed, sealed.

Delivered.

Carl marveled at how smoothly this hidden truth had revealed itself. He was watching a movie about his own life. A documentary. It had not been a tragic accident claiming his parents lives at too young an age. Carl's father had murdered Carl's mother in one of his frequent, horrifying, drunken rages. Young Carl had killed his dad. Young Carl had been raised by his aunt and uncle.

Carl Horner had filed it all away. To survive. He found a corner of his brain, put the awful reality in there, locked the door, sealed it off and thrown away the key. His mind turned the reality into a memory, then blunted the memory. Then washed the memory.

Now, the heartrending truth had broken out. Beginning on the airplane. Finishing right here in the rental car. In the parking lot of the cheap motel. In the dead city. Yes. The airplane dream had been part one. This, was part two.

Carl took a deep, deep breath. Wow. The picture was complete. He was complete. More than anything else, Carl knew the mantle had indeed been correctly passed on to him, so long ago. To serve and protect.

Carl thought some more, quite intrigued at this development.

Was Mr. Tom Forbes about to see his own truth? Was it his time? Interesting, if not for the awful fact that a little girl's life had been snuffed away.

Outside the sedan, the snow fell. The night was as black as Carl had ever seen. He was experiencing a different tingle, an external tingle. Perhaps the time off in the northlands had opened him up to better reception, because Carl felt as if he was now tapping into the illusory vibes of Jamestown.

Yes, something out of his reach was at play in this forsaken town. Hopefully, after all of these years, he could finally engage it.

The temperature dropped further. Carl adjusted the heater up and stretched some more. He had nothing to do but wait.

And digest this revelation.

CHAPTER 27

TOM FELT LIKE A RAT CRAWLING OUT OF ITS SEWER HOLE. DESPITE THE dull morning sky, his eyes smarted at the weak daylight filtering in through the shabby window curtains.

Tom heard Joe say he was going for coffee, and to meet him outside.
Then the door shut.

It felt cold in the room. Tom pushed his breath out, expecting to see it hanging in the air. He saw nothing. It was not quite so cold then. Must be the omnipresent humidity around the lake.

Tom slowly began to move his body parts. If he got up as a normal person would, he might possibly die. Right now, deliberate maneuvering and a steady hand were called for.

Last night was a rough one. The homecoming. The story of Joe. The skeleton people and the sinister atmosphere of Jamestown. The total decay of the city, which jarringly matched the total decay of Tom's life.

All the talk about Tiffany. After so many years, it was still so bleeding raw. A wound that would never heal. Could never heal.

What about this talk of sacrifices? Holy hell. Why did there have to be sacrifices? The madness of it all. The madness of him.

He was able to prop himself up on an elbow. His skull pounded with hangover troubles. Tom spied the aspirin bottle sitting on the cheap card table. About twenty of the aspirin might begin to take some of the edge off. Actually, thirty might be a better place to start. The table looked so far away. Sure Tommy, it was all of four feet, from your bed to the table.

Tom carefully sat the rest of the way up. A rush of discomfort crashed against his skull. Swirling his brain matter as if caught in an Aussie toilet, the swirl going the wrong way. He grabbed the bed and held on. The nausea grew and subsided, grew again, and subsided, back and forth, to and fro, all around, where do we go?

Finally, the nausea began to ebb.

Finally, the nausea stopped.

He was ready.

Ready to stand up and face another day. Sort of.

Tom shuffled slowly away from his bed, coming around the tacky, pressboard, privacy partition. On the floor, at the foot of Joe's bed, he spotted an open gym bag. Pictures of some sort, sticking out the top. Tom picked up the bag and set it down on the bed. More dust rose off the top blanket. He pulled out the pictures. The pictures were printed from newspapers or tabloids, or magazines. He wasn't sure.

The first picture was the aftermath of an explosion. Tom was barely able to read the text below the picture. A grocery store had been bombed in Athens. Corpses lay on the sidewalk amid broken glass and produce.

The second picture was a sinking ferry boat in the Philippines. A cavernous hole had been ripped in the side of the Manila Transfer. The picture had been taken from a news station helicopter. The ferry had been terribly overloaded with passengers. The picture froze some of the passengers either leaping or falling from the boat towards the angry water.

The third picture was a fire at something called Le Club Sociale, in Paris. Some sort of rave club had burned. Kids were running into the street, hair on fire, clothing on fire, skin on fire.

Horrible.

Tom shook his head. What a macabre collection.

The fourth picture caught the L.A. Times banner and showed a burning church. Walking out of the church were three people clad in what appeared to be hooded robes. To Tom, the people resembled monks. However, the robes weren't hanging long to the ground. The robes were styled more along the lines of hood jackets.

The fifth picture was a close up of the monks. The sixth picture was a magnified version of the close up. One monk had his hand raised. His hood had begun to push back from his face. Shadows interfered with the face. Tom stared hard. The picture was focused on the man's wrist. As best as Tom could tell, the wrist had a tattoo. The tattoo may or may not have been a lightening bolt. Tom was less interested in the wrist. He was looking at what he could see of the monk's face.

Tom sensed...........he didn't know what he sensed.

Something.

The face seemed to ring of familiarity. Something about the shadowed face.

Was it dirt? Singe marks from the fire? A beard? What?

Damn those shadows.

Tom shuffled back to the first picture of the church. Flames were shooting through broken stain glass windows. Flames were shooting through the front wooded doors from which the monks were emerging. The monks seemed to be caught up in the fire, but they weren't running or in any sort of panic.

What the hell was going on?

Who's face was the under the hood?

Questions. Questions.

Tom returned the pictures to the gym bag. Zipped the bag. Since he was fully dressed from the night before, he needed only to throw on the dirty jacket he had brought from the desert. Tom uncapped the aspirin bottle and poured out a handful. Capped the bottle, put it in his jacket. Grabbed his duffle along with Joe's and stepped outside.

The snow had stopped and the parking lot was quickly reducing to wet slush. The white, blanketed peace of evening last was now sloppy and dirty gray. Tom craned his neck around, searching the desolate lot. The black sedan from last night was nowhere to be seen. Tom couldn't even see tire treads in the slush. Had the car been there in the first place?

Joe was rummaging through the back of the Jeep. Tom walked over and set the bags down on the tailgate. He grabbed a coffee from the vehicle's roof, filled his mouth with pills and washed them down with a gulp. The coffee was hot and tasted bitter. The bitter taste of the coffee complemented the wafting smell of sewage permeating the city. What a nice combo, he thought.

Joe pushed a heavy blanket aside, revealing an olive green footlocker. Where did the damn footlocker come from?

Joe looked at Tom.

"You may need some of this today."

Joe lifted the lid to reveal the contents.

"Call it courage."

Tom opened his eyes. Wide.

Even this tiny bit of motion hurt his head.

Inside the footlocker was a sawed off shotgun, binoculars, a pistol, a metal flashlight and a gray hunting jacket. A box of shotgun shells and a box of pistol ammo completed the contents. A small arsenal. Joe set the lid back down. Tom whistled and stepped away from the vehicle. Joe slid the bags on top of the footlocker, tipped up the tailgate and slammed the window shut.

Now, where on earth had Mr. Danton gotten these weapons? They sure weren't in the Jeep when it was in Arizona. This *was* Jamestown, and there were probably guns everywhere.

"Going to war, are we?" Tom asked, partly taken aback by the firepower, and partly kidding, because he could not think of a scenario requiring him to use a gun.

Joe looked Tom square in the eyes.

"I believe we are."

The outside dampness and the tone of Joe's voice combined to send shivers through Tom. He drank more hot coffee, trying to warm his carcass.

"Let's take a look around Jamestown. See what we can find."

Tom was stiff, sore and hanging. The coffee tasted of gasoline. He figured it was a necessary start if he was going to accomplish anything this day. Sure Tommy, *accomplishment*. What did that mean again?

Nothing to him, the Isolation Man.

It had zero meaning.

Back in the Jeep, with guns and coffee.

They drove on through the downtown.

Last night when they had arrived, it was already dusk. Here in the daylight, they could see much more. Much more of the devastation.

The majestic, downtown Miracle Mile had been a veritable hive of commerce and activity. Today, very few businesses remained. In fact, Tom counted a gas station, a small engine repair shop, a second greasy spoon diner, a bowling alley, a liquor store, a triple XXX video store and a Seven Eleven. Add Champ's and the Flamingo Inn, and that was it. Of a city whose population was once near seventy thousand people.

Unbelievable.

These last holdout establishments were fortified with steel bars on the doors and steel caging on the windows. Tom wasn't a hundred per cent sure these places were actually open, as he was seeing no customers and no lit up signage.

Unless.

Unless those freaky skeletal things were the customers.

He shuddered at the thought.

As they passed the Seven Eleven, Tom saw movement.

A security guard, stationed inside the store. The guard was wearing a flak jacket, baseball cap and dark sunglasses. A sidearm was strapped to his hip. The guy looked real enough. Tom had guns in his Jeep. The security guard had a gun on his hip. Maybe they *were* in a true war zone. Besides the absence of pedestrians and cars, Tom had not yet seen any cops, firemen, city workers or EMT's.

Perhaps the guns were not such a bad idea.

They drove on.

Graffiti covered dirty brick. Broken or boarded up windows adorned the vacant buildings. The streets were badly potholed. Dead weeds lay rooted in sidewalk cracks. More abandoned cars littered the streets. Bent parking meters stood with their heads long ripped off. More hydro poles cut or chopped near ground level. Crushed grocery store buggies. Dirt and garbage mixed with the wet snow.

Everywhere, Tom saw the lightening bolts. Spray painted on walls and sidewalks.

"I see them too," Joe commented, reading Tom's mind.

Nowhere did they see any people.

Other than the armed guard at the Seven Eleven, and Benny the Innkeeper, and the fat waitress, and the punks in the diner. This made a total of nine people. Don't forget the guy in the parking lot last night, sitting in the idling car. Ten people. Ten live people so far, in all of Jamestown. Tom wasn't sure if the waitress and the teenagers were the real deal.

They drove past the cordoned off subdivision. Row after row after row of three bedroom brick bungalows, with attached garages. Beautiful neighborhoods, once. Full of families and kids. With pets and splash pools. With bicycles and green lawns. With cars and trucks and shrubs and flowers. With shade trees.

With life.

Once.

All gone.

So badly gone. Was it ever here?

Tom had Joe stop the Jeep and they both got out. Tom gawked at the incredulous ruins spread out in front of them. Windows were gone from these homes, taken away, smashed in or boarded over. Most front doors were also gone, as were the garage doors. Many roof tiles were missing and eaves troughs hung to the ground. Bricking had been removed, siding had been removed. Chimneys had been pulled down.

Tom could see right into the nearest homes. The interiors walls were gutted and the houses had been stripped of pipe, wiring, and light fixtures, anything once holding value. A few dead trees stuck out of dead front lawns. Fences had caved in, or been beaten down and removed, probably for firewood. Again, the lightening bolts were everywhere.

What the hell had happened?

Tom's destitute trailer park back in Arizona had the look of middle class housing compared to this.

He was seeing the perfect storm of destruction. Total abandonment, followed by an illegal salvage operation, followed by vandalism. The American Dream was now the American Nightmare and here he was, at ground zero of the disaster.

Because of his lack of information and his enforced isolation, Tom did not know the disease had spread from coast to coast, and border to border. Who would have thought the richest country in the world would be on its knees, buckling. The boom times of the seventies and eighties were long gone. The era of greed and larceny versus bare survivability was upon us. The haves against the have nots. Gated compounds and private security. Undermanned, inept law enforcement. Guns, guns, guns. Food stamps and food riots. Gasoline shortages and SUV's. The Isolation Man knew nothing of this.

There was even more than the destruction and the despair at play here. Through his massive headache and messed up skull, Tom was sensing a presence. Something was afoot, all around them. Tom looked up and down the empty street. He looked beyond to the streets behind. He was looking at hundreds of abandoned homes. The homes didn't *feel* abandoned. Whispers again. The same whispers he had heard in the restaurant. Sensations of substance. People seemed to be occupying these homes. People seemed to be walking right past him on the sidewalk.

Tom reached out, opening his hands, then closing them. He thought he might be able to grasp something, the feeling was so thick. It was a cloying feeling. An 'almost' feeling.

Shadows of people.

From before.

People everywhere. People nowhere.

A people wandering.

A people lost. Forever lost.

"Tom?" Joe asked. "What are you sensing?"

Tom could not begin to articulate any of this. It would sound too crazy.

"Not sure. Something though. I don't think we are alone."

They returned to the Jeep and drove on. They cruised passed the high school. Steel barricades and ten foot high chain link fencing had been erected around the school. The fencing was torn, dented and rusting badly. Huge, orange signs designating 'Toxic Waste' were bolted along the barricades. 'Do Not Enter' and 'No Trespassing' warnings abounded. Somebody had not listened. The school beyond the fence was smashed, bashed and tagged.

They drove on, coming to the former pillar of Jamestown, the gigantic St. Mary's Cathedral. The Jeep slowed to a stop.

Tom's guts wrenched as he trailed back through time. To his last night in Jamestown.

His late night meeting with Father Paulo. Tom drunk or stoned, or both. Banging on the rectory door, way past midnight. Father Paulo, allowing Tom into the sacred building. The two men making their way through the dark, following the low lighting and flickering candles.

They stopped in front of the altar, taking seats on the front pew. Here Tom was, in the House of the Lord, surrounded by the opulent trappings of religion. The deep, mahogany benches, the thick, regal carpet underfoot, the magnificent paintings, sculptures and stained glass art. The hushed quiet of the place. The reverent quiet of the place. Tom Forbes, destroyed, looking for help. Looking for answers. Looking for salvation.

Looking for the way home.

Father Paulo, nearly seventy years old, white haired, erect, firm of handshake, a font of religion and belief, the man with all the right words.

Fear not my son, for she is in a better place.

'Come again?' was all Tom could register in his brain.

She is in a better place. She is with the Lord.

She is in a better place?

What the fuck does that even mean?

What better place?

What better place could there be, than right here with her parents?

What is this magical fairytale land, this better place?

What the hell are you talking about, old man?

Do you mean she is dead?

Do you know this for sure?

How do you know this?

Nobody else does. Not the cops. Not even the FBI.

But you do. God knows. God knows *everything.*

So you *are* telling me she is dead.

Because, don't you have to be dead to get to this 'better place'?

You know what? Give me four weeks and a case of whiskey, and I too will come up with a great bunch of bullshit like yours.

Tom walked away from the big church. His chat with Father Paulo had not ended well. Nothing in his life had ended well. Not since 1987.

Tom had other memories of the church. The many weddings, funerals, Christmas midnight masses and Sunday services. The tolling of the bells, every day at noon and six, lunch and supper time. The tolling of the bells every Sunday at mass times, calling the worshippers to their duty. The church represented so many gatherings of people. Good people, relatives, neighbors and townsfolk.

No more thought Tom. No more.

The travelers could only stare.

The church was smashed, bashed and tagged. Lightening bolts had been sprayed all over. There were giant holes in the walls, as if a massive battering ram had been launched at the building. Tom could see right into the church. The chairs and pews had been obliterated in some manic fury.

The violence wrought against the church was staggering. It almost seemed *personal*. Tom was not a religious man, but he felt a sense of violation as he looked at the shattered House of God.

Holy shit. There was nothing sacred in Jamestown. Nothing had been off limits to the tidal wave of vandalism and destruction.

They drove on towards the older residential areas. Here they found many of the houses had been lifted and moved out of the city, leaving bare basement foundations behind. Some of the remaining homes must have held squatters. Smoke curled out of the odd chimney. Tom rolled his window down and smelled the air. Definitely wood smoke. To go with the sewage.

The homes showed no signs of maintenance, nor pride of ownership. The homes had the expected broken windows, doors hanging on hinges, peeling roof tiles, failed siding and plenty of garbage strewn everywhere. Beat to crap cars sat on cracked driveways or across bare, slush spotted front yards.

Tom saw a few large dogs, Rottys and Dobermans, chained to front porches. He knew what this was all about. The official guard dog of the frightened little drug dealer. Who was coming for you, Mr. Drug Dealer? The cops? A rival gang? One of your own to pop a cap in your ass and take over your business? Better make sure you keep some goodies for me. Tom tried to make a mental note of these abodes. His stash was gone and he was going to need more.

Probably today.

Tom's mind was pulled back to the pictures in Joe's bag. Who *was* the hooded man, at the Los Angeles church? Tom churned the picture over and over in his mind. Someone he knew? There was definitely a familiarity. He was about to ask Joe about it when he felt an uncomfortable tightening in his chest.

It caused him to sit straight up in his seat and forget about everything else. Tom braced himself against the dashboard.

What the hell was happening?

He could not draw a breath. There was no air in his system. He was completely empty.

A powerful hand settled over his heart, making ready to crush the life out of him.

"Are you okay?" Joe asked.

Tom gasped for a deep breath. Where had the oxygen gone?

The Jeep pulled to the curb and stopped. Joe shut it off. The wind blew outside and the warm engine ticked.

Tom finally found his breath, then grabbed another.

He settled a bit. Took some more air. Settled some more. Heading back to normal.

He was okay.

Jesus. What a terrifying experience.

"Fine. I'm fine," he mumbled.

Tom wiped at the sweat on his forehead. Was this the first shot at him? The first warning of an impending coronary attack? Why not? Why the *hell* not?

He was able to focus his eyes and look through his side window.

Now he understood the hand over his heart.

Up the driveway.

Towards the front door.

It was the Busy Bee.

1987.

God sakes.

He was here.

CHAPTER 28

THE LARGE BUMBLE BEE ABOVE THE ENTRANCE WAS UNRECOGNIZABLE. The bright yellow happy face adorning the double front doors had faded to gray. Tom closed his eyes. He could see Tiffy running up to the big happy face, planting smacking kisses on it, blonde hair flying, the bright red elephant tucked under her arm.

Back to reality.

Tom opened his eyes. The happy face was still smiling; however the smile was colorless and joyless. The smile had been drained by neglect and tragedy. It too had died.

Tom's skull began to pound. He felt the sweat bead on his forehead.

A gust of wind rocked the Jeep. Black clouds were rushing across the sky, seemingly converging on the airspace right above the day care.

Joe turned in his seat.

"Tom. This is going to be the hardest thing you have ever done. In your life."

More harsh wind. More dark clouds.

"You can do this, Tom. For you. More, for her."

Joe reached inside his jacket pocket.

"There is one more picture you need to see."

Did Joe know he had been snooping at the pictures from the duffle bag?

Joe pulled out a crumpled color photo. He smoothed the photo, and handed it to Tom. Tom took the picture from Joe. It was Tiffy. The picture Tom had kept on his desktop. Beside the big trophy. In the gold frame. With the spider cracked glass.

How did this picture end up with Joe Danton?

"For her Tom. Let's do this for her."

Tom stared at the picture, long and hard. It didn't matter how the picture ended up with Joe Danton. The picture was here. Right now. Tom's hand began to tremble. The picture. The beautiful little face. The blonde hair. The eyes. Glowing at him, from twenty-five years ago.

What in the living hell was he supposed to do?

Why was he even here?

Tom was overwhelmed. A lost little boy. He felt the tears welling. Tom knew if he started to cry now, he would cry for the rest of his life.

"It is time," Joe interrupted.

Tom tried to summon his courage.

The courage that would be needed to face……?

To face what?

His past? His failure? His demons? His future?

What he was doing here?

This courage would come from a lifetime investment in strength, morals, commitment, belief, honesty, passion, integrity, and good old fashioned guts. Investments he had not made.

Really, he hadn't been such a bad guy. Had he?

A little white dust. A little bit of gambling. Always losing of course. A little bit of flirting. Okay, a lot of flirting.

Was this the punishment for those small infractions? For shit sakes, if it was, then punish away, but punish me. Not Tiffy. Tiffy had committed no crimes. She had not sinned.

She was a kid.

An innocent, little kid.

She was two years old.

Tom let out a long sigh.

He thought about the lost decades of his life. The wasted years in the wasteland. All alone. Doing nothing. Nothing for himself and nothing for anyone else. The authentic, true, Isolation Man.

Shit.

There had been none of the aforementioned deposits made into the courage bank of his life. Rightly so, there could be no withdrawals from said bank. Tom figured he was pretty much insolvent. Therefore, completely unprepared to face what was coming.

This was last call. Last call for Tom Forbes, for the rest of his life.

He placed the picture on the dashboard.

For his little girl, Tom would do this. Whatever 'this' was.

Joe picked up the picture, and slid it back inside his jacket.

"I will have it right here."

Joe patted his jacket.

"Safekeeping."

The two men left the Jeep and stood on the sidewalk. Again, the smell of raw sewage permeated the air. Again, Tom felt as if people were drifting by him, beside him and in front of him. He sensed people in the driveway ahead. There were more whispers from the folks of Absentia.

Tom and Joe slowly walked up the driveway. They stopped at the front door of the Busy Bee. The door and windows had been boarded up from the inside with heavy plywood. Tom took a few steps back and scanned the building.

What was different about this place?

He scanned some more and tried to think through the drug-alcohol curtain surrounding his brain. He looked at Joe. Joe seemed to be caught up in the same riddle. Joe was looking up and down the building, and all around.

What was it?

For sure, something was different. Something so large and obvious, the two travelers were looking right past it.

Suddenly, Tom clued in.

Yes he did.

Holy.

Shit.

There was no graffiti on the walls.

None.

No lightening bolts.

Not a mark.

Not a single window he could see was broken.

There were absolutely no signs of vandalism. Garbage wasn't accumulating on or even blowing across this property. Not a single thing was damaged or out of place. The building reminded Tom of a black and white photograph, the original color draining away over time. Other than the fading colors and the fading brick, the building looked remarkable.

What were the odds of the vandals completely missing the Busy Bee?

Christ, look at what they had done to the fucking church.

The two men looked at each other.

Dumfounded.

Not one sign of disrespect could they see on this property.

Not one.

This one building, in all of Jamestown, was completely untouched by the tsunami of destruction overrunning the city.

Was this place sacred?

Or was this place feared?

Even the garbage was scared to trespass.

For sure, it was one more thing making zero sense.

Joe tugged at the door handle. It was locked. A cool breeze blew around the building carrying tiny laughter from the backyard. Again, the two men looked at one another.

What the?

"Did you hear that?" Tom asked.

Joe nodded.

They walked quickly around the building and scaled the chain link fence.

There was no laughter.

There were no kids.

The grass was tall and weedy. They waded through the yard. They caught glimpses of dirty, washed out toys here and there. Jesus. They hadn't even taken the toys. They simply padlocked the place and left.

In a damn hurry.

The decayed swings creaked in the wind, slightly swaying, as if little riders were present. Tom looked intently at the swings.

What was he expecting to see?

Little skeleton kids? Swinging and laughing?

Where was the sunlight when you needed it?

The sunlight had been here in all its glory back in 1987, in the morning, during the big drop off. Yes it had. The sunlight of the last Indian summer day.

Right now, the mottled sky above them was not allowing any sunlight through.

Tom was really thinking.

If the sun was shining, *would* he actually be seeing those skeleton creatures on the swings? Running around and playing? Out on the driveway and on the sidewalk? Beside the burnt fence? In the Champ's Chicken joint? Back in those abandoned homes? In the candle lit apartments above the stores on the Miracle Mile?

Or, was it real people, people the same as him and Joe, and Benny the Innkeeper, who lived in those candle lit apartments? Tom wasn't sure whether he would want to see Jamestown brightly lit, or not.

Probably not.

Especially if Tiffy was one of them.

Stop right there, buddy. This thought path is a dead end street. Tom tried to expel the ugly thought path right out of his being. Tiffy was *not* one of those things. No way.

Tom moved past the swing set, wandering on over to the center of the yard. Joe joined him under the ancient oak. The oak was bare. There were no colored leaves on the grass below. The tree had died years ago, another casualty of the Jamestown disease. Tom stared up at the great tree. It was massive. The tree stretched to the sky with petrifying, clawing limbs.

Why did the tree have to die?

Why did it *all* have to go and die?

Tom's head thump, thumped away. Damn those drugs. Damn the booze. Damn himself.

He turned away from the tree, and ventured towards the plank fence. Miniscule tatters of worn police tape remained stapled to the decaying wood. The fence was charred and terribly weathered. There was no pattern of anything on the fence. No lightening bolts, nothing but worn, beaten, moldering, dead wood.

Talk about sacred.

This was the last place his little girl had been seen alive.

Right here.

Tom prayed for a sliver of light. Just in case she was still here.

Playing.

Laughing.

Running.

Full of energy. The tiny tornado.

With the red elephant.

Two years old.

It would be *so* good to see her. Even if she was *one of them*.

Wouldn't it?

Yes, it would.

The cool wind had stopped.

All was still.

All was quiet.

She had been taken from this exact spot.

By a man in a hood. Or a robe. With a shadowed face.

The man coming out of the Los Angeles church had a shadowed face.

Tom once owned a long hooded sweatshirt. Dark in color. For pickup football games in the fall, over at Lion's Park. The hood was handy when the wind blew in off the lake. Tom used to charcoal below his eyes for the games. Made him feel like a pro. A Cleveland Brown. The charcoal mixed with his sweat and spread across his face, smearing on his stubble.

The perspiration smeared charcoal would probably resemble a shadow.

Tom's guts began to turn. He covered his mouth with his hand. The nausea passed and settled at a lower level. The nausea did not go away.

"Tom, look!" Joe interrupted.

Tom looked at Joe.

When had Joe changed?

Why was he wearing a hood jacket?

Wasn't he wearing a regular jacket, a minute ago?

Sure he was. Tiffy's picture was in his jacket pocket. For safekeeping.

Right?

So when had Joe changed?

As Tom tried to think, Joe flipped his hood up to brace against the cold damp. Joe's thin beard made it appear as if a shadow had been cast across his face.

What the hell?

Tom with his charcoal face. Joe with his beard. Both hooded. The backyard of the day care. September 11th, 1987. Tom's guts began to roil, again. *Both men hooded. Can you see what I see?*

"Look," Joe said again.

Tom stared at Joe, who was pointing towards the sky. Tom followed the direction with his eyes.

Tom saw......

Holy crap.

"What the.........?"

Tom was stopped cold.

It couldn't be.

It was not possible.

A thin wisp of smoke was curling out of one of the long dormant, factory stacks. Of Morgan Iron and Steel. Tom trailed the smoke skywards. Impossible. It couldn't be. He had to be hallucinating again.

The factory had been closed for over two decades. 1989 it went down. It must be vandals burning the place, or squatters trying to stay warm. The smoke stopped rising and began to spread, as if being held down by an invisible ceiling.

Suddenly, the ground shook beneath their feet. Tom actually thought he might fall. He puts his arms out to balance himself. Joe was doing the same. The ground was trembling in unison with the thumping in Tom's head. Earthquake? No. The mighty forges in the factory were coming to life.

What the hell was going on?

This was not vandals.

Nor was it squatters.

Tom could not find the words.

The shaking in the ground screamed proof positive, the factory was operational.

Today.

Right now.

Operational.

The lightening strike. Mist and heavy smoke. Two men in hoods. Tom and Joe. Tiffany gone. Taken by men in hoods.

Can you see what I see?

Sept 11, 1987, all over again.

Abruptly, Joe was right beside Tom. Tom nearly shit himself. Another unseen, ghostly movement by Joe Danton.

Joe was excited. He was on to something.

"Tom. The day Tiffany disappeared, Marie and I walked out the back door. We went past the big oak tree. The tree wasn't bare. It was covered with leaves. We looked at the sky above the factory. We were amazed at how blue the sky was, and how bright the sun was shining. The ground was reverberating, as it is right now. But. There was no smoke coming from the stacks. No smoke at all."

Tom could say nothing. His brain was tangled up in the hood jackets.

Was *he*, Tom Forbes, one of the men in hoods? With a shadowed face? Was he?

Was Joe Danton the other?

Had they teamed up to……?

No way! No *fucking* way! Impossible! Why would they?

What was he thinking? Damn stupid drugs.

Joe was now talking to himself as much as he was to Tom, trying to make a connection.

"September the eleventh, back in '87, the factory was firing. Firing, with no smoke. Today we know the factory is dead, but it is smoking. I think we have somehow closed a loop."

Tom and Joe were quiet.

Tom was pondering the hooded shadow men. His brain was melting, his skull was pulsating. The waves were coming at him from all directions. Thick smoke was rising from the dormant factory. He was clean out of smack. Where was his next blast going to come from? He was in a dead town. With seventy thousand dead things. His little girl might be one of those dead things.

Joe was busy pondering the loop. The loop was indeed closing. Joe felt whatever happened back in 1987 was going to happen again. Soon. Very soon. This was a giant Ferris wheel. The riding cabin from 1987 had nearly circled all the way around, and now it was about to pass right in front of them. They had a chance. A chance to jump on. A chance to make this right.

Joe looked at Tom.

"You know where you have to go, don't you?"

CHAPTER 29

There was movement out of the corner of Tom's eye. Someone was loitering on the sidewalk out front. A real person. It was the first pedestrian they had seen since they arrived in desolate, barren Jamestown. The man on the sidewalk came to a full stop, turned and looked towards them. Tom realized he and Joe might arouse a little suspicion. Rummaging around in the backyard of a building long closed down. The man continued to stare. A long trench coat flapped around his legs. What looked to be a cowboy hat, sat on his head.

The wind carried over to where Tom and Joe stood. The wind was cold. The man continued to stare. Whispers. The man turned, and slowly walked away. The wind died down as did the whispers. The man seemed to be in no hurry as he left. Why would anyone be in a hurry in Jamestown? Other than to leave?

There was something familiar about the man. The trench coat. Somebody from the past? From Tom's other life? Where?

"Strange," Joe said.

"Amen to that," agreed Tom, as he tried to recollect the idling car in the Flamingo parking lot last night. Was it the guy from the dark sedan?

Unexpectedly, Tom and Joe experienced the same creeping sensation.

Together, they turned, looking back towards the plank fence. Back to where it all began. At the base of the fence, a white mist began to rise up off the grass. They walked towards the fence. Closer. Closer. Close.

The smell caught them both. They stepped back with watery eyes. Joe remembered this smell. He sure did. Tom remembered this smell. It was worse than tear gas. It was the smell of rot and death.

The mist began to thicken considerably. It rolled across their feet and legs. The mist was alive.

Suddenly, Joe was amped up. On edge. Tuned. He had figured something out!

Something important.

"Tom. This is it. The Ferris wheel has stopped. We don't have much time. I'm going in the front. Right now. I will create a diversion. You go in the back way."

Back way?

Front?

What the hell was Joe talking about?

Diversion?

A diversion for what?

What the fuck did any of this have to do with a Ferris wheel?

Before Tom's mouth could catch up with his brain, Joe reached out and clasped Tom's hand.

"This is it Tom. The biggest fight of your life. Take what you need from the Jeep. Go in the back way. You know where it is. Surprise them, Tom. Find Tiffany. Bring her home."

Joe shook Tom's hand, Tom responding numbly in kind.

Find Tiffany? Bring her home?

There is no Tiffany. There hasn't been a Tiffany for a quarter of a century. What there has been is a phalanx of drugs and liquor with extreme visions and apparitions. Now, add in crazy stories and conspiracies and priests, and nut houses and the end of the world. Add in hooded men and sawed off shotguns. Add in a whole world of grotesque creatures alive and well in Jamestown. Creatures Tom could almost see.

And now, there was mist.

Yes, for sure, this is quite the trip you are on, Tommy boy.

Joe's grip tightened on Tom's hand. Tiny jolts of energy surged up Tom's forearm and spread across his chest. The death grip over his heart, welcoming him with pain and panic to the Busy Bee, was melting away. The jolts of energy curled down Tom's spine, surging through his legs, spreading throughout his torso. Strength was filling him up. In his mind, Tom could read his gas gauge swinging from dead empty, even negative territory, towards full, in a hurry.

Wow, what a rush! This was almost as good as the drugs. What was happening to him?

Joe released the handshake and walked closer to the fence. He began to disappear in the thick, white mist. Tom could only see Joe's head and shoulders. How could you disappear into mist? How?

Tom was beginning to panic.

Joe turned once more.

"Tom. You can do this. Believe in yourself."

The mist surrounded Joe and he was gone.

Tom's panic grew.

What on earth?

Tom closed his eyes. As he had when he was a little kid. You bet. When scared, close eyes. Count to ten. When eyes are opened, scary thing will be gone.

Tom knew when he opened his eyes, Joe would be standing there. Yes he would. So settle down. Nobody disappears into mist. Not Joe, not his Tiffy.

At the very least, he would be back in the crappy Flamingo Inn. Or more likely, back in his Arizona tin coffin. The tin coffin was real. The blasting heat was real, as was the desolation and the foul mouthed black bird.

Joe's handshake had been powerful. It had felt good. Really good. Tom went there instead. Toward the good. The energy transfer from Joe had been amazing. Yes it had. This is the way he wanted to feel. Not the stupid panic, or the near heart attack, or the fear, or the helplessness, or the sorrow, or the never ending tears and despair. Tom wanted better.

A strange calmness began to wash over him. The calmness felt good, and was so welcome, but carried with it a quality which was hard to explain. The calmness carried a falseness about it, or more, a time limit on it. You are welcome to the calmness Mr. Forbes, but only for a limited time. Now pick up your balls and your guts, and you may pass Go.

Tom opened his eyes.

Joe was *not* there.

Tom was not in the Flamingo Inn. Tom was not in his boiling coffin. Great.

Now what?

This left him no choice, he figured. He had to go for it. Finish the ride. He knew this was going to be one crazy ride when he had left the desert. He sure wasn't being disappointed.

Tom turned once more toward the factory. The reverberation moved the ground under his feet. He sure remembered this sensation. There was a time when everyone in Jamestown could tell you what the reverberation was. A healthy, booming factory firing on all cylinders, bringing wealth, goodness and happiness to all. Right. How had that worked out for everybody?

The smokestack continued to pour soot into the sky above the factory. The sky was now black ink. Evil. The factory was the place. Tom knew it in his heart.

He had always known it, hadn't he?

Tom walked through the tall grass and climbed back over the chain link fence. He trod carefully, trying not to run over the folks he thought might be on the sidewalk. What folks Tommy? Buddies of those things eating at the fast food place? Geez, be careful, your daughter could be one of them. What if she sees you right now?

What if she is calling for you?

Calling as she had, way back in 1987?

You *know* she had been calling for you, don't you, *dad*?

Calling for help. Calling to be saved.

Was this the new reality for Tom Forbes?

Starring in some kind of horror video game?

Kind of his own, private Silent Hill?

Tom sighed.

He refocused on the calmness. It was still with him. For how long, he didn't know. One thing for sure, he had done nothing to earn the calmness, so it could evaporate at any time.

Out on the sidewalk, Tom did not see the loiterer who had been staring at them. There was nothing and no one. The wonderful, wafting smell of Jamestown sewage continued to permeate the air. What were the chances any of this was really happening anyway?

At the Jeep, Tom lifted the back window. He pushed aside the two duffle bags and opened the footlocker. He took out the flashlight, the sawed off shotgun and a box of shells. He looked closely at the shells. They were very heavy, and had red, rounded tips. Tom had never seen this particular type of shotgun shell. The shells looked to be small grenades. He plugged the shells into the gun. Set the gun down.

Tom removed the aspirin bottle from his raggedy light coat. Then took the coat off. Chucked it in the Jeep. He pulled out the long hunting jacket and put it on. The shotgun went into an inside pocket. The flashlight went into another. The extra, red-tipped shells went in as well. Tom transferred his aspirin bottle to the hunting jacket. The pistol he decided, in this crazy reality, would be too small. Tom didn't know why he decided this.

We know why.

Video game, remember.

Big guns, big bangs.

Tom looked back through the chain link, towards the burnt, rotted plank fence and the thick swirling mist. Joe was still gone. Was he ever there?

It was time to roll. Tom slammed the back window shut and walked around to the driver side. He knew exactly where he was going, but he had no idea what he would find.

Or.

Did he?

CHAPTER 30

CARL HAD RISKED LITTLE BY WALKING PAST THE SHUTTERED DAY CARE. He didn't care if the druggie had seen him out on the sidewalk or not. Tom Forbes was so strung out; he wouldn't know if he was looking at a human being or an alien. Besides, Carl didn't believe anything could look out of the ordinary in this town.

What a freak show.

Jamestown possessed the same sinister, screwed up vibe as Farmington, Tennessee. The village of Farmington was a backwater toilet in the remote hills, disconnected from the Volunteer state. A sick, sick evil place. Carl had gone down to Farmington to smoke out Billy Ray Eaton. Eaton had killed thirty-six travelers and two cops, attacking indiscriminately over the southern interstate grid.

Eaton had been dubbed, 'The Rest Stop Killer' by the press. The piece of shit killed who ever trespassed his zone of operation. Besides the two cops, Eaton had slaughtered seven truckers, four college kids and members of eight different families. Including nine children. Billy Ray had slithered out of the hills and interacted with the real world. It hadn't worked out too well for anybody.

The population of Farmington consisted of nearly four hundred, severely inbred citizens. Everyone looked the same; it didn't matter if you were male or female. The only distinguishing characteristics were the birth defects. The inbreeding had been way over the top. The people were so sick. Only a few of them were allowed out to procure goods for the rest of the community.

The place was run along the lines of a commune or a cult, but without a clear leader. No one person or committee or group was in charge. It was if a single mentality ran the village. To hook into this mentality, you had to be a local. Carl could find no way to get in.

The ignorance of the citizenry was appalling. They spoke some bastardized version of English, with some ridiculous twangy accent. They all wore the same clothes and the same hair styles. The adults all reeked of moonshine, which did not quite cover their body odor. None of them had ever been to a dentist. Why would anybody choose to exist in this manner? Raise their kids in this squalor and sickness?

Finding Billy Ray had been a nightmare. Carl was unable to fold into the flow of the place, so he started shooting. Carl killed four look-a-likes before he finally tagged the correct Billy Ray. What a mess. The Bureau cleaners had to sweep in, spend some money and make a lot of threats, the usual. The cover up had been very efficient.

Jamestown channeled the same ominous vibes as Farmington. Jamestown equaled rot and death and something more. Almost a shadow world seemed to exist. The external tingling Carl had felt was getting stronger. He still couldn't put his finger on it. He was missing something, something right here and all around him. Something important.

And what about Forbes?

Forbes was proving to be a piece of work.

Pacing in the motel last night. A worried, nervous man? Or tripping out? Looking out the window how many times? Paranoia setting in on the druggie?

This morning, Forbes was rummaging through the backyard of the day care, the last place his little girl was seen alive. Reliving the day of infamy, was he?

Now, the bastard was armed. It appeared to be a sawed off shotgun.

Exactly what the country needed, another lunatic with a gun.

CHAPTER 31

Tom drove north towards the factory. There were no further signs of life. Not a single, solitary pedestrian, and not a single moving vehicle could be seen. No dogs, no stray cats, no birds. The streets were desolate. The carnage he was seeing continued to astonish. The city was a ruin. He imagined Beirut or Baghdad or Kabul looked much the same. Actually, they probably looked better. At least there would be some activity in those far away places. Bazaars, food markets, money markets, trade. Explosions. Machine gun fire. Colorful clothing. Real voices. Flesh and blood. Something.

Tom's skull ached, ebbing and flowing in rhythm with the reverberating output from the steel works. What a bizarre sensation. Why was this happening? Tom had known this sound, this Jamestownian fact of life, since he was a small child. The pounding of the forges. It was ingrained in him. It was ingrained in all of the locals. It was working, and living, and breathing.

In fact, when Tom moved to the desert, this was one of the things he missed about his hometown. Actually, he didn't really 'miss' it. The deep, perpetual, ground shaking rhythm was not there, it was no longer a part of him. In the desert, he listened to the wind blow and the sand rattle against his trailer. Nothing at all moved under his feet.

Now, here he was, back in Jamestown. Once again, the ground was throbbing. His headache was throbbing in perfect sync with the powerful energy pulse being emitted from the big factory.

Besides the headache, Tom was struggling mightily with the hooded men and the darkened faces. Were the darkened faces dirt? Or stubble growth? Or charcoal slashes? Tom could not pull anything past the crap he had been feeding himself for two and a half decades. He had indeed constructed a thick wall to contain the horror of the awful day. He was no longer sure what lay behind that wall.

Tom drove on through the emptiness of the dead city. As he drove, somebody else was having the exact, same thoughts. About the wall.

The dark, four door sedan followed the erratic driving of the Jeep. The Jeep slowed, sped up, swerved. Good thing there was no other traffic. Carl Horner wondered what his quarry was up to. Discovering what was behind his wall of denial? A wall thrown up by decades of drug abuse? Was Forbes returning to the scene of the crime?

The anger began to rise in Carl. If this was the case, he would soon be busy. There would be no arrest made this day. It had never been his job to arrest people. Carl never carried handcuffs or filed paperwork or followed protocol. Carl only worked on the green light formula. Acquire target, receive green light, and liquidate. For Mr. Tom Forbes, the green light was on. The green light had been issued by Carl Horner, to Carl Horner. There was a first time for everything.

Tom pulled up to the main gates of the Morgan Iron and Steel Works. Tangles of chain strapped the gates shut, all secured by a large, heavy duty, but very rusty old padlock. Tom drove forward, engaging the four wheel drive. He pressed the front bumper against the gates. The Jeep began to push. The metal gates squealed in protest. The weathered chain began to stretch as he increased the forward pressure. He felt the weakness ahead of him, and stomped the accelerator. The Jeep bit into the road surface, finding a footing. The resistance shattered. The gates blew open and the Jeep shot forward. Steel links ripped off the chain, cracking against the windshield. Tom ducked in panic. Sounded too much like gunfire.

He was through.

Morgan Iron and Steel.

The factory grounds.

Dead, since 1989.

Now with a pulse?

Tom could hear the vibration all around him. Feel the thumping in the ground, right through the seat beneath his ass. The thumping seemed to originate in the old forge, straight ahead. Black smoke was oozing, liquid and heavy, out of a tall, decrepit stack. The stack was filthy with carbon, missing many of its bricks, and was well into its leaning phase. The sky was inky black, the smoke swirling around with the dead gray cloud cover.

Tom drove towards the forge, on a laneway flanked with the carcasses of deceased buildings and rusted out service trucks. The factory grounds were much like the day care. Old and falling to ruin, but unaided by vandals and graffiti artists.

Was this another sacred place?

Tom parked in front of the giant building. The factory grounds were the same as the city. Dead empty. The grounds were no longer a synergistic mass of humanity and machine, working, producing and building a nation. The Morgan Iron and Steel Works was now an American graveyard. Dark, cold and devoid of life.

Except for the reverberation coiling through the earth, so strong and so alive, continuing to amplify the pounding in his head.

Tom pushed open the door of the Jeep, inhaled deeply, then exhaled and watched his breath float away. He was out of the Jeep now, walking towards the man door located at the corner of the forge. Tom stopped at the door and took another deep breath. What would he find behind this door? A working factory full of men and machinery? A factory full of skeletons? What the hell was going on in the forge?

He tugged on the door. The door was locked or seized over time. The ground was really shaking now. Everything was happening, beyond this ancient, metal barrier to entry.

The dark sedan rolled silently through the yawning gates, following its target. The tingling was assaulting Carl from outside and from within. The game was on. It was time for some good old fashioned American justice. Carl was right about the sinister current running through Jamestown. The current had been strong at the day care, and at the factory gates. It was getting stronger, now that he had breached those gates.

Tom picked up a steel rod and wedged it between the door and the jamb. He reefed on it until the forge door opened. Tom slipped inside. The door slowly squeaked with metallic resistance as it shut behind him.

There was silence.

The reverberation, the factory thumping, had disappeared.

Completely.

Not Tom's headache though.

His head continued to pound. In silence.

The ground under his feet had gone perfectly still.

Crap.

It was time for another gut check.

Why was it so quiet all of a sudden? It wasn't, a second ago.

Where on earth was Joe Danton, the story teller?

Never mind with that stupid question. Because what could the answer be?

Crap, was right.

Tom looked around in the gloom. No skeletons working. No forge operating. No machinery moving. Empty. Void. Nothing going on. Deader than dead. Dead for a long, long time.

His eyes began to focus in the dusky forge. Tom was in the oldest part of the factory, circa pre World War One. The high glass windows were mostly broken out, victimized by wind and time. Massive cobwebs hung from the rafters. On the cracked and broken shop floor, work stations stood as sentries from the past. Relics of history lay strewn about. Old fabricating molds, paint cans with brushes seized in them, scheduling chalkboards showing ancient quotas, layers and layers of rust and dust. The overhead crane bore a huge American flag. The flag was stained and filthy. The red and blue had drained from Old Glory. As life had drained from Tom. As everything had drained from Jamestown.

Tom had worked two teenage summers in this factory. He closed his eyes and was able to reverse the clock, grabbing at bits of memory. There he was, a strapping lad, seventeen years old, wearing his helmet and earplugs, goggles, heavy jeans, work boots, plaid shirt and strong gloves.

Tom opened his mind. The drugs let you open up; they let you open up so wide you might float away forever. The roar immediately filled his ears. Tom actually ducked, it was so real. Pipes clanged down the gang ramps, stacking up while still steaming hot. Overhead cranes whooshed by, hauling heavy bundles of steel. Forklifts belching diesel exhaust trundled past him. Fluorescent orange molten steel was snaking out of furnace shoots. Men were hollering clipped instructions at one another, using a universal language patched together to satisfy the many European dialects represented on the shop floor. Always, the continuous drone of machinery and productivity filled the background with sound.

The summer heat was almost beyond comprehension. Water buckets with ladles sat beside the work stations. Dehydrated men gulped the stuff down. Thousands of workers hit the showers at shift end. They chain pulled their dirty work clothes to the ceiling of the change room, making ready for their next shift. The flood of incoming humanity passed the outgoing. The mass exodus from the parking lots created a mini traffic jam at the main plant gates three times every twenty-four hours. After the day and afternoon shifts, the mad charge would begin to the corner bars and watering holes.

Twenty-four hours a day, seven days a week, when Jamestown worked hard. The best city, in the best country in the whole wide world. The wealthiest city, in the wealthiest country in the whole wide world. The most respected country in the world. The toughest country in the world.

Tom opened his eyes. It was quiet again on the factory floor. Everything had gone. Or died. Everything.

It was ominous quiet.

A shiver ran down Tom's spine.

Then the whispers began.

Thousands upon thousands of men, and a few women. Years and years and generations of service. Fathers working with sons, grandfathers working with grandsons. Countless triumphs and tragedies. Celebrations and solemn times. High points, low points, hard work and good reward. The workforce, so varied, so European. So hungry to make a better life in the land of America. The women, taking up shifts during the war years. The sons, leaving the plant to fight in Vietnam and Korea. So many experiences. So much living. So many lives. The eternal imprint of mankind was all over this space. Embedded in the concrete floor, the metal walls, the roof structure, and the dead air filling this gigantic forge.

Tom concentrated. He could almost make out what the whispers were saying. He was so close.

A fluttering sound in the high rafters startled him.

Tom reached inside his jacket, pulling out the flashlight. He clicked the 'on' button and pointed up. The light caught a glint of a bird's eye. A raven or a crow or something. It was a black bird, but it wasn't the ugly, foul mouthed bitch who had been sitting on the scraggly tree in the desert, eyeballing him, talking to him, mocking him. The same bird following him from Arizona to Jamestown would have been far too much for Tom to handle.

Well, at least he wasn't alone.

Isn't that what he thought when he and Joe began this trip?

Where the hell was Joe now?

Tommy, you are alone, and even if the black bird up there is real, you are *still* alone. So no comfort there, buddy boy.

Tom took a deep breath. The whispers were gone again. Good grief, what next? Whispers. No whispers. Make up your fucking mind.

It was getting noticeably colder. All of Tom's senses switched to overload. What were those damned whispers anyway? A message? A warning? Insanity knocking at the door? Was it time to wake up in the sweltering tin trailer?

Or, how about this?

He was *already* dead, his corpse sizzled and charred in the boiling tin trailer, days or months or years ago. Nobody bothering to check on him. Nobody caring. Why would anybody give a shit about him? He didn't give two shits about anybody else. Quid pro quo, my friend. The Isolation Man.

Yes, he could very well be dead. Why not? How could he tell? Maybe the nightmares and hallucinations carried on into death. Nobody had ever come back from the dead to explain things, now had they? Not even this Jesus dude.

Ah, but death would be too easy for Tom Forbes. When you were a drug addicted, piece of shit loser, well, you were truly a loser. Nothing would ever be easy, and nothing would ever work out in your favor.

Ever.

So he wasn't dead. Yet.

The cloudy day, mixing with the black smoke stack effluent, was offering scant light into the building. Tom could see the ugly swirls of smoke pressing in on the forge windows. Some of the black evil was licking through the empty panes, seemingly undecided about flooding in or not.

There *was* enough light for Tom to see mist rising out of a stairwell, up ahead.

His heart rose to his mouth, as he dropped his thoughts about the dark smoke pouring from a chimney in a dead factory, and whether he was dead or alive.

How many gut checks could one man take in a day?

Tom gaped at the mist. The Mist. A Stephen King novel.

Hopefully, Tom's ending would be a little more satisfying.

Slowly, he walked towards the mist, watching it roll gently up onto the factory floor. The mist was so soft, and delicate. So welcoming.

So peaceful.

Possibly, crazy Joe Danton was right. Joe had walked into thick mist at the Busy Bee. What he called the front door. Was Tom looking at the back door? Standing at the top of the stairs, Tom trained the flashlight beam downward. The mist was so thick, he couldn't tell if it was five steps, or five hundred steps to the bottom. And down there, the mist did not look so welcoming, or so peaceful.

No.

The mist was busy.

The mist was roiling.

The mist looked angry.

The back door. Right. Tom took the first step down. Then another. Something was changing. Another step down. Tom could feel the air cooling further. As if a giant air conditioner had switched on. Another step down. Another. The mist was much thicker. He couldn't see his boots. Another step. The mist grew yet thicker, and the air was getting colder. Tom stopped. He took a back step towards the top. The mist lightened, the air warmed slightly.

Jesus. What discipline of science was this?

What had Joe blathered about back in the motel?

Unwavering belief would see him through?

Right. Fuck that.

Tom quickly rifled through his jacket pockets. He had no more booze on him, and no good drugs. Therefore, no faith. He had a shotgun, some spare shells and a bottle of headache pills, the after-binge remedy. The headache pills were not going to cut it now.

Tom moved on down, slowly taking the steps. Two more steps, six steps, ten steps. It was freezing. He turned and looked back up. He could barely make out the high windows, the old beam roof supports and the long extinguished ceiling lamps. The black bird was nowhere to be seen. The bastard had abandoned him after all. So he would be going it alone. Why not. The Isolation Man in action. Four more steps down. Tom looked back up.

The world above was gone.

The uncomfortable feeling Tom felt in the Busy Bee driveway was back. His heart and soul were firmly in the clutches of something dreadful. He felt powerless. The strength he acquired after shaking Joe's hand, the feeling of a full tank of juice and inner calmness tethered to a time limit, well, the time limit must have expired. Because Tom felt weak, and sad, and pathetic, and scared. He figured one good squeeze on his heart would finish him for good. Maybe it was time to embrace the end.

Yes, it probably was.

Tom moved on, two more steps. Then another two more steps down.

Would this descent never end?

Would *his* descent, never end?

CHAPTER 32

Four more steps and Tom bottomed out. Finally, he was at the base of the stairs. The flashlight beam caught his heavy exhalations mixing with the soupy, swirling mist. The mist was indeed roiling. What was moving the mist? What was giving it such fury? Tom figured the answer to these questions would be coming soon enough. Or, same as everything else since he had left the desert, the answers did not exist.

Tom was facing a solid, concrete block wall. The bottom of the stairwell was completely sealed off. This was a dead end. The stairwell had probably been a cleanout for a long abandoned furnace. Cemented up when the furnace was decommissioned. Tom turned and leaned his back against the wall to think. As if intelligent thought, as if any kind of thinking at all, was possible. He wondered how many functioning brains cells remained in his skull.

Tom closed his eyes, rubbed at his pulsating temples and tried to concentrate. Concentrate on what? He had no idea what he was doing. With a loaded shotgun. In an abandoned factory. In a dead town. If the damn tunnel was sealed, where was this thick mist coming from?

Something.

Tom opened his eyes. He was sensing a weakness in the wall. As if the wall wasn't as solid as it should be. Tom felt a bone chilling cold on his back. A prickling communication, kind of, 'Hello, it's me the wall'.

Tom turned and faced the blocks. Looked closely. The concrete blocks were damp. Rivulets of water were condensing on their faces. With the handle of the flashlight, he rapped on a block. The contact produced a hollow sound. Tom turned and put his back to the wall. He bent his knees for leverage and pushed. To his surprise, the wall moved. He pushed again. The wall moved. He could see dim light inside. Tom heaved against the wall. The wall moved a good foot. There was enough room for him to squeeze through. He slipped in, straining to adjust his eyes. He didn't bother thinking how he could move a concrete block wall eighteen inches.

Immediately, Tom was overwhelmed with the exact same stench he had smelled moments ago near the plank fence. His eyes watered. It was the horrid smell from twenty-five years ago. The smell of death. He covered his mouth to keep from gagging.

Did Joe Danton actually know what he was talking about? He might. Because if nothing else, the loop of smell was now closed.

Tom looked to be in some sort of subterranean passageway. Thick mist curled along the floor. Think, idiot. What the hell was this? Think. Think. Of course. He remembered his dad, a lifetime union man, talking about the tunnel rats of Morgan Steel. The tunnel system had been built during World War Two. In fact, a complete underground factory had been assembled to build bomb casings, tank parts, mortars and ammunition for the U.S. Army. The legendary reputation of the German Air Force, with the rumored trans-Atlantic range of their bombers, led to this precaution. Roosevelt figured if England fell, the Luftwaffe could take off from bases on the furthest west coast of Europe. So, contingencies were explored. Underground manufacturing was one of those contingencies. This was American ingenuity at its finest.

After the war, the tunnels were expanded to ease service repairs on below ground systems. With the massive snowfalls of the 1950's and 1960's, the tunnels became a production saver, transporting workers and supplies to perimeter buildings spread across the vast complex.

In the 1970's, systems changed at the factories. New production platforms were portable and sat above ground. Something was afoot in the manufacturing world. The platforms were easy to set up, and as the workers would find out later in the eighties, easier to take down. As the climate changed, the massive snowfalls of winter became folklore for the history books. The tunnels became obsolete. They were abandoned and sealed.

Tom was in the legendary Morgan tunnel system. One of only three tunnel systems built in the entire country. The other two were in Buffalo and Pittsburgh, the big brothers to Jamestown. These three All American cities drove the war effort and then built this country.

However.

Tunnel system meant underground system. As in, the ground ran above the tunnels. Earth and stone and buildings and vehicles and things with lots of weight. Fresh air and oxygen and breathing. All sitting above Tom's head. This did not bode well with him. At best, Tom was borderline claustrophobic.

His stomach was doing leapfrogs. The upset stomach could be from the claustrophobia. More likely, it was from the drugs, the booze, the deteriorated physical condition he was in, the visit to the Busy Bee, the apparition known as Joe Danton and the shadow lives of the skeleton people in Jamestown. Or a million other things. Don't forget the men in hoods. Men in hoods with shadow faces. And don't forget the sacrifices.

Despite the sub zero cold, Tom was working up a good sweat. Bad vibes were rolling at him from all directions. The strong clutch on his heart could be the next symptom of his first official coronary. Hopefully, it would be his last, and it would take him away from this wonderful life. This was all so beautiful, wasn't it?

When quite suddenly, a new, different, sickening feeling gripped Tom.

He *had* been down here before.

He thought for a second, and then discarded the notion.

Impossible.

He had never been down here before. Never. He had *heard* the stories. From his dad and the other factory veterans. So forget about it. Move on. What was next?

Tom was ready to walk. First he cringed. He was trying to make himself small, so the walls and ceiling wouldn't feel so oppressive. The nasty clutch on his heart, along with the smothering claustrophobia, along with his flipping, burning stomach, all finally registered in his brain.

Correctly triggering a response. The correct response was now filtering through him. The correct response, was fear.

This was all getting far too ominous.

Tom felt for the shotgun inside his jacket. No reassurance there. He had not fired a gun since he was a teenager. The dads and their boys on the great deer hunter walk through the Ohio countryside. A right of passage into manhood, way back when. Tom was drawing a bead on the magnificent buck. A rack of antlers such as he had never seen in his life. Tom closed in on the animal through the rifle sight.

The deer represented all things right about this world.

Grace. Beauty. Strength. Majesty. With a backdrop of lush green pine, and softly falling snow, this was God's country. Through the curved glass of the rifle sight, the scene resembled the fairy tale land of a snow globe.

The hunters were chasing a trophy. How stupid. How obscene. How pompously human.

Crack!

Through his scope, Tom could see the blood spurt from the buck's neck. Its head twisted in agony and shock. The convulsions, as the mighty beast hit the ground, legs still fighting for purchase, eyes blinking in disbelief. Then death came. A shadow across the forest. Tom had not been the triggerman, but he was as guilty as the executioner. The target shooting, the skeet shooting, had been fun. This wasn't.

A cloud passed over Tom's heart, that day in the forest.

His hunting career was over.

Where were all of these memories coming from?

The deer hunting. The history of the factory. His two summers working in the factory.

Why was this all so clear to him?

He had rarely a clear thought for more than two long, interminable decades.

What was happening now?

A lovely stroll down memory fucking lane.

Maybe the drug abuse and the alcohol abuse messed your brain, then straightened you right back up, and then killed you.

Is this how it worked?

Probably. Why not.

CHAPTER 33

FROM ACROSS THE FACTORY FLOOR, CARL HORNER HAD SEEN HIS TARGET descend into the underground. Carl was at the top of a similar set of stairs. Why was Forbes sneaking into this long dead factory? Was this the nest? The place where he had done his grisly work?

Carl's growing anger was deadening the humanity he had rebuilt since his retirement. The internal juices were flowing. He was back. External juices were flowing as well; Carl was tapping into the other dimension engulfing this messed up place. Yes he was. Up top in the city, Carl was sure the few of them were not alone. Down here in the underground, he had to be prepared for that as well. For a city without hydro electricity, without cell towers and without the multitude of emanations from living people, there was definitely an energy pulse of some kind. Permeating everything.

The only problems Carl foresaw were the awful buzzing in his ear and his layoff from the game. These would be definite handicaps. The buzzing in his ear was much more pronounced, this deep inside the factory gates. A foreign static was running through the air, and Carl's injured ear was acting as a receiving dish. The buzzing would definitely mask any stealth approach from his right. He would have to make adjustments. He would have to be razor sharp.

The layoff meant he would not be at his best. Carl had played the game against faster men, tougher men, bigger men, meaner men and desperate men. Dedicated fanatics, lunatics, body builders, martial arts experts, professional hit men, assassins, rapists, child killers. With a few evil women thrown in for good measure. Carl had been successful, not because he was some kind of superman. He was successful because he forced his opponents to play their weaknesses. In this game, at this level, with these stakes, it was weakness that got you killed.

There *was* one other reason why Carl Horner had been so successful.

He might be, the craziest s.o.b. to ever walk this earth.

This was the conclusion drawn from his FBI psyche exam.

CHAPTER 34

Tom dug down deep inside. He was searching for a reason to carry on, a reason to not end this madness, right this second. He needed a reason to *not* reverse back up these steps to hell, a reason to *not* drive straight back to the desert. A reason to not turn the stupid shotgun on his own dripping brain box.

The reason he knew, was his little girl. He had to be punished for what happened to her. For not being there. For not finding her. For not bringing her home to safety. For not protecting her. For wasting those days on stupid crap.

For seeing, but not reading the look in her eyes.

Part of the punishment was exactly this kind of thing, whatever he was now experiencing. Whether it was a bad trip or a figment of his diseased mind or a nasty hallucination, it all added up to punishment. The main punishment though, was the voice. Every single day, he heard the voice. Once, sometimes twice if he was lucky. Despite the torture of hearing it, and the torture of reliving the awful day, and the torture of seeing his life with Karen disintegrate, it was worth hearing her voice. Because it was Tiffy's voice. The only thing of hers he had left.

Forever and ever, two years old.

His baby girl.

Tom's headache was not relenting. Again he rubbed at his temples. He tried to breathe but it smelled awful down here. So he might as well move.

There were two ways he could go in his tunnel. One direction led to pure blackness. The other direction seemed to lighten in the distance. This decision was easy.

Tom made his way towards the light.

He moved quietly, walking on what appeared to be a concrete floor. Hard to tell, because the floor was carpeted with decades of dust. The flashlight showed this part of the tunnel had not been used for a long, long time. Between swirls of mist, he saw no footprints or rat tracks or anything that had disturbed the thick softness of the dust.

Tom ran the flashlight up and over the tunnel walls. Graffiti, dating back sixty years remained etched on those walls. 'Kill the Nazi's'. 'VICTORY'. 'Out of Vietnam'. Tom walked on, reading. 'Sergeant Pepper'. 'Stairway to Heaven'. 'United Steelworkers'. Many poetic slogans, of course various people sucked, and for a good time call, etc., etc. The passing generations all represented.

Now he was seeing everywhere, the ragged lightening bolts. Tom's heart grew colder. The mist thickened around his feet and knees. The stench intensified. He walked on.

His foot hit a lump on the floor, nearly causing him to trip!

Christ!

That scared the crap right out of him!

Tom angled the flashlight down to the ground. With his free hand he tried to waft the mist out of the way. He had to kneel down to get a proper look.

Dirty bones. Long bones. Human bones. Scraps of clothing. Tom bent closer to investigate, waving away at the inexplicable mist. Bits of rotting flesh remained on the bones.

The flesh was moving!

Tom waited for his breath and the mist to clear in the flashlight beam.

Maggots!

Tom fully understood the reason for the stench. He stood back quickly, reaching inside his coat to withdraw the shotgun. Calm down, Tommy. Get a grip. It is probably a homeless person. Or a druggie.

Wow. Could be me, Tom thought. Could be me. Although, I do have a home, if you call that piece of shit trailer I live in, a home.

Definitely, not the way to go. Dead and rotting in a cold, smelly, underground tunnel. Dead and being consumed by maggots, in a cold, smelly, underground tunnel.

The ground was disturbed ahead of the remains. The body appeared to have been dragged through the dust and dumped. Faint footprints led towards and away from the body, and then on in the direction of the light.

Footprints.

Which meant humans.

In the tunnel.

Humans who had moved this carcass.

Maybe those skeletal humans. From the restaurants.

Great.

The caution light began to blink in Tom's mind.

He moved on.

The flashlight caught a second pile on the ground. The mist was swirling up and over this pile as well. Another blast of rot hit Tom's nose. Stronger rot. A second body, except more flesh and many more squirming maggots.

A fresher kill, and now, distinct footprints.

Coming and going.

Multiple sets of footprints.

Tom noticed his hands shaking on the shotgun. He very carefully began to rack a shell. The shell dropped into the chamber and Tom willed silence as he pushed the shell on through the firing position.

Crack!

To Tom, it sounded as if lightening had struck. He winced and stood deathly still, except for his shaking hands. In the cold, perspiration ran down his spine. Tom looked down at the remains. The homeless theory, the drug overdose theory, had vanished.

This was plain and simple and obvious.

This was murder.

Off went the flashlight. Tom slid the metal tube into a pocket. There was now enough light to see without it. He moved forward, taking a personal inventory. He was freezing, but sweating. His head was throbbing. His hands shook as he squeezed the shotgun. His eyes watered with the stench around him. He was completely scared out of his wits. How he longed for his next fix. How he longed for the dry, hot sunshine of the desert. The fleeting calmness jumping into him from Joe's contact up on the surface had abandoned him completely. Speaking of, where the hell did Joe disappear to?

Was there even a Joe?

Tom's quick accounting of facts determined only one thing. Trouble. Real trouble. Because the mist was roiling now. The mist was angry.

The mist was spitting out dead bodies.

Tom could hear whispers again. Of course. Why not? The same whispers from the greasy chicken place. The same whispers from up above on the factory floor. The same whispers he had heard in the wind at the Busy Bee.

He moved on, literally shaking in his boots. He was shaking because these whispers had to be real.

Because there was no wind down here.

The whispers became low voices. The voices grew louder as Tom continued on. Some sort of chant. Tom's tunnel was coming to an end. He could see a circular courtyard, or chamber, up ahead. There was activity in the center of the chamber. Tom scanned around the walls, seeing many other tunnels radiating away into darkness. The legendary tunnel system indeed, dispersing to all sections of the vast factory grounds. Tom focused his eyes back on the activity.

Wall torches provided flickering illumination. A large man in a hooded robe was leading the chanting. Tom had seen this robe before. From the burning church in Los Angeles. Joe's macabre collection of pictures.

A group of people, hooded as well, about twelve or fifteen of them, knelt in front of a crudely constructed altar. The thick mist was everywhere. A phenomenon Tom could not hope to explain. Three other lumps lay strewn against the chamber walls near other tunnel openings. The lumps were larger than the ones he had stumbled over.

Tom knew what they were.

Beside the altar, a man was lashed to a wooden cross. The cross was made of two heavy railway ties. The top of the cross was emblazoned with a lightening bolt. Blood from the man's forehead dripped down onto his shirt. Tom narrowed his eyes. The man had been savagely beaten.

His features were swollen and distorted. His beard was matted with blood. It appeared to be Jesus Christ himself, nailed to the cross.

Jesus indeed!

It was Joe Danton!

Joe's eyes rolled open and he looked above the kneeling followers, across the chamber, making contact with Tom. A twisted smile formed on Joe's face.

Hell of a distraction there, Tom reflected.

The large hooded man picked a gleaming knife off the altar, holding it high in the air. His chants were being answered by his disciples. To Tom, the disciples seemed to be answering a reverent 'Amen', but in a language he did not know.

Something caught the corner of Tom's eye.

There was movement on the ground behind the altar.

More than the swirling mist.

Dirty blonde hair.

A small body.

Something red.

Every single part of Tom's being froze!

It looked………

It was………….

A child.

Could it really be?

After all these years?

She wouldn't be a child anymore, would she?

How many years had passed by?

She would be a young woman now.

Was it his Tiffany?

Where had she been all these years? With those things at the fast food place? The punk at the diner? The shadow people in the subdivisions? My god, was she one of them?

This was insane. Tom couldn't do it. He could not process this information, or this impossible situation. His brain couldn't work. The final break was happening, right now.

Tom Forbes had finally gone around the bend. The despair, the depression, the booze, the drugs. Tom was done.

The hooded man turned towards Joe, moving the knife down. With his free hand, he tore open Joe's shirt. The hooded man placed his hand over Joe's heart. The leader's chants intensified, as did the response from the followers. The chanting stopped. The sounds of silence filled the underground. These bastards were sacrificing more than children.

Courage. Belief. Faith. Tom had none of these.

He had nothing, period.

Therefore. He had nothing to lose.

It was strange how the dying brain rationalized things, but it did make some sense. And it no longer mattered. Because if he truly had nothing, then he also had *nothing* to lose. Who cared what happened on this bad trip? How many times had he died in his dreams, or nightmares? So what if he died once more? He would live or die for another dream. Or, he would die for real.

Again, who cared?

Not him.

Tom pushed his stomach down, sucked up his guts and stepped out of the shadows.

Into the light.

His boots crunched on loose gravel, the sound echoing around the circular chamber. Tom walked toward the gathering, watching as the hooded disciples rose as one, turning to face him, murmuring, forming a defensive pack around their leader.

"HALT!" boomed the leader, in a nauseating, terrifying voice.

Tom winced, but continued forward.

"WHO ARE YOU?" thundered the voice.

Tom couldn't see faces. He could only see shadows, under all the hoods. Shadows and hoods, similar to Joe's picture, from the burning church. Similar to Joe with his beard and his hood. Similar to Tom with his charcoaled face and football hoodie.

"WHAT ARE YOU DOING IN MY CHAMBER?"

Tom stepped past one of the lumps. Covering the lump was a worn tarp, emblazoned with the Morgan Iron and Steel logo. A hand protruded from under the tarp. The hand was badly charred. Tom had seen this before. A long, long time ago. What were these people doing? Dead bodies. Burnt bodies. Torture. Sacrifices.

And.

A small child behind this altar?

"She's here Tom! She's here!" Joe called, through swollen, bloody lips.

The leader bashed Joe across the mouth with the handle of the knife. Fresh blood spilled. A disciple's hand reached towards a back pocket. Shoved the tail of the hood jacket up. Chrome flashed in his hand as he pulled something out.

A blaze of light and a loud crack!

Tom felt the heat whiz by his ear and thud against the concrete wall behind him. Cement and dust rained against his back.

Holy shit!

They were shooting at him!

For real!

Tom leveled the shotgun.

Hesitated.

The torches dimmed. He could see his breath in the air. The chamber took on a white, wintry appearance. The snow globe. The majestic buck walked across his sightline. Tom stared in awe at the radiance, the beauty of it all. He could not pull the trigger.

One last gasp from Joe, "She's here...."

Courage.

Faith.

The deer disappeared.

More fire streaked towards him from many guns being held by hooded disciples.

This is bullshit, Tom surmised.

Bullshit.

It's a dream, right?

This is all fantasy, right?

So let's play!

A steady stream of fire was pouring at him, as gun shots echoed around the closed-in chamber.

Right back at you, assholes!

Tom pulled the trigger.

A deafening blast accompanied the firestorm leaving the barrel. The red tipped shell blew through the chest of the first disciple. The shell exited the first disciple and took the arm off a second. The shell then tore into the shoulder of a third. Three of the pricks were down. On one shot. A comic book shot. A movie theater shot. A video game shot. The type of shot only occurring in the twisted, drug soaked mind of Tom Forbes.

The kickback from the shortened barrel was nasty. Tom thought he might have dislocated his shoulder. Loud barking sounds, as more fire streaked towards him. Missiles ripped by his head. Chunks of concrete tore off the walls. No time to think. Tom pumped the shotgun, grabbed on tight, and let blast number two go. A horrific neck shot spurted blood, followed on through, tearing a hood to pieces. Two more down. Blast number three took out a stomach and knee.

Disciples dropped as Tom began to walk towards the altar. Something amazing was happening. He was *in* the movie now. Christian Bale or Daniel Craig. Untouchable. Unwavering faith, Joe had called it. Unwavering faith felt pretty damn good. Tom was fast approaching superman status. The disciples were raining fire at him, but Tom the super hero was bulletproof.

Because his little girl was here!

Right behind the altar!

Nothing would stop him this time!

Nothing!

Blast number four, then five, then six, dropped more disciples to the ground. The destruction pouring out the end of the shotgun barrel was awe inspiring. Unwavering faith, indeed. All of the disciples were now splattered on the ground, badly wounded, dead or soon to be dead. The leader released the knife, allowing it to clatter to the ground. His hands rose slowly, above and then behind his hooded head.

Tom was closer now.

Close enough to see, it *was* a child lying on the ground!

The substantial mist continued to swirl around the child. He was catching glimpses of blonde hair. And something red. He knew what the red thing was.

Tom's heart beat faster.

He definitely knew what the red thing was. If the red thing was here, then yes, do the math. One plus one. The red stuffed elephant meant Tiffy was here. Tom's eyes raced from the hooded leader, to the child, and back, desperately trying to watch the madman. More desperately, Tom was trying to identify the child. She looked young, very young and, was he really seeing blonde hair?

Could it be?

Stop procrastinating idiot! Shoot the fucking leader and go to her! Now!

Tom cranked the shotgun.

Aimed.

The leader drew back his hood.

Tom saw.

No!

It couldn't be!

The dark shadows. The stubble. The beard. The charcoal?

All mixed together?

The leader's face!

Was Tom's!

Or?

Was it Joe's?

Who the hell was it?

Had Tom been down here before?

Two and a half long decades ago?

With Joe?

Is that what was behind the wall he had constructed out of the alcohol and drugs?

The charcoal smudging. The beard. The dark hoods. Tunnels and sacrifices.

Bewilderment. Disbelief.

The leader understood. The leader began to laugh. A deep hearty laugh, filling the chamber. Echoing around the chamber. Echoing and folding and swirling and maddening.

Confusion reigned.

Tom Forbes was stunned into immobility.

Had he been down here before?

What……………what had he done?

In a rapid flash of movement, the leader's hands came down, throwing lightening bolts, or fire, or some kind of flash powder, at the ground. An ugly growl of sound accompanied the blazing light streaks.

Immediately, a wall of fire rose in front of Tom.

He jumped back as the flames shot to the ceiling. Tom could feel the intense heat of the unnatural looking fire. Blue at the bottom, then deep orange, topped with searing yellow. Tom had never experienced this type of heat, not even in his Arizona coffin. The fire formed a precise circle, surrounding the altar, the dying disciples, Joe, the maniacal leader, the child and the red thing. The red stuffed toy.

They were on one side.

Tom was on the other.

An ocean of fire separated them.

Tom tracked around the perimeter of the fire, looking for a way in. He could hear Joe struggling behind the flames.

"Walk through the fire Tom! Walk through...."

A sickening thud cut Joe off.

The fire began to roar in the underground chamber, sucking oxygen out of the tunnels. Tom felt the wind blow right past him, feeding the hungry, screaming conflagration. Dust, garbage and small chunks of god knows what were fed to the beast, incinerating on contact. Black smoke rose from the top of the fire, spreading across the chamber ceiling. The same black smoke Tom had seen from the backyard of the day care. The same black smoke that used to blanket Jamestown every single day. Tom felt a tug on his body, similar to a huge magnet. He was being drawn towards the inferno.

He had to try. She was on the other side.

Quickly, Tom yanked the flashlight out of his pocket and set it on the ground. Then the bottle of aspirin. He stepped back from the fire and set the shotgun down. Spilled out the extra shells. He sure as hell didn't want the fire to grab the ammunition and start blasting it around the chamber.

He peeled off his hunting jacket, bundled it up and edged back toward the flames, bracing himself against the strong drag. Tom tossed the jacket in. The jacket exploded in a fireball. It took less than half a second to incinerate. He carefully reached his hand toward the fire. Half a foot away the skin on the palm of his hand began to sizzle. He yanked his hand back. There was no way he would survive the ring of fire.

Courage. There was none.

Tom couldn't walk through the flames. This was no Tony Robbins fire walk. He was not superman, after all. He wasn't Daniel Craig, or Christian Bale either. He was nobody.

He wasn't even sure it was his girl on the other side.

Belief. There was none.

How could it be her? She was no longer a child. She would be almost thirty years old if she was still alive. Alive. Tiffany alive. What a concept.

Faith. There was none.

He was defeated.

Tom knelt down to the ground to escape the sucking vortex. Heat and smoke stung his face and eyes.

With a death raging, ear splitting roar, the fire vanished. The heavy black smoke cleared in an instant, as if it had never been there.

Tom stood up and looked across the circle.

Unbelievable.

There was nothing. No hooded men. No Joe Danton. No cross. No wooden altar. No little girl. Tom looked behind and along the walls of the chamber. No dead bodies. No sacrifices. No mist. No wall torches. Tom saw plenty of dust. Decades of dust. Tom saw one set of footprints leading from a tunnel, tracking to where he stood. His footprints.

Tom was alone.

Not even a black bird.

The room darkened.

There was nothing.

At the end of his tunnel, Carl Horner stopped. He snapped off his flashlight. Carl's tunnel opened to a central chamber. The chamber was lit by a tiny bit of illumination filtering down from above, via some old vent pipes. He saw Forbes standing in the chamber.

Standing there.

Staring at. Nothing.

Doing. Nothing.

Carl Horner held back in the mouth of the dark tunnel. Watching.

CHAPTER 35

Tom could not fathom the depths to which he had sunk. Was he even in the tunnels? Under the shuttered factory? In Ohio? Was he even alive? Was he stoned out of his brains in the desert? His situation was getting worse and worse all the time. If this brand of trip was what he had to look forward to, then he was definitely in the danger zone.

But this had felt so real. Without a doubt, the last few minutes of his life had seemed so incredibly existent. Amazingly true. As life should be lived. With a purpose.

He had been so close to her.

Hadn't he?

Was it her?

Only steps away?

After all these years?

Still two years old and blonde curls?

Where had she been for twenty-five years? In this town? With those things?

Joe Danton had said it was her.

There *was* no Joe Danton.

Was there?

Joe Danton, the bastard, disappeared the same day Tiffany did. So this was a new addition to his torture. Joe Danton now added to the mix. Hooded people added to the mix. Murdered people added to the mix.

Maggots and skeleton people added to the mix. Swirling mist and tunnels added to the mix. Sacrifices, added to the mix.

What next?

Tom continued standing in the gloom. Truly lost. Nowhere to go. Couldn't even begin to take the next step. Because there was no next step. There was nothing for him. An infinity of nothing. He was stuck somewhere he didn't know. There was no possible way out. A true nightmare.

A never ending nightmare.

He looked around the cleared circular chamber. On the floor he saw the flashlight, the shotgun, his pill bottle and some scattered shells.

A little further away, something else.

That something else was on the ground in the exact center of the chamber. When Tom had set his flashlight down, it must have clicked on. Because the sharp beam was pointing through the gloom, landing on the object sitting on the floor. Tom groped down and retrieved the flashlight. The beam danced as he straightened up. It was freezing cold again. The fire or the imagined fire, had nearly seared him, but now he was chilly. The flashlight beam showed his warm breath.

Tom walked to the very center of the chamber. The object on the floor was covered in dust. The object was showing red underneath the dust. Tom thought he had seen something red beside the little girl. The little girl who he also thought he had seen. Too confusing.

He reached down.

Picked up.

An elephant.

A dirty, red elephant.

Big nose and floppy ears. Soft belly. Battered. Stitched up.

A child's toy.

A *certain* child's toy.

His child's toy.

How could it be down here?

Why would it be down here?

Discolored and filthy and so old.

Tom carefully wiped the dust off the toy. When he was done, he clutched the elephant to his chest. He could see her, smell her, hear her and feel her.

And, it was good.

Memoires he had buried, emotions he had forgotten, came forward.

Rivers of emotion.

Tom wept.

Despite the stupid setback in his hockey career, despite his failure to achieve the big dream, Tom Forbes had been a very lucky man. He had found Karen, and together they had made Tiffany. Really, what else mattered? Those had been fantastic choices.

Then the bad choices. He began to stray. To walk on the wild side. Call it greed. Call it stupidity. Ignorance. Temptation. Call it weakness.

Call it human frailty.

Tom understood he had failed the test of faith.

Not only this night, but more importantly, twenty-five years ago.

If only.

If only he could get it back.

If only he could go back and do it again.

CHAPTER 36

From the opposite side of the chamber, Carl Horner emerged from the black mouth of his tunnel. He had seen enough. Enough of the nothing.

"Forbes."

Tom was startled.

A large man, dressed in a black trench coat and cowboy hat, was standing across the circle, nearly thirty feet away. Another lunatic? Another fanatic? Had they returned? Were there more of them? Tom began to back up. Backed up some more. He watched the big man move towards him. The guy was so bloody silent. He covered the distance as if he were a ghost. Tom began to reach down to the floor for the shotgun.

"Don't."

The big man opened his trench coat, revealing two side arms strapped to his waist.

Cowboy style.

"Who the hell are you?" Tom managed.

"FBI."

More insanity for Tom. He had seen this man before. Where? From twenty-five years ago? From earlier in the day? At the day care? Was this the guy who was standing on the sidewalk watching them? Was this the guy from the dark sedan in the parking lot? Last night at the crap motel?

"Where is she, Forbes?"

The FBI man pulled both pistols from the holsters, raised his arms toward Tom, and continued to approach.

"Tell me, before you die."

Tom tried to think. He could sense an anger, a hatred of monumental ferocity radiating from the FBI man. Tom stared at his adversary.

Where had he seen this man before?

"Who?" Tom stumbled. "Where is who? What on earth are you talking about?"

Something was very, very wrong.

The FBI man stopped about six feet from Tom. Tom continued staring at his opponent. A gold cop badge was pinned to the lapel of the man's coat. Tom squinted, but could not hope to read anything on it. Tom's eyes ran up to the man's face. Blurry. Focusing in and out. Shit. Was the guy's ear missing? What kind of freak was this?

This wasn't one of those skeleton things, was it?

"You've been a busy man, Forbes. I've seen the body count."

Tom was reeling.

Body count?

The disciples?

They had vanished!

The decayed bodies at the tunnel entrances?

He had nothing to do with those! Nothing! Those bodies were also gone.

The bodies he had stumbled over back in the tunnel?

He didn't know if those were still there or not.

Tom's diseased mind was swimming.

"So this was your old dumping ground? No wonder it was never found. Clever."

Dumping ground?

For what?

He had never been in these tunnels before. He had only heard about them. From his father.

Why did this all seem so familiar though?

Why did he so feel as if he had been down here before?

What was with the men in the hoods?

Carl Horner was fast running out of patience.

"What did you do with the girl?"

Who the hell was the FBI man talking about? His girl?

Tom grasped.

"Tiffany? My girl?"

"Tiffany."

"We came here to find her!" Tom spit out.

"We?"

Tom sensed this was more than a bad dream, more than a bad trip, more than insanity. He could not get a grip. He fumbled badly, trying to put something together that would make even a shred of sense. Tom opened his mouth to speak. Was his mouth still attached to his face? Still somehow connected to his brain?

"Joe Danton came to Arizona. To my place. We drove back together. Joe was up in the yard, in the mist, then down here, tied up to a......"

Joe was what? Tied up to a cross? Trussed up, a sacrifice, surrounded by gun toting maniacs? Then everyone and everything magically disappeared in a ball of fire? And rivers flowed backwards and shit actually tasted good? Tom realized how ludicrous the Joe Danton story would sound.

Except.

His little girl's red stuffed elephant. Which he held in his arm. Right now. The elephant was real enough.

Carl interrupted.

"Joe Danton? You're kidding right? Here? With you?"

"Yes. Joe was ......"

"The motel last night Forbes. I was in the parking lot. Watching you. All night long. Today, I followed you to the day care. Watched you in the backyard. I followed you to this factory. Down the stairs. Through the tunnels. Here we are. Look around. It's you and me. Nobody else. No Joe Danton. You. Me. And your little girl's toy. Interesting, wouldn't you say, you still have that toy?"

Carl could see the look of utter bewilderment on Forbes's face. The druggie had to be insane.

"You're all alone Forbes. You drove from Arizona. Alone. You ate dinner in the chicken house. Alone. A plate of microwave and two beers. You stayed at the motel last night. Signed the register. Alone. You went to the day care. Alone. You came here alone. You have your little girl's stuffed toy, right under your arm. There is only one thing missing from this picture."

Still nothing from dead brained, drug addled, Tom Forbes.

"WHAT THE *FUCK* DID YOU DO WITH THE GIRL?"

Tom cringed. His mind tripped.

What the hell was the FBI man getting at?

What was he saying?

Where was *my* girl? What did I do with *my* girl? Tiffany?

Is *that* what he was asking?

And Joe Danton wasn't real? The trip from the desert? Dinner at Champ's? The night in the motel? The incredible story? The shotgun on the floor of this chamber? None of it real?

Apparently not, according to the FBI man.

Joe not in the driver's seat of the Jeep. Joe walking right through the big waitress at the diner. Joe fading into the mist at the Busy Bee. Joe gone and never here.

Tom didn't know what was real anymore. Or what to believe. He sure couldn't express it in any language he knew.

Carl Horner re-holstered his weapons, something he had never before done in his career.

"You know what Forbes?"

What Carl had gone through on the airplane and in his rental car had been a powerful revelation. The mind could keep secrets for only so long. Eventually, life chipped away, pebble by pebble, brick by brick. Whatever was built would return from where it came.

Ashes to ashes.

"I am not going to kill you. You deserve to die a slow, painful, tortured death. Your wall of denial is starting to crumble. You keep plowing those drugs into your brain. They are not going to rebuild the wall. Not any more. You can't contain what has happened, can you? She's in your head, isn't she? Every day. Every single day. Every night. Calling. Calling for you. Soon it will be every hour and every minute of every day. You will not rest. You will never know peace."

The FBI man came forward, stopping right in front of Tom. The FBI man reached into his coat, withdrawing an old photograph. A glint of light on the agent's ring finger as he pushed the photograph towards Tom's face.

"Take it," Carl commanded.

Tom was holding the elephant tight against his chest. He tucked the flashlight under his arm and took the picture. He already knew what it was. The picture from his office. From his desk top. The picture beneath the cracked glass in the gold frame. How did the FBI man get the picture from Joe? Had the FBI man already killed Joe? What the hell was happening?

Tom free fell to a level of despair he had never thought possible.

Carl stepped back.

"I will find her Forbes."

Carl swept the chamber with his arms extended.

"You brought me here. I *will* find her."

Carl dropped one hand to his side. The other hand pointed right at Tom.

"*Not* you. You are already dead. You just don't know it."

The FBI man turned on Tom and silently walked back to his tunnel. He was gone.

Tom was stunned.

What had he done?

He crumpled to the ground, clutching the red elephant, the picture and the flashlight.

He remained motionless.

Time passed.

The footprints leading out of and back into the FBI man's tunnel disappeared.

Dust to dust

One gigantic question remained. Above all other questions.

What, had he done?

CHAPTER 37

Tom Forbes calculated, only two choices remained. One was to knock down the rest of the bricks. To look behind the walls. At the truth. To see what he had done. To finally find his little girl. Did he dare? Did he have the courage?

Courage. Faith. He knew what his reserves in these categories were. Zero. Tom was terrified of this option. Option two would take no faith.

Option two it would be.

Tom played the flashlight onto the old picture. The blonde hair, the beautiful face, the innocence. The eyes. The eyes that would haunt him forever.

Tom tucked the picture into his shirt pocket. Stood up. Stepped over to the shotgun. Reached down and picked it up off the dusty floor. He cracked the barrel and checked. Yes, there was one round sitting in the chamber. He closed the gun. He didn't bother with the extra shells or the pill bottle. He wouldn't need those any more. Soon, there would be no more headaches. No more waves. No more drowning. No more speeding bullet trains. No more falling buildings. No more Joe Danton. No more skeletons. No more of the rot and gray clouds and dust and death of Jamestown. No more of anything. No more of him.

And the voice would be silenced forever.

Tom retraced his path through the tunnel. The two lumps of bone and rotting flesh he had stumbled upon were gone. The graffiti was still on the walls, but the mist along the floor was also gone. As well, the awful putrid smell was gone. He squeezed through the opening in the concrete block wall. At the bottom of the steps Tom looked up. Things were only slightly brighter up there. He climbed the steps out of the tunnel system.

At the top of the steps Tom paused. He had counted only ten steps on his way up. Had he not gone down twenty, or thirty steps? Sure he had. Tom turned the flashlight on the concrete block wall at the bottom. The wall was already closed, once again sealing the tunnels.

How had the wall closed?

By itself?

Tom remembered leaning hard against the wall to open it. Now it was closed. Had the wall even *been* open? Had he just emerged from those tunnels? Or had he been in those tunnels a long time ago? Twenty-five years ago? Were the stories from his dad coming to life in his burnt out brain?

Unexplainable.

Tom looked closer at the steps. Layers and layers of dust had somehow recovered the steps.

There were no footprints.

No sign of disturbance.

He had not even been down there.

Holy hell.

This was too unreal.

Tom set the flashlight on the ground. He didn't need it anymore. He walked across the factory floor. The black bird was back in the rafters, watching the solemn figure troop by below. The bird looked sad, if it was possible for a bird to look sad. Tom went through the steel man door, creaking it open, the door creaking shut behind him. Outside, the early evening had arrived.

He clutched the red elephant and the shotgun.

The elephant was real.

The shotgun was real.

The picture in his pocket was real.

These things were as real as anything he had ever known in his life.

Snow was falling again. Wet, slushy snow. Dirty snow. Gray snow.

Tom's skull throbbed.

His body ached.

His soul screamed.

It was time.

He fumbled back into the Jeep. Placed the shotgun and the elephant on the seat beside him. The keys were still in the ignition. Tom cranked over the motor.

The Jeep seemed to drive of its own volition, taking Tom Forbes with it. Rolling south away from the factory and the lake. The Jeep bumped up over a set of ancient railroad tracks. And stopped. Tom looked left down the tracks, and then he looked right. He could sit on these tracks and wait for his turn. The rails were rusted and flaked. The heavy, tarred wooden ties were crumbling. Dead weeds poked out of the gravel between the ties. No. It wasn't going to happen here. The time of the speeding bullet train was over. The bullet train had been replaced by the ghost called Joe Danton, and hooded men, and lightening bolts and horrible past deeds.

Tom drove on through the barren subdivisions and past the abandoned high school. There was no need to stop at the day care. He had already checked the day care off his bucket list. The Jeep plowed on, moving through the lifeless downtown core, following the Miracle Mile. There were no other passing vehicles and no pedestrians. There was more decay, more destruction, and good old despair.

The Jeep pulled off the Miracle Mile, stopping in the garbage strewn alley behind the former Burns, Henderson Accounting building. Tom could park anywhere he chose because the lot was dead empty. He could use slot one or slot two or his old slot eight, it didn't matter. There was no more totem poll of power at Burns Henderson. There wasn't even a red Ford Escort in the parking lot. All so sad. The once magnificent brick structure was weather beaten and graffiti smeared. What a mess.

Tom got out and walked toward the rear entrance. He was carrying both the shotgun and the red elephant. He checked the chamber of the shotgun once more. The final shell remained. Perfect. One shell is all it was going to take. He tried the door. Locked. Locked for years. Tom stepped back, then placed a hard kick against the door. Again. The aged lock mechanism held firm, fending against any illegal entry. There was no way he was getting past this door.

Tom took the narrow walkway between buildings. Came out on the front sidewalk. Things were as gloomy and foreboding out here as they were in the alley. Tom looked around the street front. Nothing and nobody as far as he could see. He moved under the overhang of the main entrance. He assaulted the front door with his boot.

Again.

A third time.

The door gave way, swinging in.

Tom stepped into his old workplace and into the past.

Déjà vu swept over him, a powerful tidal wave. It wasn't déjà vu, was it? Couldn't be. He had definitely been here before. In his other life.

Same set up, same décor. So very little had changed after he left for the desert. In the gloom under the cloudy sky, it was all blacks and grays.

Tom's great returning memory allowed the hustle and bustle of the past to file back in. Echoes of a time before. Some talking, some laughter. The sensual, fresh, lilting, girly voice that once drove him crazy. Over by the coffeemaker, Lisa. So young. So hot. So alive. Wiggling her ass in his direction, pretty much sending him into apoplexy. Smiling at Tommy, the private smile she saved exclusively for him. Right. She was probably forty-five, and married with children. Or divorced and starting over. Or a skeleton creature. Or not. What a fool he had been.

The place was dusty and held a damp, mildewed perfume. The mildewed perfume was tinted with the smell of raw sewage. There was definitely a commonality amongst the smells of Jamestown. Sewage, maggot-rotted flesh, poison tear gas and white mist. They all shared the theme of corrosive death.

Tom made his way towards his old office. The last office before the washrooms. Number eight on the depth chart. He stopped at the door. There was a different name plate bolted to the door. Of course, he had been replaced. He pushed open his old door.

Tom felt the breath being sucked right out of his lungs. The same chair. The same desk. He stepped up to the desk and rolled out his dusty old chair. Tom sat. Even the computer monitor was still there. Covered in dust, not hooked up to anything. Looks as if the fancy machine of the future never did make it at Burns Henderson.

A mess of papers was strewn on the desk. Somebody else's papers. Somebody else's life. Tom let out a heavy sigh. Now, nobody's papers. Once again, tears welled in his eyes. He could sure use a fix. Guess what? Now, he would take that fix. His final fix. An avalanche of despair was smothering him. Burying him. The end was here. It was definitely his time.

Tom cleared some of the dusty papers out of the way. As he did so, mites, pollen, fluff and what had to be decades of gray ash, all swirled in the air. Tom placed the red elephant on the desk. Beside the elephant, he laid the photograph. He sat back in the chair, cradling the shotgun.

There was nothing left in Tom Forbes.

Bankrupt.

It *really* was time.

CHAPTER 38

Carl was making his way through the underground tunnel system. There had been some thin light in the large circular chamber, but now his flashlight was once again required. Back thirty yards or so on his way in, Carl had passed a fork in his tunnel. He happened to guess the correct path in his pursuit of Tom Forbes. Now he would explore the other fork. On the off chance there was something further down here. There had to be something more down here, right Mr. Forbes?

The prickly sensation of 'more than meets the eye' was extremely strong.

Carl stopped at the fork.

There were actually *two* other tunnels he could take. Strange. He could have sworn there was a perfect 'Y' when he first came in. Carl had taken the right fork of the 'Y'. Now there were two left forks. How had he missed such an important detail? Such a giant detail? Had he languished too long in retirement? Had his skills dulled so quickly?

Carl picked the next tunnel. He slowly made his way, the flashlight beam playing from the dust caked floor, up the walls to the ceiling and back to the floor. At the thirty pace mark, the end of the tunnel lightened. Ten more yards and he was right back in the chamber.

How weird was this?

Forbes was gone from the space. The red toy he had been carrying was also gone. As was the shotgun. Carl walked to the center of the chamber and looked down. Left behind were some shotgun shells and a large bottle of white pills. Carl bent and picked up one of the shells. He brought his flashlight to bear. The shell was heavy, and did not resemble any shotgun ammo he had ever seen. Carl had seen all kinds of shotgun ammo in his career. This was really different. The business end of the shell was red and rounded smooth. It resembled a small missile. What was this? Chinese made? Russian made? Carl looked at the other shells. They were all the same. Carl pocketed the shell and returned to the tunnel. He backtracked forty paces to the now three way intersection.

Carl stopped dead in his tracks.

Shit.

There were now *four* tunnels branching from the main line, not three.

And not two, as he had seen on his first trip in.

What the hell was going on?

Okay, okay, something was happening.

The tingles were running wild through Carl. As if a current of water was blowing through the tunnel system.

Was there some sort of gas or contaminant?

Something playing with his mind?

Carl looked at the dust on the ground. The two tunnels he had traversed which led him to the chamber showed clear footprints. His footprints. Carl looked back down the main tunnel at the way he had come in. Clear footprints in the dust as well. So he wasn't hallucinating.

All right. He would try the third tunnel. Thirty more paces. The flashlight beam bouncing through the dust. The tunnel lightened a touch. Ten more paces. He was back in the chamber.

Shit mother goose.

What on earth was this, Groundhog Day?

The chamber was still empty, save the pill bottle and the remaining shotgun shells.

Was this some sort of purposeful design by the factory engineers?

For what possible reason?

Three tunnels leading to the exact same chamber, all from the same intersection?

This made no sense.

Carl could at least test the theory. He began walking around the chamber, examining the floor where each of the tunnels converged. Carl counted sixteen entrances to the chamber. Therefore, four of them should have footprints coming in. The three he had made, and the one Tom Forbes used.

Carl inspected the tunnel entrances. He found the first set of footprints. Had to be Forbes', it was on the opposite side of the chamber Carl had originally entered, and it was a different set of tread marks. Carl circled, looking, looking. Not that one. Nor that one. Nor that one. There. Footprint set number two. The tunnel he a moment ago, had emerged from.

Carl then circled all the way round the chamber, back to Forbes's tunnel. Only the two tunnels showed footprints. This was Carl's third trip in. There *had* to be two more tunnels showing footprints. There wasn't. Carl keenly suspected he had finally tapped into the sinister river running through Jamestown, both above ground and in these tunnels.

Carl retreated back through his latest tunnel to the junction. He sort of expected, but realistically, he didn't.

He wasn't disappointed.

There were now *five* branches off the main line tunnel.

Carl contemplated. This is probably not the place to be. Caught up in this river, this river of what?

A thought rattled around his brain. This is going to sound crazy, but it seems as if someone or something is throwing up barriers to prevent me from reaching the last tunnel. If I keep selecting the next tunnel, nothing will change; I will always reach the empty chamber. When I get back to the junction, there will be yet another tunnel added to the mix. And so on and so on, forever and ever, but with no amen.

What to do?

Get out of this current of insanity and get topside. The smart thing to do. The prudent thing to do. Or, finish the job, skip ahead and grab the furthest tunnel. For these delay tactics to be happening, there must be something mighty important in that far tunnel.

All makes sense, right? Only in Jamestown.

Carl would indeed skip the fourth, and take the fifth tunnel. He stepped into the furthest left hand branch and began to make his way through the dark. Flashlight working. Thirty paces. Nothing but virgin dust on the floor. He should be seeing the darkness alleviate any second.

Ten more paces. He should be at the chamber. He wasn't. Ten more paces. Carl kept going. Ten more paces. Ten more paces. Twenty more paces. Thirty more paces.

He was in deep. Very deep.

Finally, stop.

A dead end.

A solid block wall.

Shit.

Carl sniffed at the air. The air smelled musty and old and uncirculated, but he couldn't detect any contaminants. This meant squat, because so many contaminants were odorless. Carl leaned against the wall. When he realized, the tingling sensation was gone. Completely. It had faded to nothing.

Wait a minute.

Something was at his back. Carl pressed himself against the wall. The wall seemed to shimmer. Only slightly. Carl turned and looked at the wall. The blocks and the mortar looked ancient. He moved the flashlight beam over the surface.

Some of the mortar wasn't as ancient as the rest.

Carl pulled out his knife. Hit the release switch. A five inch blade snapped out. Carl dug the blade into the mortar. The mortar chipped and began to crumble. Carl worked faster. More mortar fell. He was able to dig enough mortar out to get a finger hold. Carl broke the mortar at all four corners to weaken the security of the block. Then he returned to the finger hold and carved out a hand hold. Then a second hand hold.

The blade was clicked back into its body and put away. Carl fit as many fingers as he could in the shallow space he had carved out, gripped hard, and began to pull. The block was heavy, but it started to give. Crumbled mortar fell as the block slid forward. Another few inches and the block was pulled completely free.

Carl dropped the block on the ground and aimed his flashlight in.

Not good.

A cop always hopes for closure in this type of case. However. In a case such as this, closure is the last thing a cop wants to find. Because closure means the case is actually finished. Done. Over. Unsolved becomes solved.

The paperwork goes in a drawer or in a file cabinet. Or in a storage room.

And hope has died.

Carl set the flashlight down. Frustration. Gloom. Disappointment. Internal temperature percolating. He heaved the second block out. His anger began to simmer. Then the third block. Then the fourth. Ten blocks were soon piled on the floor. The anger was becoming a rage. Decades of dust rose up and swirled in the tight air. Carl hewed the ugly concrete wall down, using the power he had developed from chopping all of that Canadian wood. He felt his biceps and forearms and shoulders flexing and knotting, supplying an enormous amount of force. When he was finished, he was perspiring mightily. He gasped for air to inflate his chest. He coughed loudly as the dust joined the air filling his lungs. Finally, he returned to equilibrium.

Carl looked behind him at the mountain of blocks he had built. This was no figurative wall. This had been a very real wall. It didn't get any realer than concrete blocks and mortar. Carl stepped forward into the void he had created. The flashlight was back in his hand. He moved the light around.

Candles and matches.

Carl found them both.

He looked at the match book. A popular brand. Once. Made in America too. He lit four candles with the old matches. Both candles and matches worked. Yes, we used to make good stuff in this country. Carl took a step back as the candles reached their zenith.

Bringing bright light to a place of darkness.

No.

Not good.

Not good at all.

Carl felt every gasket in his body begin to weaken. The pressure inside him was mounting. Something was about to blow.

He blinked his eyes.

He was seeing remnants of colored clothing.

A handful of small toys.

He paused. His mind working hard.

Then Carl saw the small package.

He came to a full stop.

Just as he had, back in his cabin in the woods. When he read the email. The email from his old buddy at the bureau, Jack Ramsey. The email had been the accelerant, the match, lighting this entire, sorry journey.

Carl was staring at the package.

The package was *about two years old in size.*

Carefully wrapped in swaddles of blankets.

Everything layered in fine dust.

Carl took a deep, deep breath.

A loud exhalation.

A terrible sigh.

He couldn't even think. His whole being had gone mute. He *still* had the capacity to be surprised, after all these years. More than surprised. Shocked. More than shocked. Run over by a transport truck doing seventy fucking miles an hour.

In his shock, his thirty three years of training took over.

The guns on his belt were calling.

He knew what he had to do.

Carl backed away.

He let the candles burn in the shrine. He would return later and deal with this.

First, the loose end he had allowed to exit these catacombs?

Had to be tied up.

Carl slowly retraced his steps out of the long tunnel. It was a never ending journey, because he was bearing such a heavy burden. Grief. Yes, that old chestnut.

Mysteriously enough, the footprints he had made on the way into this tunnel had already begun to fade. The further he pushed from the shrine, the weaker his footprints got. The current of Jamestown was returning, stronger than ever. Carl was thinking about the possibility of being trapped underground forever. Lost in this maze of magically appearing tunnels.

Finally, he arrived at the 'Y' intersection.

Carl stopped.

Once again, there were only two forks.

Not five, not four, not three. Two. The original two. Yes indeed, this place is truly fucked up.

Carl walked on down the main line, reaching the staircase he had descended. His guns were calling. The guns were putting life back in his steps. He bounded up the concrete, coming onto the empty plant floor. He was striding now, purpose was returning, gliding past the remaining relics of industrial history. He exited the forge on the opposite side of the building Forbes had used.

Outside, it was gray gloom, and sewage air, and wet flakes were falling. Another shitty weather day in the shithole of Jamestown. Carl fired up the rental car and drove away from the forge.

It shouldn't be hard to find Tom Forbes. Daddy. You bastard.

There were Jeep tracks in the slush showing Carl the way. Across the plant property, through the blown out gates, over a set of railroad tracks, through the subdivisions, past the condemned high school. The Jeep tracks were holding. On towards the downtown, finally picking up the Miracle Mile. Not a single pedestrian could be seen. Not a single car was moving. Not a single set of vehicle prints other than the Jeep's, were showing. This was a movie set in the days right before or right after the shooting was complete. Dead empty. A ghost town, but full of ghosts.

The Jeep had veered off the Miracle Mile up ahead. Then turned left into a garbage strewn alleyway. Carl saw the Jeep parked up behind a formerly grand brick building. The back door of the building had been booted, a few times. The back door had held. Carl saw the remnants of man tracks leading to a narrow walkway between the brick buildings.

Forbes.

Carl simply killed the rental car's engine in the middle of the alleyway. He exited the vehicle. The big guns were out in a flash.

Carl walked across the slushy parking lot to the back door. Definitely, no entry here. Carl moved to the walkway. Followed it to the front street. The dead front street. Not a soul in sight. Carl saw the front door, violated and ajar. With his foot he pushed the door further, enough so he could slip in.

An office suite, it once was.

A funeral home, it would soon become.

CHAPTER 39

Tom pumped the shotgun, chambering the final round, and turned the weapon towards him. He wedged the gunstock against the desk. Opened his mouth.

The feelings of cowardice he had been carrying, were gone. The weakness preventing this from happening all of these years, was gone. It was indeed, over. Tom tasted acrid gun residue as his mouth slipped over the barrel. His thumb found the trigger. Ten seconds left in the game. Ten seconds to die. Tom began to apply pressure to the trigger. This was going to be ugly. Real ugly. The kickback of the shotgun had nearly dislocated his shoulder. What would it do to his head? No matter. Nobody would ever find him, in this place of nothing.

The countdown began.

Ten.

Tom closed his eyes. Inhaled his final breath. A kaleidoscope of his life began to flash across his mind.

Nine.

His parents. Golden. Seen through little baby Tommy's eyes. Unquestioned joy. Unquestioned love. Unquestioned everything.

Eight.

So excited, running down the stairs at Christmas, dad leading, then Tommy, then mom. The thick, bushy green tree, covered in colored lights and decorations. The splash of fancy wrapped presents underneath the tree.

Seven.

The winning goal for his high school hockey team. His first girlfriend. His first kiss. The NCAA championships. College and fraternity brothers. The big trophy.

Six.

The first day he laid eyes on Karen. The magic of the moment. Wedding day. His beaming, ecstatic grandparents. His proud mom and dad. The fabulous honeymoon in Barbados. The incredible sunsets with Karen at the patio bar. Her white bikini and her copper skin.

Five.

The moment his humanity shook, the arrival of Tiffy. The new queen of his castle. Kicking and screaming her way into the world. The tiny bundle of energy. Already moving.

Four.

Tears fell freely now. Deep, deep inside, Tom knew this was wrong. This was not the way out. He had no right to waste a precious life. His precious life. What about his girl's precious life? How was he honoring her?

Three.

He wasn't. By taking this way out, he was shitting all over her grave. Where ever her grave might be. He was *dishonoring* her memory, dishonoring her two short years of living.

Two.

Tom wasn't yet sure what unwavering faith was, but he understood without faith, there remained only despair. He was so sick and tired of despair. *Could* he make something out of his miserable existence?

One.

Tom saw it in his subconscious.

The flash on the FBI man's finger! A ring! An emblem on the ring!

A lightening bolt!

Zero.

Wait..............!

Too late.

The forward kinetic pressure on the trigger was past the point of no return. Tom could sense this through his thumb. He tightened his eyes further to embrace the end.

CHAPTER 40

Carl heard the shotgun being pumped. The crack reverberated right through the office. Carl froze inside the doorway. The piece of shit druggie might be making a last stand. Hard to believe. Drugs could make you do anything. Add to it the sick place they were in, and the possibilities became endless.

Fine with Carl.

Let's dance, asshole.

Carl scanned the gray office.

He saw desks, chairs, computer monitors, plastic plants, garbage cans and rows of filing cabinets. Papers were scattered everywhere. Dust covering everything. Twenty-five years of dust. There had been no attempt to clean up, no attempt to sell off. Nothing. Turn out the lights, lock the door and walk away. Get the hell out of Dodge.

Carl was looking for signs of Tom Forbes. Because of his hearing impediment, Carl could not pinpoint the exact location of the shotgun pump.

As his eyes adapted to the gray gloom, Carl could see the trail of footprints heading to the rear of the office. The rear of the office held the individual cubicles, and Tom Forbes. Moving quietly, a large cat stalking with skills honed in the Canadian forest, Carl followed the footprints back. He arrived at a hallway with four offices branching to the left, and five offices branching to the right. At the very end of the hallway were the washrooms. The big shot offices would be first, the prime real estate with the window views. The small shots and secretaries would be further back in the windowless cubes. Tom Forbes was a small shot. His office was probably the last one. Nearest the shitter.

Carl continued back. Both of his big guns were leading the way. Sweeping a field of fire in front of him. As expected, the first two offices were spacious, with their own windows. These would have held the big bosses. The fancy shelving and wardrobes complemented the large, manly desks.

The next three offices were smaller and darker. No windows. Less impressive furniture. Smaller desks. The final three offices were smaller yet, with inexpensive, throwaway furniture. Carl picked up a strong tension coming out of the very last office. As if a major mental or supernatural battle was being waged. Carl focused. Was it the buzzing in his ear, or was there some type of white noise coming from the last room?

He crept up to the final doorway.

It was wide open.

Occupied.

This was it.

There was no magic way to enter this room in perfect safety. If Forbes was awake and aware and pointing the jacked shotgun at the doorway, the chances weren't good for Carl. The shot would easily spray the entire entrance, from top to bottom, from side to side. The shot would be coming hard, because this last room would be tiny. There was no point in doing the floor roll or sticking one hand in and firing. That was television crap. Scripted and acted. Not Carl Horner, real world methodology.

Carl was ready. He checked himself. He didn't know if his ear was tricking him, but he was sure the tension in this last room was audible. What the hell was going on in there?

On three then.

One.

Two.

With hair trigger pressure on the pistol firing pins, Carl stepped into the doorway.

Forbes was sitting in a chair.

At a desk.

With his back to the doorway.

Totally unaware of Carl's presence.

A red toy elephant and the picture of the little girl sat on the desk. Forbes was sitting stock still, humming, in some sort of trance. What the hell? Carl stepped in closer. Arms straight out, weapons trained on the skull of his target. The carpeting underfoot made his approach soundless. As did the twenty-six years of insulating dust layered over top. Carl was close enough to tap Forbes on the back of the head with his pistols.

Shit!

A shotgun was wedged against the edge of the desk, the barrel in Forbes' mouth!

The gun was probably loaded with one of those mean looking, red tipped shells.

Forbes' finger was on the trigger, white with pressure.

He was squeezing the fucking trigger!

Carl's brain raced.

If the druggie pulled through on the trigger, he would splatter his own skull to bits. The push through of the shot would rip through Carl's midsection. Could get extremely nasty.

No time for that game.

Shoot to kill.

Play to thrill.

Carl stepped in close.

For the little girl.

Carl pulled the trigger.

Both of them.

CHAPTER 41

A BLAZING WHITE LIGHT FLASHED.

Silence followed.

It was over.

There was no sound.

No heartbeat.

No breathing.

No sight.

No thought.

No hope.

No chance.

Nothing.

Was this death?

Was it?

If it was, how could he still be having thoughts?

Tom's eyes opened. He could see nothing but remnants of the sun, or a blinding light being reflected off of metal. A ring? A badge? A mirror? What was it? His imagination again? Tom's eyes cleared. He could see the long steel barrel running from his mouth to the desk. On the desk, sat the elephant and the picture of his girl.

Something else.

Something was commanding his attention.

All of his attention. As if his life depended on it.

Which it did.

Under the desk.

An overflowing trash can had tipped two decades ago, spitting crumpled papers onto the floor. Sticking out from under the papers, Tom saw the glint of a dirty, gold shape. Something twigged, deep, deep inside him. It couldn't be. The picture. The picture was on the desk. Right in front of him. The FBI man had given it to him. Taken it from Joe. How could the picture frame be under this desk? It had to be a different picture. It couldn't be his. It must belong to the next guy who had sat at this desk. Tom's thumb was frozen on the trigger. His eyes flickered to the desk top.

The picture of his angel *was* on the desk, beside the red elephant.

But wait!

The picture was being reduced to gray ash, right before his eyes!

The picture was *gone*.

The elephant began to crumble next. A small pile of ash was replacing the stuffed toy. The pile leveled off on its own. The ash became dust. It mixed with all the other dust on the desk.

The elephant was *gone*.

Did that really happen?

Did it?

What did this mean?

Did it mean, that underneath this desk, the picture was……..?

Tom willed the pressure off the trigger.

Perspiration poured off his forehead.

The trigger remained in no man's land, preparing to strike the hammer.

Tom's mind was suddenly clear. Crystal clear. Tuned. Razor sharp. Even clearer than when he was blowing the disciples to kingdom come.

Tom could see the trigger move forward, a micron.

Tom could hear his heart beat. Thud, thud thud.

He willed his heart to a near stop. The trigger came to a near stop. Then a *full* stop.

Tom heard his heart start up again. Thud, thud thud.

Or was it the damn police helicopter from so long ago, beating in his ears? Or was it the ominous thumping of the steel works, reverberating in the ground?

For a second time in the past two seconds, Tom willed his heart beat silent.

Silence. Silence. Heart not beating. More silence.

A miracle was required. A miracle was delivered.

The trigger moved back a micron. Back another micron. Then back a little more. Finally. Click! As the trigger reset. The thumping returned to Tom's ears. He took his mouth off the barrel and exhaled the biggest breath of his life. He moved the shotgun away from his face, placing it on the desk.

An incredible dry flush ran through his body. A thousand spiders skipped down his spine. Tom felt a tapping on the back of his skull. A hard, metallic tapping.

He whipped his head around!

What the hell was that massive sensation? *Right at his back?* What the *fuck?*

Then it was gone.

Vanished.

Holy shit. That, was insane.

Tom turned back and faced his desk. His eyes went under the desk. He bent forward, sliding to the edge of his chair, the ancient spring creaking in protest as it compressed for the first time in twenty-five years. Tom reached under the desk, stretching, stretching his fingers. His fingers walked over dust and old papers and cobwebs. He was able to grasp the corner of the gold frame.

Tom lifted the frame and pulled it towards him. He ran his fingers underneath and could feel the cracked glass surface. He paused. Cracked glass? What was it about a cracked glass covered picture? Dare he? Ever so slowly, he turned the picture over. He stared hard.

It was too dark under the desk, so he backed out.

Wham!

Tom felt an immense jolt to the back of his skull!

The ancient chair spring had boomeranged, sending Tom's head straight up against the heavy wood desk.

Perspiration broke out on his forehead, ran down his back and soaked his arm pits. His body began to tingle. Tom was on his way to passing out. He managed to secure his ass in the chair as he thrashed in and out of the black, teetering at the edge of consciousness. The lump was already growing on his head.

Wow! Did that ever sting!

The pain roared in his skull as he fought to stay out of the black. The pain seemed to be far too amplified for what he had done to himself. It was almost as if he had been slammed really hard on top of an existing injury.

Barely, Tom was able to move towards a more stable, but extremely groggy and disoriented state. As if he was waking from a long hibernation and possessed minimal cognitive skills, and limited motor skills. He shook the staleness out. The motion didn't help his headache.

Tom stared at the picture he had managed to hold on to through his latest folly. Good grief. It *was* her picture after all. The picture swam in and out of focus. The cracks he had felt in the glass receded and the face of his beautiful little girl appeared. The glass was smooth and perfect, and wow, what a shot. Sharp and clear, wrinkle free, no dust or dirt, a magnificent photo. How did the picture get from Joe in the Jeep, to the FBI man in the tunnel, to the top of this very desk, and then into this picture frame under the desk? How indeed? More questions.

Suddenly!

The sinister cracks returned, covering the glass and obliterating Tiffy's face. The cracks receded. Returned. Receded. Returned.

Something was wrong!

The bottom of Tom's stomach dropped out. He felt the cold sweat spreading all over his body. Panic took hold. Tom looked at his hockey trophy, perched proudly on the desk.

What the hell!

The trophy wasn't there, a minute ago, was it?

Had he not taken the trophy? When he cleaned out his office? Twenty-five years ago?

Sure he had.

Why on earth would Tom's replacement keep the trophy?

No way. The trophy was Tom's pride and joy. He would *not* have left it behind.

However, in his despair and loss, had he left the trophy behind? He could have. Tom had been pretty messed up when he blew out of

Jamestown. The trophy would have been a sad memory of a much better time. So possibly, he had left the trophy. He couldn't picture it anywhere in his Arizona trailer. Yet, the earlier question remained. Why would Tom's replacement keep his trophy?

Tom didn't have enough remaining brainpower to add this mystery to his file. He eyeballed the trophy. The dusty, golden hockey sticks were badly bent. The fine cherry wood base was cracked and chipped. It appeared as if the trophy had fallen, or been whacked about. Not maintained as he had. Polished and clean and proud.

Tom rubbed his skull and sat in his own sweat. He was a sick, sick man. He needed a fix, a shot, a beer, a case of beer, a hug, a friend, something. He was tired. He was sore. He was a mess. Holy crap.

Tom stared at the trophy, confused by the world he had created.

Whispers.

Tom could hear them.

Again.

Growing louder.

Why not?

Maybe the skeleton folks were coming for him. Maybe this was the reason he had left the desert. To come home. To be with the skeleton people.

What could possibly happen next?

CHAPTER 42

What could possibly happen next?

Before Tom's unbelieving eyes, the dust on the desk began to melt away. What? The hell?

Papers on the desk top began to arrange themselves in order, settling in neat piles.

Shivers racked Tom from toe to head.

How was this possible?

More whispers.

They were louder.

Almost speaking.

The trash can under his desk flipped over and stood up!

"Jesus!" Tom barked aloud.

The garbage ran up the sides of the can and settled inside.

No! That did not just happen! Could not have happened!

Lights clicked on throughout the long deserted office. Tom grabbed the arms of his chair and held on for the ride.

The golden hockey sticks on the trophy straightened.

Unbelievable!

The cherry wood returned to its original polished glory.

What had to be a lightening strike, Tom jumped, as the four-pack fluorescents above his old desk roared to life!

Color flushed up the office walls and across the carpet.

Whoa!

This was too much.

Just say no to drugs, people.

The phone on his desk was clean, shiny and black. It beckoned Tom. He relinquished his grip on the arm of the chair and reached to pick up the phone. Tom heard a dial tone. He quickly replaced the phone in the cradle, as if the thing was possessed.

A dial tone? In Jamestown? *Nothing* worked in Jamestown.

The floor under his desk was now spotless carpet. Even the clear, plastic rug protector was back under his roller chair.

His trousers?

Clean and pressed!

His shoes?

Black and shiny!

His white shirt?

Crisp and bright.

A red tie hung below his neck.

Clean and snappy.

His jacket, fitted and pressed.

He opened and closed drawers. Everything was in place. His brand spanking new computer monitor sat on the desk. Waiting for the tech people. Yes, everything was in perfect order.

For a second, Tom had no idea who he was, where he was, or even *what* he was. Something about a dark corridor with deep rooms and skating. And sick people, looking out of the rooms as he skated past.

The second passed.

The clock on his desk.

One minute past two p.m.! Could it be?

The big event was starting!

Where had the time gone?

Tom stood quickly. Blood rushed to his brain, magnifying his headache. The throbbing spiked sharply, catching him unprepared. Tom's stomach flew into his mouth. The taste of fire and venom smothered his tongue. He reached for his trash can. Too late. He wretched violently, splashing the top of his desk. With a putrid mix of breakfast, coffee and stale whiskey. Tom looked at the mess. The barf of all ages. He couldn't believe so much crap was in him.

The loud whispers.

Were now voices.

Tom whipped his head around, searching. Who the hell was talking? He saw no one. There was no one at his open door. No one in the hallway. What on earth were these voices? Tom nearly vomited again. The smell of the mess on his desk. Putrid. Nasty. The smell of death.

Tom stared at the disgusting sight. The mess had come from inside him. Inside his being. Is this what he was doing to himself? Brutal.

He couldn't do it any more. He brushed the puke covered files and papers into the trash can. Placed a binder over top to seal the stench in. He would deal with this later.

Tom opened his bottom desk drawer and withdrew the whiskey flask. He straightened up, fishing in his jacket pocket for the drugs. His hand found the glass vial. Tom looked at the small flask and the smaller vial. Small but powerful. Small, but very consequential. They had both seemed to be good ideas, but they weren't. This was not a road he wanted to go down. These two habits had to go. Right now.

The phone began to ring. Tom looked at it with dread. The ringing continued. Calling for him. Ringing, demanding his attention. He shifted the vial and the flask into his jacket pockets. Tentatively, he picked the phone up.

"Forbes," he answered in a small voice.

"Tommy baby! It's Mike at the bar! I need your picks for the weekend games! Go Twins!"

Tom dropped the receiver on the desk. This habit was also being moved to the trash bin of history. How stupid was he? Christ. Karen and he were working hard, working long, to support the lifestyle they hoped to build. The consequence of their choice had Tiffy in the day care. So, he was ready to piss away money on booze and drugs and betting? What an idiot. Time to man up, Tommy boy.

Tom made his way to the office washroom. Pushed through the door. Slammed the shitter stall door shut behind him. Pulled out the whiskey bottle. Twisted the cap off. Poured the golden liquid into the toilet. Tom tried to drop the vial of powder in the bowl, but it stuck to his hand. He tried again, but still it stuck. Stuck in his brain were the beautiful highs he was getting off the stuff, plus the considerable financial investment.

Where could this magic powder take him? Where indeed? Don't be a moron. Do not throw it out. Why don't you finish the stuff? You already paid for it. It's non-addictive, totally harmless, and anyway, you can't get your money back. Don't waste it!

Voices.

Talking to him?

On the third try, his hand let the vial go. He pushed the toilet tank lever and watched the swirling waters take his poisons away. The flush echoed in his brain, an overpowering cleansing sensation running through him. Tom exited the stall and dropped the empty booze bottle in the garbage can. Over to the sink, he splashed cold water onto his face and into his stinking mouth. Gargle, gargle and spit. Repeat. Cold water over the back of his skull. Damn did that hurt. A quick dry with paper towels and out of the washroom he went.

Bam!

Right into Lisa.

The perky smile left her face when she saw him.

"Mr. Forbes? Are you okay?"

He looked a frightful mess. He smelled of rotting ass.

Lisa stepped towards him, alarmed. Then she stepped back, repelled.

"Tom?"

Tom needed to exorcise this girl from his life. He held up his hands to ward her off. He was done with this habit as well. Tom blew through the rear office door, exiting into the alley. The alley looked surprisingly clean and neat. Fresh brick buildings. Smooth clean asphalt. The sun was shining and the sky was blue.

For some reason, this is not what he was expecting.

What was he expecting?

He wasn't sure. There was no graffiti or garbage or decay anywhere.

Why would he be expecting graffiti and garbage and decay? The boom times were here.

There sat his Jeep, sparkling emerald green, brand new, the forty-eight month lease beginning. The manly, sporting truck which he needed to project his image to the world. Or rather, to the citizens of Jamestown.

Right. As if anybody cared about such nonsense. The Jeep sat in a row with many other clean, sparkling new vehicles. Including a red Ford Escort. The eighties were proving to be good times all around. Everybody working. Everybody spending. Everybody searching for more.

Tom sat down in his Jeep and tried to collect his bearings. The feeling in his gut had not subsided after throwing up. In fact, it was getting worse. His head pounded, throbbing with new abandon. He shivered and reached for the heater control. The gagging sensation was roaring back. Tom got the window down and gulped fresh air. He stomped on the accelerator and blasted out of the alley.

The Jeep careened onto the main drag and raced towards the Tribune. He didn't get far. Cars and trucks were everywhere, people were everywhere, real people, shopping, spending, engaging in commerce.

What did you mean by 'real people', Tommy?

Tom shook his head. Ouch, the headache, remember?

He stopped the Jeep. Started again. Stop. Start. Stop. Start. The roads were packed with shoppers. The city was rocking. Gridlock. Flags fluttering everywhere. Red white and blue. So festive. So alive.

Before his eyes, the sun began to fade. Clouds raced in, stopping in the sky ahead of him. An overpowering feeling of foreboding filled his soul.

Karen was waiting on the sidewalk in front of the Tribune, chatting with a co-worker. Amazing, she looked so young, and so beautiful. Those legs. The thin, body hugging dress. The strappy sandals, rescued from storage for this last magnificent day of Indian summer.

Tom screeched to a halt, fish tailing the Jeep up to the curb.

"Karen! Get in! Quick!" Tom shouted.

"We're going to be late!"

Karen climbed in the passenger side.

"Easy, easy. It's okay honey. We'll be fine."

Karen reached across with her hand to touch his thigh. Tom felt a sense of dread, knowing exactly what she would say next.

"Tom, she'll be so excited to see us. It should be fun."

Tom shook his head. Why was this all so bloody familiar?

Tom sped the Jeep the last six blocks and stopped as close to the Busy Bee as he could get. What he knew he would see, he was not ready to see.

What he did not want to see.

Traffic and commotion plugged the street in front of the day care. Red and blue beacon lights strobed the building and trees.

"Tom?"

Karen was alarmed.

"Why are there emergency vehicles here?"

Tom was past the alarmed phase. They got out of the Jeep. Tom grabbed Karen's hand and led her towards the Busy Bee. They marched up the sidewalk with a false determination, uneasy and unknowing. Anxious parents hugged their kids. Tightly, and with relief.

Suddenly, the air drained out of the world, a giant balloon sucking down to nothing.

Time slowed.

Slowed some more.

Slowed even more.

Nearly stopping.

On the front driveway, an ambulance crew was trying to set up a wheeled stretcher. Why were they taking so long? It was a simple task to raise the bed and click it into place. Two second operation guys. Not rocket science. This was going to take ten minutes.

Their next door neighbor separated from the scrum of people and slogged towards them, as if her feet were encased in concrete blocks. The look on her face screamed urgency, but she was actually slowing down.

Tom could see two police officers recognize him, and then begin their tedious move towards him. Why were the cops so slow? They were cops, trained for situations such as this. Trained to react with speed and agility. Not so, apparently.

Tom veered into the crowd, slashing, trying to find his way through. It was taking forever, he seemed to be moving in quicksand. He struggled, shoving and dodging his way, the thick mass of humanity enveloping him. Tom turned and looked back above the crowd. Sure enough, the neighbor was about to hug Karen, but attempting to do it in an agonizingly measured fashion. A look of confusion and dread was distorting Karen's beautiful face.

Tom saw the red and blue lights barely crawling across the dark sky, slowly projecting against the day care building. The police were pointing at him, moving their mouths as if they had walked out of a dentist's office stuffed with Novocain, trying to form words he could not hear or understand.

Was the whole world on valium?

A slow thump, thump, thump showered down on Tom from above. He strained to look up. A helicopter hovered above, its rotors barely turning. Jesus! Was the thing going to crash land right on top of him?

Suddenly, the world re-flated.

Tom blasted through the remainder of the crowd to the front of the day care. He tore at the yellow happy face door, nearly ripping it off the hinges. Tom raced through the darkened, empty building and out the back door. Emergency personnel milled around the yard. Bright colored toys littered the green, green grass. A large yellow digging machine was parked near the fence. Perfectly shiny and yellow. Almost cartoonish. A gigantic Tonka toy. So out of place in the backyard of a day care. Smoke, or mist was curling up from the ground near the machine's front bucket. A mound of earth was piled to the side. Mist was rising off the mound.

What was with the mist?

Police tape cordoned off the area. A dark gray tarp covered a lump on the ground. Tom could see a hand with burnt, charred flesh sticking out from underneath the tarp. How many more times did he have to watch this horror play out?

Color began to drain from the backyard.

The grass, the enormous oak tree, the toys, the sky; everything turned to blacks and grays. Everything began to die. In mere seconds. Tom's battered jeans were filthy, as were his old boots and ratty sweater. His head pounded, his body ached and he smelled of liquor and old man sweat. The whispers encircled him. The ground reverberated underneath his feet. The teeter totter moved up and down, the swings swayed with tiny riders. Skeleton riders.

Tom closed his eyes.

Holy.

It had happened.

Again.

Tom sunk to his knees. He bent down, covering his face with his hands. He was convinced he was planted firmly in hell.

One thought filled his being.

What have I done?
And there it was.
"Daaaaaaaaaaaaaaaaaaaaaaaaaaa……….."
The call from the ages.
The call from the other world.
Only a matter of time, wasn't it?
Then silence.

CHAPTER 43

"Tom?"

A different voice. Familiar. Silky. Beautiful. From his other life. From his good life. How he missed this voice, as much as he missed his little girl's. He missed his old life like there was no tomorrow. Which there wasn't. Thanks to his stupidity and his bullshit.

"Tom?"

Karen walked out to the backyard, accompanied by the two police officers. Ambulance personnel were heading towards the tarp covered body, pushing their wheeled stretcher.

Tom raised his head, removed his hands from his face. He stared straight ahead at the plank fence. Not daring to look anywhere else. He stood, and walked closer, looking for? Looking for what? Tom stared hard. Burnt into the fence. Was it a pattern of some sort? It almost looked to be a zig zag pattern. A lightening bolt. The pattern swam before Tom's eyes, fading in the wood grain and the charred mess. The pattern was gone. Damn, it was so hard to determine anything, when everything was black and gray and charcoal and burnt. And dead.

But not his girl's little voice. Her voice echoed in his brain. Alive. Alive forever. The voice that would torture him for all eternity. The voice of an angel.

"DAAAAAAAAAAADDDDDDDY……………."

This time, so much stronger! Tom shook from head to toe. *So much stronger.* And twice in a row! He had *never* heard the voice twice in a row. Never. Tom's world was changing again.

He backed away from the fence, terrified at what new form of torture lay behind him. Tom had to look. Yes, he had to. It was part of his crazy penance. He turned slowly, towards the voice.

A ray of blinding white sunlight hit him. Tom had to shade his eyes with both hands.

The sunlight blasted through the gray clouds, splashing against the magnificent oak tree. One at a time, slowly, then quickly, then at lightening speed, the leaves began to change. From dead gray. To live colors. Life colors. Producing a riot of magical fall shades. Brown. Beige. Tan. Red. Orange. Yellow. True fall colors. The tree trunk turned a deep, majestic brown, the bark rippling with texture, producing a musty, healthy smell of nature. This was unbelievable.

Tom followed the powerful sunlight beam from the tree to the ground.

Joe Danton!

Holding a red elephant!

Jesus! Where had he come from?

And.

And.

Tom's phasors were on stun!

Tiffany?

Standing in the light, the two of them, hand in hand?

Joe and Tiffy? Were they leaving? Or had they just returned?

Tom could not even breathe!

Could this be?

The grass began to green up, deep and rich and emerald. The grass lengthened. In his peripheral vision, Tom could actually see the grass blades growing! Birds chirped from their perches in the big oak. The sky exploded in the most brilliant blue Tom had ever seen.

Again, could this be?

In that second, Tiffy broke from Joe and ran towards her daddy.

"Daddy, daddy!" she called.

Tom watched the little girl run, slow, slow, slower. He didn't see his shirt whiten, his tie flatten down and turn red, his dirty jeans and boots replaced. No, he was mesmerized, staring at the little girl running his way. She churned through the grass, flailing, fighting her way towards him, straining, the effort considerable, as if she was finishing a long journey.

The blonde hair.

The little bundle of blonde business.

He bent down and snatched her up off the ground.

Tom could not believe it!

He thought he might squeeze the life out of her. Ugly waves of horror, dread, insecurity, doubt, depression and despair blew out of his body. In the form of tears. Karen ran to join them. They hugged together. Karen looked at her husband, not quite understanding the emotion pouring out of him. They held tight as three, letting the minutes pass.

Tom's brain was going about a billion miles an hour. It screeched to a halt in the right here, and the right now. Tiffany. His Tiffany. Karen. His beautiful Karen. The Busy Bee. 9/11. 1987.

It was all good.

If, this was all true.

A gigantic if.

But it had to be. What else could it be? Where? Or what? Had happened? Tiffany. Karen. Here and now. For real.

It *was* all good.

Joe Danton joined the happy reunion. Tom was able to peel his eyes off his little girl to look at Joe. Joe handed the red elephant to Tiffy. She grabbed the stuffed toy and folded it into herself.

"Joe, what happened?"

"We phoned the city about a smell by the back fence. Actually, Tiffany discovered it. We couldn't figure out what it was, so we called it in."

Joe was pointing towards the yellow Caterpillar machine.

"They sent a back hoe to dig. The operator hit a power line running into the Burlington property. There used to be a switching station behind our place. The station is long gone, but the line was still live. Poor guy. He stepped down to check a problem with his bucket and was electrocuted. A bunch of us saw the accident. Including Tiffany. I think we will all be traumatized for a long time."

"God Joe, that's awful. Terrible. The poor workman."

Tom broke his embrace on his daughter. He didn't want to let her go, but everything was okay. He was okay. More important, she was okay. There was something else going on. Questions. Questions. Questions. Why questions?

Tom handed Tiffy over to Karen.

"Hey babe, can you take her to the Jeep? I'll be one minute."

Karen smiled and looked at Tom with questioning wonderment. Something was going on with her man. She would find out later. Something was changing. She sensed it was something good.

Tom took Joe's elbow and steered him towards the back fence. What a mess. The back hoe had singe marks on its steel bucket. Shredded electrical cable remained tangled in the bucket's teeth. Burn marks blackened the grass where the operator had made contact with the ground. The flashpoint of electricity had started a grass fire which then spread to the plank fence. The fire was out, but wisps of smoke curled off the ground and fence.

Tom felt a tingling sensation in his body. Something about 9/11. Not today, but a different 9/11. A coming 9/11. Falling buildings. Fast trains. Empty houses. Vacant streets. Sick people. Dark tunnels. He stopped dead in his tracks.

His eyes began to water.

"Holy crap! What an awful smell!"

"You know it," Joe agreed. "They still haven't determined the source."

Joe nodded at the idled machine.

"The digging stopped when this happened."

Tom found himself staring at the fence. His mind swirled. There was something else here, achingly out of reach. Graffiti spray paint. Wrecked cars. Garbage and rot. The smell and taste of sewage. A filthy diner. Skating.

Fading. Fading. So close, but so far.

Tom turned and looked at Joe. The day's events had taken their toll on Joe Danton. The man had been his usual energetic, happy self when Tom had dropped Tiffy off this morning. He recalled their handshake at the drop off, and the relief he had felt when his little girl climbed onto Joe. Now, Joe looked trodden and tired.

Tom caught a glimpse of a scar underneath Joe's beard. The scar seemed to run across his neck, and up to his ear. How strange. Tom had never noticed it before. Also, there seemed to be bruising around Joe's eyes and mouth. A lot of bruising. The long hair and bushy beard hid so much. For a young man, Joe Danton possessed a very old, very worldly appearance.

More pin pricks of what seemed to be memories, stabbed at Tom's brain. He reached for them, but could not grasp. The memories were ice, melting quickly on an unexpectedly warm, sunny day. An ice rink melting beneath his feet.

"Joe? Is there something I am missing?"

Joe extended his hand to Tom.

"No, I think you've got it all. Probably good to get Tiffany home. She has been through a lot."

Tom took Joe's hand. The two men shook. Tom felt a surge of energy pulse from Joe's hand, into his own. It ran up Tom's arm and spread across his chest. Minuscule electric shocks were spreading throughout his being. How weird.

Joe pointed to the back door of the Busy Bee, where Karen was toting Tiffy and the red elephant. Karen had stopped and was waving back at them. Tom headed for his wife and daughter. Marie was now walking out of the day care, stopping to talk with Karen. For some reason, Tom felt an enormous relief seeing Joe's wife. She looked good. Healthy, vibrant and alive.

Why wouldn't she?

What were these parallel sensations he was experiencing?

"Hey Tom," Joe said, "I think you found what you were looking for."

What the hell did that mean? Found what he was looking for?

Tom stopped. Turned back to Joe. What did Joe mean by that? Tom had many more questions besides this one. He immediately forgot about his questions, because Joe's fatigue and aging had vanished! The bruising and the nasty scar Tom had noticed a moment ago? Gone. Completely.

What a strange day.

CHAPTER 44

The Jamestown County Sheriff walked across the backyard. He nodded towards Tom and Joe, then checked with the ambulance attendants. The EMT's were making ready to remove the body. The sheriff lifted the green wool blanket now covering the corpse. He took a quick look. He replaced the blanket, nodded. The ambulance attendants began to move out.

Tom always marveled at how suited the sheriff was to his calling. A huge man. Long white hair. Handlebar mustache. Cowboy hat. Flowing black car coat with the gold law badge affixed to the lapel. The sheriff was from out west. New Mexico, or Arizona, they said. One of the Sunbelt states. The sheriff looked to be a throwback, certainly out of touch with today's fashion. For sure, a guy you would want on your side when the shit hit the fan. The man made the boomtown of Jamestown the safest city in the nation.

More pinpricks of memory.

Something continued to be out of Tom's reach.

Tom saw the crumpled tarp lying on the ground, cast aside. The tarp had been hastily thrown over the machine operator, out of respect for the dead, and to save the children from nightmares. He could see the Morgan Iron and Steel Works logo on the tarp. Why would their tarp be way over here, miles from the factory, at the Busy Bee?

Or *did* he see the Morgan logo?

The more Tom stared at the lettering, the more he realized he could not make out those particular words. Anyway, it made little sense. How could a Morgan tarp migrate all the way across the city? How could the tarp find its way into the backyard of the day care? Why did he think a secret tunnel existed, joining the day care with the steel plant? How ridiculous. What a stupid thought. More pin pricks of memory.

The sheriff stepped under the police tape to examine the accident site. The big man walked around the excavation, staring at the ground. Why was this so familiar to Tom? Tom could picture a large man, standing on a sidewalk, with a dark car coat whipping around his legs. Staring at *him*. On a dark, cold, wet day. Had Tom seen this man, from this exact spot, in this backyard? When would that have happened? Exactly. It never did. Because it made zero sense.

Wherever the sheriff stepped, the smoke would curl up in wisps, the grass happy to shed the foulness of it all. The sheriff stopped in front of the fence. Slowly, his eyes trailed up from the ground. He stepped closer to the fence. He reached out one hand. To Tom, the sheriff was tracing an imaginary figure, almost a zig zag pattern. Another round of pin pricks stabbed at Tom's brain. A blown out church. Battering ram size holes in the wall. Pews and chairs trashed to pieces. *She is in a better place.*

The sheriff backed up a few steps, ducking under the police tape. He walked over to where Joe and Tom were standing. The three men formed three points of a perfect triangle where they stood, all looking at one another.

Under the massive oak tree.

Tom noticed the deformity about the right ear of the lawman. At least it appeared to be a deformity, or perhaps, questionable surgery. Long white hair covered most of the ear.

Pinpricks.

Tom's gaze fell to the gold badge of the County Sheriff's Office. The badge reflected sharp glints of sunlight. Flashing the reflected light across Tom's eyes.

The sheriff was about to speak, when a stiff breeze rattled the oak.

A shower of colored leaves drifted to the ground, framing the three men, almost in a cone. An unnatural silence muted the outside world. Together, they looked up, watching nature's performance.

The breeze stopped.

The leaves seemed to be hanging, suspended in the air.

Not falling.

Not moving.

Not doing anything.

A true freeze frame.

A low static crackled through the air.

The leaves were speaking, in muted whispers. The men looked at each other. They all heard the whispers. The leaves began to fall again, and when the last leaf touched the ground, the whispers stopped.

Silence. Uncanny and eerie. Almost, supernatural. The calm before the storm.

The seconds passed, and the regular sounds of the day crept back. The birds chirping. The wind touching the leaves. The kids and parents out front of the day care, readying to go home. The emergency personnel doing their jobs. A siren, as another rescue vehicle arrived. The reverberation was back in the ground. The factory thumped in the distance. Joe was staring, as if in a trance, in the direction of the factory. The sheriff followed Joe's gaze, with the same hypnotic reaction.

Tom was about to look.

A million pin pricks of memory flared across his mind. A mini slideshow of sorrow and fear and desperation and decrepitude. He decided, no. Not a choice he was going to make. Karen and Tiffy were waiting for him.

Tom walked away from under the oak tree.

Through the rich green grass.

Past the brightly colored toys.

Past the dotted soccer ball.

Past the gently swaying swing set.

The swing set was empty.

END

COMING NEXT,

from William Jeffrey Patus.

DARK HEART

THE TWO OF CLUBS. ROOM TEN.

THE EYE IN THE SKY. NAZI GERMANY.

COMPUTER SEARCH BUGS.

THE SHROUD OF TURIN. THE GATES OF SHAME.

THE LORD'S RESISTANCE ARMY. THE ROCK OF EVIL.

FEATURING: Dr. Llubo Bordant, Professor Richard Donofrio and Agent Jackie Johnson WITH: Peter Moldivar, Jesus Desoto, Sir Allan Grant, Big John Smith, Miles Davidson, Marilyn Donofrio, Johann Wiens, Franz Metcalfe, Sir Robert Raleigh, Jurgen Heinz, Dieter Shrenk, Evan Hunt, Alfred Jackson, James 'Jimmy' Schmidt, Mr. Chen, the Freak, and the Russians

CPSIA information can be obtained at www.ICGtesting.com
Printed in the USA
LVOW08*1036270913

354316LV00001B/1/P